Lyn Hughes is the author of the critically acclaimed novels *The Factory* (1990), shortlisted for the National Book Council's New Writing Award, *One Way Mirrors* (1993), *The Bright House* (2000) and *Flock* (2011). Lyn was born in Wales in 1952 and spent some years in South Africa before moving to Sydney in 1982. She now divides her time between the Northern Illawarra and the Blue Mountains.

MR CARVER'S WHALE

LYN HUGHES

Fourth Estate

Fourth Estate
An imprint of HarperCollins*Publishers*

HarperCollins*Publishers*
Australia • Brazil • Canada • France • Germany • Holland • India
Italy • Japan • Mexico • New Zealand • Poland • Spain • Sweden
Switzerland • United Kingdom • United States of America

HarperCollins acknowledges the Traditional Custodians
of the land upon which we live and work, and pays respect
to Elders past and present.

First published in Australia in 2022
by HarperCollins*Publishers* Australia Pty Limited
Gadigal Country
Level 13, 201 Elizabeth Street, Sydney NSW 2000
ABN 36 009 913 517
harpercollins.com.au

Copyright © Lyn Hughes 2022

The right of Lyn Hughes to be identified as the author of this work has been asserted by her in accordance with the *Copyright Amendment (Moral Rights) Act 2000*.

This work is copyright. Apart from any use as permitted under the *Copyright Act 1968*, no part may be reproduced, copied, scanned, stored in a retrieval system, recorded, or transmitted, in any form or by any means, without the prior written permission of the publisher.

A catalogue record for this book is available from the National Library of Australia

ISBN 978 1 4607 6295 0 (paperback)
ISBN 978 1 4607 1553 6 (ebook)

Cover design by Darren Holt, HarperCollins Design Studio
Cover images: Humpback whale (*Megaptera versabilis*) from *Natural History of the Cetaceans and Other Marine Mammals of the Western Coast of North America* (1872) by Charles Melville Scammon (1825–1911); Ocean by David Billings on Unsplash; Sunset on ocean horizon by Soren Egeberg / stocksy.com / 206435; all other images by shutterstock.com
Typeset in Bembo Std by Kelli Lonergan
Printed and bound in Australia by McPherson's Printing Group

For Sarah, Jesse and Shelley

It's often the name of the crime upon which a life shatters, not the nameless and personal act itself...

— Rilke, *Letters to a Young Poet*
(Eighth Letter)

ADULTERY

The Sea-Chest

A whale spotter was first to sight the steamer. Peeling off, just before dawn, from the bunched-up clouds on the horizon, belching smoke. Cabin lights twinkling like so many fallen stars. Churning the waters to a froth as it closed on the small, still-sleeping island of Pico. Bringing with it who knew what troubles and joys.

A blind woman was first to come ashore. Pausing at the top of the gangway to fervently cross herself, before being led off on the arm of a nun. Followed by a young matron, big with what Rosa could only think must be twins, if not triplets. Followed, in turn, by a skinny, wan-looking girl cradling a newborn. Then everyone else, in a rush. Lurching, stumbling, weaving after days at sea.

The animals were next. A piebald mare trembling badly, hard on her heels the probable cause—two fierce-looking dogs, jaws bound with strips of cloth. Two donkeys, a cow, a couple of pigs, sheep, goats. Any number of chickens, ducks, geese, borne aloft in baskets, boxes, crates.

Finally, the luggage. Suitcases, valises, hat boxes, carpet bags, portmanteaux, packages, parcels. What looked to João to be a trombone, roughly swaddled in a blanket. All carried ashore by a band of grunting, cursing, pigtailed sailors and piled up on the dock.

No sign of a sea-chest.

They'd all but given up hope when two burly sailors suddenly appeared, a large chest carried between them.

'Carvalho?' The older of the pair squinted at the shipping label. João nodded.

'Can't think what's in it,' the sailor said, as they set it down.

'Bricks?' The younger mopped his brow.

'Just as well I brought the cart,' João said. 'And the lad,' with a nod to his elder son, Marcelinho.

'Just as well,' they agreed, with a familiar pitying glance at his younger son, Antonio.

João hunkered down beside it. Certainly nothing fancy, he thought, running a hand over the smooth, slightly domed lid. No ornate carvings, mother-of-pearl inlays, shiny brass hinges or locks. But a large, plain, workaday sea-chest, tied up with a leather strap. Faintly scuffed at the edges, the remnants of old shipping labels still attached.

Leaning on his stick, Antonio could just make out:

LO.DO.
BO.TON
B..NOS A.R.S
CAL.UTT.

Well travelled.

It was addressed to him, Antonio, the youngest of the Carvalhos. Master Antonio Mateus Carvalho Cabral. He watched open-mouthed as his father, João, checked the shipping label twice before finally undoing the strap and raising the lid.

It was full of books.

Not a brick in sight.

*

Halfway up the hill, as often lately, the old donkey, Bonita, suddenly pulled up short. João and Marcelinho got out of the cart and began to walk, Antonio taking the reins. His mother, Rosa, at his side, offering a steady stream of advice and encouragement. The beast could hardly put one hoof in front of the other by the time they crested the hill.

'Books,' João could now and again be heard to incredulously mutter. 'Books.'

'And what's wrong with books?' Rosa finally said with an edge, though herself not without misgivings. Not that she had any real quarrel with books, she thought. Why, Antonio was always with his nose in one. But a whole chest full? The trouble with books was that they always seemed to lead to questions and wanting to know more, then more, and never once satisfied. Now she came to think of it, books were probably no better than boats for spiriting people away.

'Nothing's wrong with books,' João replied to Rosa, with a shrug. 'Or with bottles of madeira. Or port. Or legs of ham, come to that.' Then, barely under his breath, 'It's not as if she's exactly short of—'

'João!' Rosa abruptly cut him off. 'Palmira's the most generous person in the whole world!'

Almost always a parcel at Christmas, Easter and Epiphany; a little something or other tucked inside a letter.

As if letters and presents could make up for the sisters' separation.

Books? Marcelinho thought, trudging beside his father. Antonio would have liked it if he'd read books. Whereas João wanted him to be just like him and work in the vineyard. Rosa had always wanted him to be an altar boy, despite his size, or sing in the church choir, when he couldn't keep a note. He'd never been one for books but he didn't mind presents. As long as it wasn't another hat on his name day to replace one lost—more a reproach than a gift—or another pair of socks, or woolly jumper knitted by his mother but something special, just for him. You could hardly blame his brother for Aunt Palmira taking a shine to him. Telling everyone he was just like their lost Uncle Luis, telling them stories of what they got up to as kids. Probably thinking how Antonio could hardly get up to anything with his leg and wanting to send him something special. Probably sour grapes, Marcelinho diagnosed of himself, this achy, forlorn feeling.

*

Word had got out. They'd barely pulled up outside the house before Madelina Pereira's big nose poked through the curtains as Ligia Gonçalves swept her front path, head jerking like a chicken pecking seed.

'They'll have been gnawing their fingers to the bone, wondering,' Rosa said to João.

It took some time to manoeuvre the chest through the front door, down the hall, into the kitchen, neighbours popping in to offer advice, encouragement, tales of other such unexpected gifts.

'Thought they were aiming to stay for supper,' João said, when the last had gone. He gave Antonio a gentle little shove. 'All yours, lad. Get to it.'

Resting his stick on the chest, Antonio picked up the first book he laid eyes on. Enticingly thick, covered in brown leather, pages edged with gilt.

'*The Mysterious World of Cetaceans*,' he read aloud, stumbling over the unfamiliar last word. He opened it to a glossy frontispiece of a sperm whale spouting in a bright blue sea, waves topped with little whitecaps, every drop of water sparkling in the sun.

'We'll be here until next Sunday, this rate,' João cleared his throat to say, as Antonio stared at the page.

Reluctantly closing the book and setting it down, he picked up another, bound in blue cloth.

Sea Serpents of the Galapagos Islands. Then another and another until the chest was emptied out, the table piled with books.

Suddenly aware that Marcelinho was left out of proceedings and leaning against a wall, hands in pockets, Antonio picked up a likely looking book, flipping through pages. 'Hey Marco, come and look at these flags!'

Walking over and laying an easy hand on his brother's shoulder, Marcelinho studied the page of brightly coloured ensigns representing some of the great maritime nations—lands he'd always dreamed of one day visiting, he thought, with a familiar yearning

'There's Argentina,' Antonio pointed it out. Pleased to feel his brother give his shoulder a friendly squeeze, in response.

'Seems I'll have to turn my hand to a bookcase,' João said, studying the towers with evident satisfaction. 'Four shelves should do it,' he muttered, already mentally measuring up. 'Five? What do you reckon, son?' Leaning over to good-naturedly ruffle Antonio's hair.

*

Almost the second he got in from school the next day, Antonio fetched the whale book. He'd been thinking about it all day, a little worm of excitement wriggling in his belly. When up until then he'd hardly given whales a thought. Well, no more, he supposed, than he had cats and cows, of which you could encounter many on Pico. And if he had, would have pronounced them, as everyone did, vicious beasts, only too happy to upend a man with a flick of a fluke. Or take him down to a gruesome death by drowning, if he had the misfortune to be fastened on when one made up its mind to sound.

He made short work of it. Within days, he had consumed every gilded page and begun over. Which even he found something of a puzzle. It wasn't as if he hadn't seen dozens, possibly hundreds, of whales. Mostly dead ones, nothing like the illustrations in the Aunt's book. Rather, they were huge ragged mounds of bloody flesh on the slipway at Lajes, like something chewed up by giant rats. Chunks of what might have been cats or cows for all he could have said, bubbling away in the big iron try pots that looked like witches' cauldrons.

Now, if kept awake at night by his leg, he passed the time trying to work out where whales came from and went to, how they slept and where, what they liked to eat—aside from whale fishermen. Whether it was true that they could sing, preferred smooth seas to rough—or, as it seemed from the way the young liked to hurl themselves above the big rolling swells off Lajes, it was a case of the stormier the better. The longest he could hold his breath was thirty seconds. Whereas sperm whales, he now discovered, could stay submerged for over an hour. And their teeth. He'd have sworn they all had giant fangs like monstrous bulldogs, when in fact some didn't have any at all, just stuff called baleen. And the young fed on mother's milk, like his new baby cousin, Filipe. However many times his mother reminded him to look at the floor or ceiling if his Aunt Serafina took out a breast, he always forgot. Not that Marcelinho helped, asking why he was so red in the face.

When he told Margarida about his new interest, she immediately began thinking up questions of her own. Did whales have favourite places, she wanted to know. Or best friends, like her and Antonio? Did they prefer Pico to Faial? Antonio wondered how much they could see out of their tiny eyes, struck by an illustration of an elephant's eye in another of Palmira's books, not just its remarkable resemblance to that of the whales but to the tiny wrinkled anus of baby Filipe, which he'd happened to notice while watching Serafina change his napkin.

He'd certainly never given a lot of thought to how it might feel to *be* a whale: chased by whale fishermen, sharks, killer whales, giant squid with enormous slippery arms, desperate to squeeze the air out of you as if you were an accordion. Marcelinho, who spent almost every waking hour carving up blubber on the dock at Lajes, wading in whales, clogs sinking into whale flesh like quicksand, said he'd hardly known a whale that didn't have scars from fighting giant squid.

And as for whales being mysterious … Why, waiting on the dock to have their heads sawn off, they seemed about as mysterious to Antonio as Ferreira's old donkey, which, having fallen off a cliff some weeks before, had spent days braying pitifully on a sliver of black sand far below, before finally falling silent. Only that Sunday, he and Margarida had gone to look at it after church, peering over the edge to find it swollen to twice its size and covered in gulls, like barnacles.

Cetaceans. He learned to pronounce it from another of Palmira's books, a dictionary. It sounded like the sea, he thought, swishing against the Ilhéus da Madalena on a still night. All the many wondrous things he now knew about whales, he'd almost give his good leg to see one close up. A live one. Not that it seemed likely. Not when Marcelinho refused to go further than the breakwater when Antonio was allowed out in the boat for the first time ever that summer, then rowed at such a leisurely pace even Antonio could have kept up.

*

The books had belonged to Palmira's late husband, Tomás de Souza. In the accompanying letter, belatedly found tucked inside the chest, Palmira explained that though Tomás had always intended them for Antonio, it was only now, two years after his death, that she felt up to tackling his formidable library.

Rosa had no trouble at all in recalling the summer Palmira fell in love with Tomás, a doctoral student of the natural sciences, who'd come to Pico in search of the skeletal remains of whales. It seemed every five minutes she'd been sent outside to play so the grown-ups could talk. Everyone whispering in corners, gossiping over walls. Rosa grateful, for once, to be invisible. What with the wedding such a rushed affair, everyone had presumed Palmira must be in the family way. Only, as later became apparent, she wasn't. Just madly in love, and determined that nothing and no-one, least of all her meddling mother, was going to prevent her marrying her Tomás. Happily settled in Lisbon, she often wrote Rosa long, newsy letters. Not a word of babies but plenty about books and plays and trips abroad. The city didn't seem to exist that she hadn't visited with her husband. She wrote, too, that Tomás had been made a tutor, then lecturer, then associate professor, then professor in zoological studies at the University of Lisbon.

And that they'd moved into a big airy apartment in the very heart of the city. Small wonder João rolled his eyes when Rosa read snippets of the letters aloud. She'd come home to visit just once, after their mother passed away. Too late for the funeral, of course, given the distance between Lisbon and Pico. Not that there'd been a lot of mourners that day, or tears, Rosa recalled, which seemed the saddest thing of all. Palmira had really taken to the boys. Particularly Antonio. She couldn't help but love him, Rosa thought; he was so much like their long-lost brother, Luis. Aside from the limp, of course. Which was precisely what Palmira said, the first time she saw him. The resemblance between the pair! Even now Rosa sometimes had to pinch herself. And the same laugh. You never forgot Luis's laugh. Even their mother couldn't help but smile when he laughed. Now all these years, Rosa thought, and not a word from him. It was worse than burying a son, a boy vanishing. When you knew bad things happened.

Like Antonio's leg. Not a sign or warning the whole nine months. Naturally, she blamed herself. The amount of tripe and bacon she'd consumed, she was surprised he hadn't grown pointy ears and a tail. She'd been short-tempered with João, what's more, and snapped Ligia Gonçalves's head off when she'd enquired once too often when the baby was due. They'd hesitated before naming him Mateus—gift of God—after João's father, who'd died of some weakness of the heart while João was still an infant. Besides, Rosa had thought, you didn't always get to keep a gift. Take her own miniature blue-painted boat with its little fisherman holding a tiny gilded fish, given to her on her name day, only to be crushed under her mother's boot. And all because, fearful of it being broken, she'd refused to let Palmira hold it. Greed, her mother had pronounced, a cardinal sin. Enough to make any woman, Rosa thought, cradling her son, promise that no child of hers, whatever their crime, would be so cruelly treated.

Antonio had mixed feelings about his leg. Mostly he worried about his parents worrying. His mother was always fussing or praying. Most nights he could hear her droning through the bedroom wall—though, in truth, he quite liked drifting off to the sound of her voice. Fortunately, he wasn't alone in being singled out in her nightly prayers, what with Mrs Gonçalves next door, a woman desperate, still, Rosa said, to shrug off an oversized nun's hood. How many wash days had she seen the poor soul hanging out Gonçalves's big baggy drawers, mumbling novenas under her breath? What had possessed her to marry the man? Any man? A former nun. Then there was the postman who'd lost his wife to a fire, and witless Manoel who wove baskets for the grapes. Family lore had it that, on first seeing her baby's foot skewed sideways with half the toes fused into a lump, Rosa had wailed like a banshee. Whereas João hadn't uttered a sound but made a beeline for the shed and began building his son a cart so he'd be able to get around, one day, all the many hills on Pico.

Almost every evening, after his mother kissed him goodnight and shut the door and he was sufficiently convinced she wasn't about to pop her head around it one last time, Antonio would slip out of bed to retrieve one of Palmira's books. Most often the whale book. He liked to feel the weight of it beside him on the coverlet, the softness of the leather binding, hear the little sigh the pages gave passing through his fingers, stroke the silkiness of the transparent sheets separating each of the many illustrations. Though he itched to trace the outline of a sperm whale (or cachalot, as he now knew) onto the gossamer-sheer paper with a pencil, he never did, only with a finger. Best of all he liked the illustration of two humpback whales together: a fine drawing of a whale skeleton set beside a glossy print of one breaching, whole body airborne. Oddly, he was reminded of himself. Not his crippled self but the one he dreamed of, had always dreamed of. Perfect. Like that breaching whale, not bloodied or bristling with metal barbs but smooth, unblemished, glistening, flying through the air as if for the fun of it.

The Stranded Whale

Most in Lajes do Pico could still recall the special cart João made for young Antonio. Margarida de Azavedo Machado pushing it full pelt down the hill, Antonio hanging on to the calico cat, Chuchuzina, for dear life. Margarida's mother, Angelina, certainly could; and the scabs on her daughter's knees, from her many falls. And how, seeing her pause mid-descent to adjust a blanket and tenderly stroke the long-suffering animal's fur, she'd thought what a fine mother her only daughter would one day make.

Whereas Margarida's sole desire had always been to be an actress, and a great one. Such was her passion, she vowed she was never truly herself but on a stage. When, in truth, most saw little difference in her on stage or off, so loud and prone to speaking her mind was she. Fortunate, perhaps, that the Machados, prominent and well-to-do, were more than usually well placed to support the ambitions of a precocious only child. Almost as soon as Margarida could walk and talk, there'd been dancing, singing, drama lessons. And if the Machados' conspicuous support of church and school seldom met with universal acclaim, most would have allowed that it wasn't just for their largesse that Margarida was awarded the lead in so many religious pageants and school plays. She had genuine talent, an admirable work ethic (first to learn her lines, last to leave rehearsals), along with an unwavering determination to succeed, and not just on the modest stages of Pico.

What, perhaps, wasn't so well known was that the Carvalho and Machado families were loosely related, with a shared, long since departed great-great-great-grandfather on far-flung Flores, and distant cousins on even more distant Corvo. There might have been more for all Angelina knew. She hadn't exactly pursued the possibility. It wasn't unheard of to lose or mislay the odd relative with families scattered across nine tiny islands set down in the middle of the Atlantic. The Carvalhos, as Angelina was only too well aware, were highly regarded in the small community of Lajes. Rosa frequently singled out for her generosity, kindness, spiritual devotion (though not a word, to Angelina's chagrin, of smugness). João, hard-working, shy of words, clever with his hands, was deemed steady as a rock (and about as animated, to Angelina's way of thinking). She wasn't too sure about the elder boy, Marcelinho—only that it took some spunk to hunt the whale. She found it hard to imagine her husband, Dom Ricardo, let loose with a harpoon. He could barely manage his member. And sadly, he'd not improved any with practice. It was rumoured that Marcelinho had the gift, that he could draw whales to him. Which left the younger boy, Antonio. No point holding the lad's leg against him, Angelina knew—it was fate, and no arguing with fate. Or with the fact that she felt queasy around the lad. He listed badly—worse by the day—his left foot more like some old vine root you might use for firewood than flesh and blood. Angelina found it hard to believe it could end well. Or more to the point, her daughter take it well. Even as a baby, Margarida need only catch sight of the boy to be burbling and blowing bubbles. Unfathomable.

Almost as unfathomable as to Antonio when, only weeks after the arrival of Palmira's books, a whale managed to strand itself one night on the town beach. Almost, he thought, as if he'd lured it there. Wanted a whale so badly that, contrary to whale instinct and reason, one had somehow been persuaded to embed itself, feet deep, in black sand.

By mid-morning half of Lajes had been out to see it. It was barely alive by the time he got there. Pure chance that he was right beside it when it drew its last breath. He heard a low, plaintive moan before a terrible smell hit him in the face, like the slap of a rotten fish. The whale's eye turned liquid, as if it were about to cry, and for a moment looked right into Antonio's, then blinked, once, twice, and closed. He was quite certain it blinked. Although, looking it up in the book afterwards, he couldn't find any reference to whales blinking. All the same, he was sure it had seen him. He knew it had. He wondered if it would have looked at him the same way if he'd been about to plunge a barb into its heart. He was strangely upset by the experience. And irritated, too, because he knew that scientists (and more than anything he one day hoped to become one) were never swayed by emotion, only by facts. Yet the fact was that, though surrounded by a small crowd, it felt to Antonio, when that whale looked at him, as if they were alone. Just the two of them. And the feeling, which should have soon faded, hourly grew stronger.

As soon as they were sure it was dead, everyone wanted to climb the beast. Antonio was surprised they didn't plant a flag in it like some mountain they'd conquered. Making his way tortuously up the hill and home, afterwards, he bumped into Marcelinho. And for some reason suddenly felt tongue-tied. He'd been really glad, he wanted to say, going down the hill that a whale had beached, but now he didn't feel glad at all. And he hadn't learned anything in the least scientific except that when something died you knew it. There was no mistaking it. It was like someone leaving the room and shutting the door.

'It's dead,' he told Marcelinho, with a shrug.

'Did you get to touch it?'

Antonio nodded. 'It felt weird. Like seaweed.'

'Good lad.' Marcelinho patted him on the back, went on his way, whistling.

Within days, it was picked clean. Everyone with whale for breakfast, lunch, supper. And a whale tale to go with it. There was much conjecture that first night, why a big young male had stranded for no apparent reason: no sign of sickness, distress, injury. A mystery. The Carvalhos were talking about it at the supper table when Gonçalves, wandering in from next door and leaning his bulk against their doorjamb, pronounced it was lice.

'Drives them half mad,' he said, furiously scratching at his chin. 'They'll rub against anything to be rid of the pests—rocks, sand, whaleboats.'

'Might have been chased in by an orca,' Marcelinho suggested tentatively.

'Or been caught in the current,' João said. 'It was coming in fast.'

Gonçalves shook his head. 'It'd be an old barb, if not lice,' he offered as an alternative. 'Might have been weeks ago. Months. Worked itself in deep, then out again. Can take a while.'

Antonio didn't know enough to make a guess. Perhaps it just got lost, he thought. Whatever the reason, he didn't much like the thought of it dying.

Which made him feel like something of a spectre at the feast that night. Because everyone else seemed pretty keen on the idea. As he would have been not so very long ago. What had happened to him? He smiled, but he didn't feel happy. Perhaps it was just that he hadn't been so close to something when it died. It might have been a cat and he'd have felt the same. Maybe it was because it was so big. Although ravenous, he had to pretend that he wasn't hungry, because he couldn't, for the life of him, have eaten any part of that whale. His mother started fussing, putting a hand to his forehead to check if he had a temperature, so he finally yawned hugely, said he was really tired and went to bed.

He dreamed that night that he was sitting at a long table among rows of men, sunburned, shirt sleeves rolled up, toasting the success of the hunt, when his brother suddenly slapped him on the back, grinning with his perfect white teeth. Teeth which grew ever larger as Marcelinho's mouth got bigger and bigger, as the room got darker and darker, until eventually Antonio was swallowed up. An image so terrifying that he woke with a horrible crick in his neck that ached all day whenever he tried to turn his head. So he could hardly look at anyone. Which he didn't really much mind. They were all still talking about the whale. You'd have thought they'd all personally had a hand in killing it when it had washed up all on its own.

Around that same time his leg started playing up worse than ever. Unable to sleep for its nagging, he took to keeping watch on the bay with João's old spyglass. What did he think, he asked himself: another whale was going to strand? And what was he going to do about it, exactly? It was impossible to see anything but the breaking phosphorescence of waves, and only then if the moon was new.

The muscles in his good limb grew alarmingly that summer, leaving him ever more lopsided. He stumbled a lot, unsure why, until he figured out that the increased weight of his growing limb was throwing him ever more off kilter. Was that where it came from, he wondered, this weird ache, whenever he thought of that dying whale?

When he tried to tell his mother she gave him a hug. She often gave out hugs unasked. If he'd tried to explain to his father, he knew João would have sat him down and tried to work it out. His father liked to do calculations. He liked things to add up. Antonio sometimes thought he was quite a lot like João, and that his father would have made a good scientist. His brother would have laughed. And tickled him. Or slapped him on the back. It was weird, but he only had to think of that dream to feel cross at Marcelinho. When his brother had only been trying to be friendly. He told Margarida. It came out pretty muddled, but she seemed to understand, nodding and looking sympathetic, not that you could ever really tell with Margarida—she might have been acting—then she suggested they put some flowers on the water for the dead whale. He said he thought that was a bit much. He just wanted to forget about the whale by then.

Sometimes he wished he hadn't read that book. That there was a way to un-know things.

The Hunt

Born and bred on an island renowned for its whale fishermen, Antonio sometimes couldn't help but imagine the hunt. Or dream about it. So vividly, some nights, he could have sworn he was there with the other young men, triumphantly rowing home, leviathan floating beside them, flag planted in its heart as on some newly discovered island. He could feel the heat of his companions' bodies, hear his own pulse thundering in his ears. As Marcelinho turned to smile at him from the prow, eyes on fire, muscles straining, hair streaming in the wind like a Viking.

Unless, that is, they lost the whale. Or got upended by it. Found themselves treading water (dream or nightmare, he always had two good legs), shivering and puking, clinging to whatever remained afloat as they waited for a boat to pick them up.

If, as on rare occasions, a boat failed to return home by nightfall, a good half of Lajes might lie sleepless, waiting for the dawn. First glimmer, men would be headed for the dock, eager to share tales of their own nights spent at sea, struggling to make way against a headwind, some monstrous beast dragging at them like a ball and chain.

Not just men, but mothers, wives, sisters, grandmothers, the infirm and lame, much like Antonio himself—all would come to stare at the horizon, exclaim at every gull, every distant whitecap. False alarms by the dozen. They only need sight a sail for men to be flinging off clogs and shoes, readying to wade in and bring the boat the last yard home. Counting heads, as it closed on the shore, trying to figure, from the way the men rowed, how the thing had gone. You could always tell when they'd lost one of their own. If it was possible to row gravely, well that's how they rowed. As if careful not to overly trouble the surface of the water, to desecrate a grave. But mostly they rowed in a state of utter exhaustion, splashing and flailing, all rhythm gone—and sometimes a whale in tow, and sometimes not.

As soon as they touched land the stories would begin. And if some were struck dumb by their encounter with the great fish, there were always those, fresh from battle, willing and able to tell the tale—and embellish it. How, in the whaleboat, they flew, fastened on, mile after mile, grinding across waves as if the sea had turned to stone, layer upon layer of varnish sanded off the vessel. And how, when the whale sounded, they hadn't even dared a whisper. Had felt a couple of lifetimes pass, unable to cough, sneeze, clear their throats, the beast right beneath them, listening through its skin. And the great roar when it rose from the deep, water exploding around them like a cannon going off! Worse than the gates of hell, that great maw looming above them. Coming from nowhere. At which, some of the old-timers might well share an amused glance, for you could always tell where a whale was about to surface—if you knew where to look. Just as astronomers were able to chart the trajectory of stars. Or a man, feeling a faint reverberation under his boots, know that Mount Pico was growing restless.

No-one knew all this starting out, of course. Marcelinho certainly hadn't. The first time he fastened on to a whale, everything happened at such a rate, he told Antonio, it was only at the very last moment that he remembered to leap to his feet, brace against the kneeboard, stand clear of the rope unreeling at breakneck speed, almost brushing his leg, all the while desperately trying to keep his balance so as not to be thrown overboard. Yet, for all that, he said, he already felt fastened to the beast as if by an invisible cord. And knew if he kept his nerve, if his eye never for a moment left the spot where he intended that barb to land, he would find his mark. That he and the whale both knew that the moment had come. And that it could go either way. And he, suddenly, without a shred of enmity for the brute. The overwhelming fear he'd felt all the time he was rowing, wishing he was somewhere, anywhere but in that boat, vanished.

'Just as well,' Marcelinho said, with a grin. 'Because where did I think I could go? Into the water, with the whale?'

Antonio laughed. 'So you threw?'

'With everything I had. It felt like my arm was about to be ripped off. I pulled a muscle in my shoulder, I threw so hard. I was so keen for that whale not to eat me. Not to get the chance.'

Antonio thought a great deal about Marcelinho's first time in the boat. Because that year some new thing seemed to happen to him almost every day. Not just the arrival of the Aunt's books. Or the dead whale. Or his leg playing up. But his parents sitting him down, one morning, to break the news that he was to go and live with Palmira, in Lisbon, to have an operation on his leg. Well, his father broke it. The look of blank innocence on his mother's face, though first to promote it to her sister, she might never have heard of the plan.

'Else you won't be able to walk at all soon,' João said. 'You'll be bedridden. A complete invalid.'

'João!' Rosa gave him a sharp nudge.

'What?' João said, bewildered. 'It's true.'

Antonio wasn't entirely surprised. At his last check-up the doctor had repeatedly asked him if his leg hurt, all the while prodding and twisting it in various directions, then sent him from the room so he could talk to his parents alone. He knew something must be out of the ordinary. But an operation? And Lisbon?

João, more than a little sheepish, revealed that not only had Palmira insisted on paying for the procedure and secured the services of a top-notch Lisbon specialist, but had enrolled him in a school close to where she lived so he wouldn't fall behind with his schoolwork.

'A first-rate establishment, from what I've heard,' João cleared his throat to add. 'Wouldn't be surprised if there weren't other lads there from the islands. Faial, São Miguel …' he trailed off. His mother took out a handkerchief and blew her nose.

It was at that moment that Antonio remembered Margarida. Though naturally eager to share the news, he was also a bit anxious. More than a bit. It might have been a whole lot easier, he thought, if it were Porto or Coimbra and not Lisbon. Lisbon was her special place. And had been since her father, in Lisbon on business, sent her a postcard of the city's new Teatro Nacional Dona Maria II. The moment she saw it, she vowed one day not just to perform there but to know everything there was to know about the great city: its many theatres, restaurants, tea-rooms, supper clubs, impressive buildings, the astonishing Tower of Belém. He supposed he could offer to climb it for her. Only to recall he could barely climb a step. All the same, he couldn't help but be thrilled at the prospect of such an adventure.

Not that he felt so thrilled or adventurous trying to ignore the throbbing of his leg in bed that night. Lisbon wouldn't be half as much fun without Margarida, he thought, suddenly sunk in gloom. The operation and its after-effects were bound to be painful. He wondered if he should ask her to wait for him. She was almost fourteen. In the Middle Ages, they'd probably already be married by now. She was sure to start looking at boys soon. And they at her. Probably already had, she was so pretty. Even when she scowled. Which she did quite a lot when he came to think about it. At least she liked his brains. She was always asking him to look up things in Palmira's books, not that there was much in them about the theatre. Strange, he thought, how everyone thought her vain when she hardly ever looked in the glass and always talked with her mouth full. You had to show off on stage, he reasoned. You couldn't just stand there, mouth agape. She was a paradox, he decided then; he'd just come across the word in Palmira's dictionary. She felt most invisible when the centre of attention. She'd always wanted to act, she'd once told him: talk with someone else's voice, think with someone else's brain. He'd got goosebumps; it had sounded like she was possessed. Though it wasn't really very different to how he felt reading a good book, when he wouldn't have noticed or cared if he had no legs.

*

The week he was to leave, João shepherded him into the front room as if he was one of the goats and gave him a lecture. It seemed that he had to be on his best behaviour in Lisbon. Not leave his clothes on the floor. Help clear the table and with the washing-up. Work hard at school. Be quiet and respectful because his Aunt Palmira wasn't used to having young people around. Antonio was crestfallen. Did his father really believe he did such things?

Though fully aware that João was worried about him, he found it surprisingly hard to shrug off his stern admonitions. Small wonder, he thought, as his father continued to enumerate his many potential offences, that Marcelinho was always reluctant to tell him he'd lost yet another of his hats, blown off on the boat. What did he think, João would bellow, they grew on trees? Antonio supposed, only half listening, that he also kept things from his parents. Though, offhand, he couldn't think what. It wasn't as if, with a limp, he could sneak around. He always tried to tell the truth. Despite Margarida, who said everyone told lies. That you could always tell, the way they kept adding superfluous (another new word) detail to the story; like bad acting.

Fortunately, his mother appeared that moment to advise him not to listen to a word his father was saying, but only to remember to keep a clean handkerchief in his pocket at all times, to say please and thank you, and say his prayers at night. He supposed he'd got off pretty lightly.

*

He had some trouble falling asleep the night before he left. He tried counting all the different sorts of whales, then porpoises, dolphins, manta rays, octopuses, sea snails. The ocean was full of strange creatures. If only he knew more, he thought; could remember more. Then wondered if the brain ever got full up. And what happened if it did. Then started fretting about the fuzz that had begun to sprout on his upper lip, and the hairs under his arms, pale orange straggly ones, as if he was turning into an orang-outang. Marcelinho said it happened to everyone, had happened to him, though Antonio couldn't ever recall his brother having orange hair. Besides, if you were six feet tall and built like Marcelinho, it probably didn't matter what colour your hair was.

Almost the best thing about Pico, he thought, was that you could see whales whenever you liked. Not that it was exactly fun, seeing them on the dock torn apart by hooks; the blood and blubber never failed to make him queasy. It was almost impossible to believe that he used to throw stones at their huge dead bodies as they waited on the dock to be flensed, aiming for the blowhole. And been thrilled whenever Marcelinho killed one. How astonishing, he thought sleepily, to be able to dive deep; to survive hundreds, perhaps a thousand feet under the sea. To live in a world where fish swam in clouds and giant squid moved like giant waves. But even if there weren't any whales in Lisbon, he thought before falling asleep, there were bound to be more books about them.

The Aunt

Books? Antonio had never seen so many as in the Aunt's apartment. They were everywhere, in every room, on every wall, arranged in neat rows in tall, elegant glass-fronted bookcases and cabinets that stretched from floor to ceiling. Piled higgledy-piggledy on every table and chair, stacked in precarious towers either side of the imposing chesterfield sofa; even, he was soon to discover, nestled in a little pile in the water closet.

Not that he had a lot of time to make their acquaintance that first night, it being extremely late by the time he arrived at the apartment. A warm, moonless Lisbon summer night, ripe with the smell of roasting meat, horse dung and the instantly haunting perfume of some unfamiliar plant in bloom.

Opening the front door, a beaming Aunt immediately pulled Antonio to her not inconsiderable bosom in a warm embrace. Mr P, close friend and colleague of the late Tomás, charged with collecting him from the port, receiving, in turn, a resounding kiss on both cheeks. Immediately upon which Palmira led the way down a hallway to a central room, pausing only to give Antonio an encouraging pat, as one might a dog. Almost overwhelmed by the presence of so many books (though conscious to keep himself from gaping), Antonio stood gazing around as Palmira and Mr P exchanged pleasantries, with the occasional discreet glance in his direction. Shortly after which, making his farewells, the obliging Mr P went out into the night.

Almost the moment the door closed, the Aunt, taking him by the arm, steered Antonio over to a table on one side of the room, where a substantial supper had been laid in a space conspicuously cleared of books. Seasick for much of the voyage and now finding himself ravenous, he ate everything he was offered, much to Palmira's obvious satisfaction. Soon after which, shepherded down another hallway to a room where a bed lay waiting for him, he turned in for the night. But it was some time before he fell asleep, head full of unfamiliar sights and sounds, snatches of half-remembered conversations, the room lurching and plunging almost as much as a ship.

Poking her head around the door to find him still awake, though cautioned by any number of friends and acquaintances against spoiling the boy, Palmira immediately went in. Spoil? The boy could hardly haul himself into bed.

'Can't sleep?' She twitched an invisible wrinkle from the counterpane. 'I'm not surprised. Do you still like to read?' she added. 'You used to, all the time.'

He nodded vigorously. 'I still do.'

'That's why I sent you the books,' she said with satisfaction. 'You liked them?'

'Oh, yes. Thank you.' Perhaps his father's words had sunk in, because he was suddenly very conscious of appearing well mannered. Had he ever thanked the Aunt? No. He presumed his mother would have on his behalf. Realising that now he would have to do his own thanking, he added, 'It was very kind of you, Aunt Palmira. I very much liked the books. Particularly the one about whales.'

'Cetaceans.'

'Yes.' He smiled eagerly, pleased to discover he'd got the pronunciation right. He hadn't wanted to practise on the Aunt.

'*The Mysterious World of Cetaceans*,' he said.

'An old favourite.' Palmira smiled. 'So, you like whales?'

'Very much. I really like the illustrations …'

'Ah.' Palmira looked pleased. 'I thought as much.'

He looked at her enquiringly.

'Your Uncle Luis liked that book. He used to read it all the time when he was your age. It's one of the few that didn't belong to Tomás.'

Antonio beamed. He was unsure why, but it made him happy to think of his uncle reading the book before him. He hadn't ever thought of anyone else reading it. It seemed to have arrived fully formed, yet untouched. But of course, books were read by lots of people. Probably dozens, even hundreds. And each held it the same way, or differently, read it slowly, or fast, dreamed as he sometimes did about what it contained.

He said as much to Palmira, surprised when she instantly responded with 'It's almost as if we should recognise them, if we bumped into them in the street. That something about a book should leave a little mark on a person. I suppose it does.'

'Perhaps we might have stamps,' Antonio said eagerly, 'on our hands.' He realised that moment that Palmira wasn't at all as he'd expected. He'd hardly noticed her, to tell the truth, when she'd come to visit on Pico. Only that she was small and round and appeared to bounce a little when she walked. If asked, he would have said that her eyes were brown. When they were green, pale green, and quite sharp, as if they might peck at him if they didn't like what they found. He hoped, suddenly, that she would like what she found in him.

'Would you like a book to read now? I still have a few left.' She smiled. 'A few rooms full. Your Uncle Tomás never ate a meal without a book beside his plate. Or on it. Even at breakfast. I would have thought him ill, if he hadn't.' Then stopped, with a sad little smile. 'But it's late. You should go to sleep. You've had a long day, a long journey.' She sounded slightly unsure, so Antonio assured her he wasn't in the least tired and would love to have a book to read.

'Oh, but now I must think of one,' she murmured, leaving his room. 'It's quite a responsibility.'

When she returned some little while later with a copy of *Treasure Island*, he was sound asleep, hands laid neatly on the coverlet.

Looking down at him, Palmira was surprised by a sudden intense pang of what might only be described as joy.

So, he's come back, she thought, laying the book gently on the bedside table. After all this time. 'Luis,' she murmured almost soundlessly, and with one last faintly indulgent glance at her sleeping nephew, straightened the covers, snuffed out the lamp and went out.

The Western Isles

If anyone in Lisbon had thought to ask Antonio where he came from, he would have said that home was the small volcanic island of Pico, a thousand miles distant, one of the nine islands to make up the archipelago of the Azores, or Western Isles. Intent on filling out the picture, he might well have added that on a summer's day the sea was so darkly blue it appeared almost black. That the volcanic bricks, of which their house and most others were made, were seemingly blacker still, especially set against their front door which was painted a brilliant scarlet. And wherever you went on the island, he might have elaborated, you could see the sea: gently cupping it when the day was calm, and grabbing and shaking it when the great Atlantic storms blew up. Bouncing it, almost as he did his baby cousin, Filipe, holding his hands and pretending to lift him into the air, but careful not to take him entirely off the floor. Nothing like the city's River Tagus, he might have added—subdued by the presence of ships, trams, buildings. Not to mention the thousands upon thousands of living, breathing beings who broke over him each morning in a consuming wave the moment he stepped out the door. Not that anyone ever did think to ask. Perhaps because, in the great bustling cosmopolitan seaport that was Lisbon, almost everyone came from someplace else.

His Aunt's apartment, on the first floor of a large, ornate building, one of a small number of such buildings fortunate enough to have survived the Great Earthquake, was itself somewhat large and ornate. A pair of handsome oversized French doors gave off the main room onto a balcony with sweeping views of the square. Standing there any length of time, you couldn't help but witness some small drama unfold, Antonio thought. As on that first morning when he'd seen a delivery boy unseated from his bicycle by a pack of yapping dogs in pursuit of a cat. Which hapless creature, taking refuge in a nearby tree, found itself, as if to add insult to injury, instantly subjected to a barrage of denunciation from a group of elderly women seated in the shade, fanning themselves against the heat.

In summer a whole forest wouldn't have been defence against that heat. Palmira felt it badly. She grew pink in the face, and sometimes a little fidgety and impatient. Positioning her chair close to the window in the late afternoon, shutters fast, she would work at her tapestry, even though she complained that the wool made her hot. She was very glad to have someone to complain to. And made something of a joke of it, as she had no desire to trouble a boy with more than enough troubles of his own. 'I feel hotter than a hamster,' she would exclaim, puffing out her cheeks and blowing out exasperated air. It seemed that as a child she'd had one for a pet. Discovering a picture of a hamster in one of the Uncle's books, Antonio thought the resemblance marked. 'I might as well put on all my furs,' she would say, rolling her eyes, 'and be done with it. Will it never end?'

She said much the same, Antonio would later come to realise, in autumn and winter, of the cold and rain. It seemed she felt the weather more than most, forever poking her head out of the drapes to see if it was about to rain, the sun go in or come out, the wind alter direction. A supply of umbrellas, coats, boots, gloves, hats was kept in a cupboard in the hallway, ready for any eventuality. Antonio wondered how she'd managed, travelling with the Uncle on his many scientific missions to exotic lands. He would have liked to ask, but had quickly grown chary of too often mentioning the Uncle, as Palmira would sometimes fall silent or even, glancing away, dab at her eyes with one of Tomás's voluminous handkerchiefs.

Having had very little to do with one another over the years, there was at first a respectful, comfortable distance between the two. Though they talked of shared relatives more frankly, perhaps, than was usual, as one might of neighbours, friends, acquaintances. Soon, with only a modicum of shared history and an abundance of goodwill on either part, they were fast friends.

*

The Aunt's apartment had a smell all its own, sweet and spicy as plum pudding, with just the merest tinge of wet dog: all of its many threadbare rugs, Antonio was later to discover, having been cleaned in honour of his arrival. If it had appeared almost fantastical that first night—glittering with chandeliers, gleaming with polished antiques, rich with brocaded drapes—by light of day, if somewhat less impressive, it still had a considerable lived-in charm. The brocade curtains had suffered moths, the parquet flooring was badly scuffed, tracks were worn between the many bookcases so you could tell at a glance Uncle Tomás's favourite books. The chandelier was missing glass, the ornate ceilings peeling, the dining room table, of ebony, sported watermarks, the Uncle in the habit of nursing a glass of port or madeira while working late at night. The red plush seats of the black-lacquered dining chairs, which afforded the room a vaguely Oriental feel, were in want of buttons: Antonio liked to sit on one, of an afternoon, to do his homework, reminded of the front door on Pico. On the sideboard, also of ebony, stood an assortment of carved animals—elephant, water buffalo, lion, a trio of camels—acquired on the Aunt and Uncle's many varied travels, along with an impressive arrangement of flowers. Lilies that first night and afterwards flowers of every kind, Palmira having something of a passion for them. Not just for their beauty and perfume, but because they so ably evoked the changing seasons: signalling that winter was almost at an end and spring soon to arrive; that summer, with its many torments for the Aunt, was mercifully drawing to a close, as autumn arrived to spread its cooling mantle over the heat-crazed city.

The Uncle

As predicted by Margarida, Antonio fell in love with Lisbon. Far from overawed by the vast, bustling, salt-laden city, he felt quite at home in it. Perhaps because they'd so often talked of its many enchantments. Or because the buildings, some almost as tall as the cliffs of Pico, turned the same amber-gold each afternoon; or simply because the incessant hum of human activity might so easily be mistaken for that of breaking waves.

That first morning, Palmira escorted him to a tailor's shop off the main square to be measured for a school uniform. Taking delivery of it some days later, he was thrilled to discover the trousers so expertly cut as to disguise, almost wholly, his disfigured leg, and the straw hat so finely woven he knew even Marcelinho would have been at pains not to lose it.

Starting school the following week, he took his cue from the other boys, knotting his tie in a vaguely cavalier fashion, perching his hat at a jaunty angle. Each morning as they left the apartment Palmira would reach to straighten it, Antonio readjusting it the moment he clambered aboard the tram. At which defiance they would exchange small gleeful smiles.

*

He'd had some practice, on Pico, at fitting in. So he knew to be helpful in class, obedient but not obsequious, willing and able to take a joke at his own expense, to pass the odd illicit note under a desk. Unable to join in games, he volunteered his services in the library, and though never having played before signed up for the chess club. Palmira taught him his first moves with Uncle Tomás's chess set, ivory pieces so finely carved he knew even his father would have been impressed. The biggest help, to his surprise, turned out to be Uncle Tomás himself—his reputation such that his teachers were in awe of him as were some of his fellow students.

He wrote to Margarida with all his news. Once, twice, then a third and final missive, in case the others had gone astray. Not that he thought for a moment that they had. But that he'd waxed far too lyrical about delectable custard tarts, fascinating books, thrilling chess tournaments and thought-provoking plays by Aristophanes, and never once thought to ask what play she was rehearsing or if Chuchu had finally caught another mouse. Though disappointed to receive no reply, he made up his mind not to take it too much to heart. After all, he reasoned, he'd be home soon enough, and able to relay for himself how the São Jorge Castle overlooking the city turned pink, blue, green, orange each evening, before becoming black and forbidding—no bad thing, to his mind, for a fort. Or how, propped at the window to watch the crowds sweep past on their way to the theatres and music halls—accompanied by the mouth-watering smells of roasting meat, the noisy clatter of glass and plate, the screech of chairs drawn back on cobblestones, and the hurdy-gurdy music of the organ grinder rising and soaring over all like birds—he never once failed to think of her.

*

Palmira thought about him from the moment she opened her eyes each morning. She sometimes wondered what she'd thought about, before him. She could spend a good half hour fussing over the afternoon tea-tray, arranging cakes temptingly on the stand. He seldom ate more than one, two at the most. She never nagged him to. Not for the first time, she thought it a blessing that she and Tomás had never managed to conceive a child. She would have made a terrible mother, she knew: having to fuss with nonsense, do and say what was expected, pretend to know everything there was to know. She'd made up her mind, from the start, not to even attempt to act the parent, but only be his friend; enjoy his company, for as long as she was blessed to receive it and ask nothing in return. And would she have done that as a mother? What she'd seen of mothers, and fathers, too, they asked the world of their children, with no idea they'd already been given it. Antonio had shown her the Praça do Rossio anew that first night, a square she hadn't properly seen in over two years. It had leaped to life. And herself, it seemed, with it.

As the Lisbon heat intensified, they acquired what quickly became the habit, in the late afternoons, of joining the ranks of the nursemaids lined up on the benches nearest the fountain in the square, where the air always seemed a little cooler. Invariably, one of the infant charges, tested beyond endurance, would attempt to scale the fountain wall, nanny in pursuit. Whatever the weather, the square was always filled with people: many, like themselves, inhabitants of the apartments that overlooked it; others for whom it seemed a second home—patrons at tables spilling out of cafes, pamphleteers, artists, speechmakers, agitators, students from the university. A good half, so it seemed to Antonio, taught by the Uncle. They'd barely be settled, some days, before some young man would suddenly appear to doff a hat, offer a bow, enquire as to Palmira's health, while she, beaming, would demand to know if he was studying hard. She liked people to study hard.

Afterwards, she would glance at the sky. Much as she did, at home, at the ceiling. As if the Uncle were up there. Antonio had been taken aback on first seeing his portrait, formerly in his rooms at the university, now in pride of place above the mantel in Palmira's room, to discover a small amiable-looking man with thinning hair. When, to hear Palmira, he might have been the handsomest, tallest, most imposing man in the whole of Lisbon. Though it was hard not to concede that, given his own glowing account of Margarida, Palmira might not have been equally surprised to see her in the flesh.

*

Secretly, both were relieved when the operation, scheduled for soon after his arrival, was delayed due to a shortage of hospital beds, the result of an unseasonal epidemic of influenza. In modest celebration, Palmira treated them to lemonade and *pastéis de nata* at one of Lisbon's finest pastelarias. Increasingly, she had come to dread Antonio's surgery. Almost nightly, in her dreams, limbs came loose, and a boy passed across her vision like a whale across the horizon. One night she even dreamed she was a lookout in one of the *vigias* on Pico, endlessly scanning the sea for whales, only to wake to find her arm crushed and bloodless under her own weight. And on the ceiling, Tomás's pale skeletal face, his hair fallen out, bald and fragile as an egg. When a vital piece of equipment failed only days before the procedure was once more to go ahead, Palmira bought them tickets to a performance of *Titus Andronicus*. When the surgeon tripped and broke a wrist, they profited from a slap-up dinner. But when a replacement surgeon was found, Palmira was filled anew with dread that she would lose him. Just as she had Luis. And Tomás. On the eve of the rescheduled operation, pacing the apartment and finding herself in Antonio's room, Palmira sank gratefully onto the bed. Only, with an upward glance, to find herself come face to face with the looming presence of the great fort. Had he ever seen these four walls as his prison, she wondered, then. Longed for Pico? He'd never seemed unhappy. Or herself heart-broken, she supposed. She sent up a prayer, to Tomás. She wasn't alone, she knew, in watching over the boy.

Perhaps she was right. The operation, a fraught and complex procedure involving an incision to the Achilles tendon, was deemed by surgeons past, putative and present a triumph. Having already imagined every possible complication, Palmira found herself immensely grateful for the superficiality of Antonio's immediate post-operative effects: a slightly elevated temperature, a minor inflammation of the stitches, a small abscess where the bandages had chafed.

In no time at all, it seemed, he was home. Yet it was a long, painful road to full recovery, and some months in a cast before he took his first step, his leg encased in an iron brace, as it would always be henceforward.

Palmira hardly left his side those first weeks: sitting up with him at night, stroking the hair back from his forehead, squeezing his hand as if to squeeze out the pain itself. She read to him for hours, so grateful to see him distracted she hardly noticed her aching back and eyes. The pain turned his eyes so black she was reminded of the pebbles on the shore at Pico, washed by the sea. How they threw those pebbles! They were always throwing things. The boys, as if instinctively practising for the hunt; it seemed in their very bones to want to hit something. But she'd just liked the way the sea gathered them up, the little sucking noise they gave before they sank. Everyone thought her hopeless at pebbles, Palmira recalled, but she'd never wanted to skim them, only hear them fall. A misapprehension, Tomás would have said. He'd thought her capable of anything, pebbles the least of it. Many a night, the boy's eyes fixed on hers as she read, she would sense him: just down the hallway, book propped before him at the table, glass of madeira at hand.

*

As Antonio soon came to realise, Palmira not only knew how to pronounce 'cetacean', she knew more about whales than anyone he'd ever met. Over the years, she'd been involved in every aspect of her husband's work. There was nothing she'd liked better than to hear his insistent cry: 'Come, Palmira! Come and see! Come and look, my love!' She'd witnessed his work unfolding. The way one thing connected to another in a little chain, like the ones she used to make from daisies as a child. The first time she looked under a microscope, Tomás's hand steadying her own, she'd shaken so much that the colours and patterns had jumped in and out of focus. She'd hardly looked at a thing since without wondering how it might appear magnified, its hidden self revealed. More than anything, she'd loved the celebratory dance that had come to mark Tomás's many discoveries, revelations, milestones, small and large. Seizing her in his arms, he would swing her around the room, avoiding tables and chairs, in a wild, pagan, see-sawing dance, entirely lacking in rhythm. An intensely private man, he'd been a fiercely romantic one. Showing Antonio the small piece of whalebone she and Tomás had together uncovered on Pico some weeks after they first met, Palmira recalled how, that very night, it had stood in for an engagement ring. And not a jot of false modesty on either part but only delight. Besides, it would have taken a will far stronger than she possessed, Palmira knew, to resist such an ardent lover of women and whales.

*

One night, Antonio asked, 'Am I really like Uncle Luis?'

'Like?' Palmira's eyes widened. 'You've got his eyes. His nose. Why, you even sound like him. If I closed my eyes, I'd say he was right here, in this very room.' She shook her head. 'You know the Egyptians believed in reincarnation? Well, I'm sure I'm at least half Egyptian.'

Antonio grinned. He'd seen pictures of pharaohs with dark kohl-ringed eyes and pink cheeks, like Palmira when she put on rouge, though she swore she'd caught the sun.

Eyes and nose? Soul and heart too, Palmira thought. She took the time, head to one side, to more fully consider the resemblance, but really she was drinking him up. For he had grown more handsome by the day since the abating pain had eased the lines from his forehead and eyes.

'Here, I'll show you.'

She bustled off to the Uncle's study, returning with a small framed likeness of a young man.

'There,' she said, handing it to him. 'Who's that, if not you?'

Antonio scrutinised the drawing. It was hard to believe that someone could be captured on a page for all time. Like that painted whale, he thought. Then felt suddenly sad to think of his

Uncle Luis trapped here and vanished to somewhere else. Perhaps he could one day find him for Palmira, he thought. But he would be old, almost as old as Palmira herself.

'He's very handsome,' he said.

'As are you, my young man,' Palmira said emphatically.

'Why did he leave?' Antonio asked. He wanted to know. And there was some subtle change between them since the operation that allowed the question. One night, coming in to find him soundlessly crying, she had soundlessly squeezed his hand in her own, all the while furiously nodding, her chin jutting. It had occurred to him, that moment, that she had also suffered. Not just with Uncle Tomás, but Uncle Luis. He'd never dared ask before.

'He had to,' she said simply. 'He had no choice.' She nodded to herself, tucking her bottom lip, which had momentarily wobbled, firmly under the top one. The time had come. There would be no lies between them. He was asking with a pure heart. She'd never known a purer. Or perhaps one.

'I'm going to tell you a story. I told it to your Uncle Tomás when we first met, but for a long time he couldn't understand. He grew into it, the way people do. Over time. When certain things happen. Well, here we go. But be warned, I'm no great shakes at telling stories.'

He nodded encouragingly.

'There was a boy, very much like yourself, who lived on the island of Pico. He had two sisters, nine cousins, and any number of uncles and aunts. And he was just like everyone else. There wasn't a thing different about him. He ate the same food, played the same games, studied the same things at school as all the other children. But with one difference. He felt things, felt them as if his skin was on fire.' Palmira paused, as if surprised at her own words. 'Yes,' she said, with growing certainty, 'on fire. Everything hurt that boy,' she went on. 'When the other children laughed to see a dog hurt or lamed, he'd cry. If a cat were caught up a tree and everyone rushing around to find the nearest slingshot, he'd be looking for the nearest ladder.

'The boy's family,' she said, 'hunted whales. Just as they do today. And like your family, mine, they used the oil to keep their lamps lit through the long stormy winter nights, and ate whale meat to feed themselves, and ground the bones fine to feed the vines in the vineyards. The boy felt badly about this. But no-one else did. No-one else seemed to even notice. His friends and sisters played hide-and-seek in the old try pots, marching around with whalebones, pretending they were rifles.' She thought a moment, then suddenly demanded, cheeks grown quite pink with passion, 'But then, what child doesn't feel? Hasn't cried to think of the Christ Child nailed to the cross, blood trickling down from all those thorns? Every child feels.' She subsided, slightly flustered, then went on. 'Of course, everyone became more and more angry as he grew up. Who did he think he was, to feel so much? Did he think he was better than everyone else? Everyone knew about pain and suffering. Just wait, the world would soon teach him a lesson. Everyone ran out of patience with that boy. His mother and father were embarrassed, even his big sister teased him.' And here Palmira gave a tremulous sigh. 'They did everything they could not to understand,' she went on. 'Because deep down they understood only too well. There is a garden of paradise, an Eden, reserved for such as that boy and it has no place on this earth. People must be fed. Children must be read to by the light of whale-oil lamps. How else will they learn?' She paused, staring unseeingly for some moments at Antonio, then seemed to come to herself. 'The boy's parents,' she continued, 'were adamant. The boy must hunt the whale. He must prove himself as flawed, stained, tainted with the misery of the world as every other boy.

'When he was fifteen, he was taken on his first hunt. He killed a whale. Well, helped kill it. He was bent, some might say broken, by the desire of his family that he become one of them. No-one wants to live, day in, day out, faced with their own innocence.'

'What did he do?' Antonio murmured, so stricken, Palmira reached out and took his hand.

'He tried. He did his best. It was something, at least, to be accepted by his family, his relatives. Everyone was pleased with him. They said he was brave. He didn't feel brave,' she added.

'When I first told your Uncle Tomás, he said that he should have faced the realities of his life and hunted the whale. That it was hubris—do you know what that means?' she paused to ask.

Antonio nodded urgently, not wanting her to stop.

'To think he could change another's heart,' Palmira continued. 'Your Uncle Tomás said that no-one killed those whales to torment them; that those whales were there to be killed. Of course, he was young then, a keen scientist, could hardly see the connection between those bones we were picking up all over the place on Pico and the creatures we used to watch from the hills, playing out in the bay. All that came later, took a long time.

'What would you have done, do you think?' Palmira asked after some moments, searching his face. 'Would you have killed the whale?'

Antonio thought long and hard. He thought of his father, who'd also helped kill whales. And Marcelinho. And Ferreira, whose eldest son, Pedro, got caught up in a line and cut almost in two, been laid out on the kitchen table. He remembered peering round his mother's skirts and seeing him there.

'I don't know,' he finally said in a small voice.

Palmira nodded, sucking on her lower lip. 'No. Of course you don't. Of course not. Not yet. Not yet. Give it time,' she murmured, almost to herself. 'Poor Luis,' she went on. 'He held out for as long as he could, a couple of months, then packed what little he had and left. On a whaleship, bound for Boston. The only boat he could find. So that was that. Vanished. And not a word since.'

'Nothing?'

Palmira hesitated. 'No. But I've always had this feeling—'

'That he's still alive?'

She nodded emphatically. 'I saw him once. It wasn't a dream because I wasn't asleep. Here, in Lisbon. I passed by him in the street. I only realised too late. Then I couldn't find him. Not anywhere. Vanished. Again.'

'How did you know it was him?' Antonio said in wonder.

'He said my name. My first name. Inácia. Even my friends here don't know it. Your Uncle Tomás said I was vain and silly, but I always loathed that name. As soon as I came to Lisbon, I took my second name, Palmira.'

Antonio gave a big sigh, as if he'd been holding his breath. 'So you still don't know for sure.'

Palmira shook her head. 'No. And probably never will. Now it's time for you to sleep. You'll be having nightmares.'

'No,' Antonio said with certainty, nestling down into the sheets. 'No, I won't.'

*

To help while away her nephew's hours in bed, Palmira shared what she knew of whales, gleaned from her travels with the Uncle, and what she herself had seen, heard, experienced, read, over the years. Antonio wrote everything down—stories, facts, suppositions, myths—in a journal especially bought for him by Palmira. Leather-bound, it was almost as handsome as the whale book. One afternoon, intent on making a fair copy of a whale as a frontispiece, he began to draw one. Tentatively at first, then with some assurance, almost as if his hand knew the shape, his inner eye able to draw on every whale he'd ever seen: in books, on the dock, out in the bay at Pico. He drew a large male sperm whale under which he wrote its scientific name, *Physeter macrocephalus*, in his best script, along with the date. Then called for Palmira to come and see. She came rushing in, inordinately pleased to hear someone urgently calling her to share a discovery, when she'd never thought to experience that again.

'Oh, bravo! Bravo!' she exclaimed, examining the drawing closely. 'Why, you've even got the blow right, a little to the left. We'll make a scientist of you yet. I wish …'

'Uncle Tomás were here?' She nodded. 'Except I think he is.' She glanced at the ceiling. 'In fact, I know it.'

The House of Palms

A lot happened on Pico while Antonio was away.

There were acquisitions. The Ferreiras finally got around to replacing their ill-fated donkey with another, kept permanently tethered. One of the larger whaling outfits in São Roque acquired a second whaleboat.

There was weather: a tropical cyclone, an underwater eruption, a bone-shaking earthquake felt all the way from São Miguel.

There were bountiful rains two years in a row, the oranges almost breaking the branches with their weight, with two bumper vintages to follow.

There was bad luck. Awarded a leading role in a local production of a play by Gil Vicente, Margarida succumbed to the chickenpox—though mercifully was left unmarked.

There were the usual births, deaths, marriages. The usual affairs, peccadillos, romances. Some fruitful, some doomed from the start.

Unaltered: the Carvalhos' annual flurry of preparation for the Festa dos Baleeiros. Rosa sewing late into the night, repairing church banners and flags, as next door, Gonçalves practised the trumpet for the processionary band.

Early on the day of the festival, piling everything into Antonio's old cart, all three Carvalhos set out to deliver the decorations to the church. And had very nearly reached it when Marcelinho was jolted from a reverie of himself taking the helm of the whaleboat as it was blessed, his manly physique on proud display, as João stopped to fish a stone from his shoe directly in front of the House of Palms.

Marcelinho bumped into him.

'Oi! Look where you're going, lad!'

'Sorry, Pa.'

Why did his father have to stop here, of all places? As if he had a sixth sense, Marcelinho thought. And not just for lost hats.

Marcelinho made to walk on, but his mother had also pulled up short. The pair stood shoulder to shoulder, peering up through the palm trees at the shuttered upper windows.

'Just look at the poor thing,' Rosa tutted, pink-faced. 'The paint's hanging off in strips. He's going to have to do something about it, sooner or later. Fix it or sell it. Or give it away,' she added darkly. 'He should give it to the church, for his sins. Think of the hospice it would make, João. What does a murderer want with a great big mansion?'

'He's probably got plans,' João said with a philosophical shrug. 'For later. For when he comes out.'

'Plans,' Rosa snorted. 'The only plan he's going to need is what to say to Saint Peter at the gates. When I think of what he did to that poor woman. Not to mention his *friend*. No-one deserves that, whatever their crime.'

'He's probably got family,' João said after a moment's thought. 'They're hardly going to give the place away. Why, it must be worth a fortune. The vineyards alone must be worth …' He shot Marcelinho an enquiring glance. 'What do you reckon, Marco? Five, six thousand réis?'

Marcelinho shrugged. His father always wanted to know how much things cost. What everything amounted to. Down to the last real. Hats included. Why couldn't he just enjoy himself? He'd be dead soon enough. They all would.

'It's hardly going to be worth a brass button, the way it's going,' Rosa said grimly.

Marcelinho shot it a backward glance, walking on. Rosa was right, he thought. The place was a wreck. At least from the outside. It might have had the pox, the amount of plaster that had fallen off. It used to be the best house on the island. What did a man get for killing a wife? Plus a best friend? Ten, twenty years? Life? Then winced. The calculation was worthy of João.

His parents always said the same things. Year in, year out. Like him and Fredo, he supposed. Whenever they passed the place, Fredo would say it was haunted, to which Marcelinho would reply 'Rubbish!' And then they'd walk on. Well, that's what used to occur.

He'd been looking forward all week to the festival, and a day off. It was hard work, whaling: dirty, dangerous, tedious. Not just the catching of the beast, but cutting it up, boiling it down. It could take days, a really big male sperm whale. He was lucky to still have all his fingers. And the smell. Even here he could seem to smell it. The best part, by far, was the hunt. You never knew how the thing would turn out. If you would catch one, or even two, though that was rare. If you'd come home, all the richer for it. Come home at all. Some whales seemed to want to give up, first lance. Others, especially if they had young, would drag you halfway to Boston, given a chance. He supposed he liked those best. The ones that fought and never gave up; the ones you were sometimes obliged to watch swim away, lost irons glinting in the last of the sun.

It wasn't as if, Marcelinho thought, they had a lot of outings. Unless you called church an outing, which he suspected Rosa would. He wouldn't have minded going to church if they could have the occasional Sunday off. Say once a month, just to catch up on some sleep. Unlike Rosa, he was sure God wouldn't object. He shot a curious glance heavenward, wondering if he'd blasphemed. But there was nothing there, not a cloud.

Glancing back again as they walked on, something caught his eye. A pile of dead palm fronds, neatly stacked against the near wall. Ana? Fredo said you'd think she owned the place, the way she carried on: nagging him to take his boots off, complaining he left fingerprints in her polish. According to Fredo, it was as good as Ana's second home. Marcelinho shot João a glance. He'd be a dead man, he thought gloomily, if his father ever discovered he'd been inside.

*

They used to hang around the place all the time as kids. Peer in at the windows, take a piss against the pink stuccoed walls. Spook themselves, thinking they'd seen someone inside. Her. The murdered one. Looking down from one of the top windows. It wasn't hard to believe when the wind rustled the palm trees, shadows moving in every corner. Fredo was good at ghost stories.

About the only thing he was good at, Marcelinho thought, with a faint grin, before he'd taken up whaling. Their first day at school, he recalled, Fredo had tripped him and sent him sprawling. The size of him, back then, Marcelinho thought, he could have sat on Fredo and squashed him. Instead he'd got up, dusted himself off, walked away. Within days, they'd been fast friends. Though he still sometimes had occasion to wonder why. It wasn't as if

Fredo had a lot going for him but bluster and charm. The girls certainly seemed to fall for it; hardly seemed to notice his arms were too long, his eyes set too close together. They'd called him the little monkey at school.

They'd been almost as bad as each other for bookwork, Marcelinho remembered ruefully. Fredo said words were worse than fish for jumping on the page. It had been a real torment, stuck in that classroom summer-long, waves just about breaking through the window. Little wonder they'd got up to mischief; tied Ferreira's old donkey's legs together more than once, not that it had complained. He'd never known beast or man more stoic, unless perhaps Fredo. On the boat, nothing could throw him off balance: ten-foot waves, forty-foot sperm whales—he could pepper them with one hand. It was only when they'd started working together on the boat that he'd finally understood why Fredo was so reluctant to take his shirt off. Not just that he was a skinny runt; he had scars all the way down his back to his bum. His old man had never been one to spare the rod. Unlike João. Funny, Marcelinho thought now, how he sometimes used to envy his friend, his punishment over and done with in one fell swoop. Or half a dozen. When he sometimes complained of his father, Fredo merely said with a shrug that João probably couldn't help but expect too much of him, given he had two good legs.

*

They'd been returning from Santa Cruz-Ribeiras, Marcelinho recalled, having delivered a cow for Fredo's uncle, when they saw that one of the downstairs windows of the House of Palms was ajar.

'You're sure it's empty?' Marcelinho asked, peering in.

'As an oyster shell, my friend.'

Almost before Marcelinho realised what his friend was up to, Fredo had hoisted himself up on the sill. And in an instant he was through. Hearing a shrill whistle moments later, Marcelinho hurried around the front of the house.

Fredo was leaning nonchalantly in the doorway. 'It's unbelievable,' he grinned. 'Like a fucking palace inside. More gold than Sé Cathedral.'

'Fredo …'

But Fredo was already taking the stairs, two at a time.

As soon as he closed the door, Marcelinho smelled polish. Fresh. Lavender, like his mother made.

'Someone's here,' he hissed into the empty stairwell.

Fredo suddenly appeared on the landing. 'That'll be Ana,' he said, with a nonchalant shrug.

'Ana?'

'Girl who cleans. I happened to bump into her the other day when she was closing up. A stunner. Good of her to leave the window open.'

'But I thought you said …'

'Always the worry-wart,' Fredo tut-tutted. Then crooked a finger. 'Come on. Up with you.'

Marcelinho paused halfway up the stairs to run a finger over the papered wall at his side. Like velvet, blood-red, threaded through with what looked like hoops of real gold. He almost cricked his neck trying to make out the pattern in the ceiling high above: flowers, birds, ribbons, gold stars glittering in the sun.

Reappearing on the landing, Fredo draped one of the red velvet curtains that hung on either side over his head, bunching the material under his chin. Then peered down, his eyes beseeching.

'My dearest Marco,' he cooed in falsetto, 'make haste, I beg you. There is nothing here to fear, I swear. Only trust your Fredo. Paradise awaits!'

Marcelinho shook his head, grinned despite himself. Fredo made about as convincing a maid, he thought, as Margarida Machado had a lad in the school play. Tripped over her cloak, all her hair, tucked under a cap, falling down.

Catching up to Fredo, he peered into a large room with an enormous carved four-poster bed hung with red velvet drapes. The cloth so thick Marcelinho knew that whoever slept there wouldn't hear a peep out of the dawn chorus of birds, nor one clamorous note of the bell tolling early morning mass.

Fredo threw himself onto the bed, luxuriantly stretching out all four limbs.

'Like a cloud,' he sighed in bliss.

Clouds

There were clouds on Margarida Machado's horizon that same year Fredo and Marcelinho discovered the House of Palms. Examining her face in the glass, chewing viciously on her lip, she wondered, as usual, what was happening to her. First blood, then hips, breasts, hair in the most unlikely places. No choice. No-one thinking to ask if she even wanted breasts. Which, for the record, she didn't. Not just that you had to bind them up to play a boy or that they made your frocks poke out, but men stared at them and not just on stage.

And now tears. She'd always been able to make herself cry. Only need think of her father incinerated by lava, or Antonio falling off a cliff like Ferreira's old donkey, to be in floods. Now, it seemed, only the thought of Chuchuzina torn apart by Gonçalves's dog worked. And so well, she immediately felt compelled to drag the cat out from under the bed where she was sleeping and hug her, inhaling warm fur. And dust. Rubbing her cheek against her pet's tawny softness, it suddenly came to her that Chuchu would one day die. That she would one day be unable to hold her, stroke her tummy to make her purr, fall asleep with the cat's small head beside her own on the pillow, paws twitching.

Tears streamed down her cheeks. Nothing lasted. Beauty. Love. Friends. Fur. Nothing.

It had begun innocuously enough. Her nose had begun to turn up. Secretly, she'd been rather fond of her nose. One of her better features: dead straight, slightly patrician. Nothing like her father's, bulbous at the tip. Or her mother's, thin and pinched. But it had tilted a fraction, then more, until now it was almost retroussé. She liked the word, but not the nose anymore. Or the mouth, either. It had lately grown so wide, so vulpine, she had to remember not to smile. And her eyebrows, shapely but querulous. Her cheekbones, high and haughty. The tools of her trade overnight grown unfamiliar, uncertain. Then, one morning, a small indentation in her chin. 'Dear God,' she prayed, and she hardly ever prayed, 'not a dimple.' Who in the wide world was ever going to entrust the role of Medea to a dimple?

Hearing her father in his study, she knocked and went in without thinking.

Dom Ricardo was stuffing papers into the top drawer of his desk, as if she didn't know he kept a stash of dirty pictures hidden there.

'Papa,' she demanded, 'how do I look to you? Do I look different?'

'Different?' His eyes darted anxiously around the room.

But she had no time, today, for pity.

'Tell me. The truth.'

He considered the ceiling, then the floor, chewing on his lip. How her father hated the truth.

'Why, my darling, you look absolutely lovely. Lovelier by the day. Why, you look …' He squinted, head to one side, before exclaiming happily, 'Like a princess!'

'Chorus girl, more like,' Margarida returned sourly.

'Chorus girl? Rubbish! Nothing like.' He seemed quite certain. 'More,' he searched, 'like an angel.'

Sighing audibly, she turned and walked out. Poor Papa, she thought. It was hardly his fault that she had a dimple. Or that he could never say the right thing. So that Angelina had to speak for him. Even when people asked after his gout.

*

Seeing Margarida in the street a year later, Marcelinho hardly recognised her. He couldn't put a finger on it, but she looked entirely altered. Taller, thinner, grown-up, the tangle of long brown hair tied neatly in a topknot. The only thing unchanged, that she looked right through him. Then, about to round the corner, she suddenly turned and smiled. Beamed at him. As if she meant it.

He saw her again that same week. She was too far away for him to clearly make out her expression, but she definitely waved. Mistaking him for someone else, he thought. She used to poke her tongue out at him, once. She must be, what, fifteen, sixteen?

It was some time before he saw her again. But he thought about her. All the time, at first. Wondering what she was up to, whether she was on Pico, Faial, São Jorge, visiting relatives or rehearsing some new play. She'd always been around as a kid. As if she didn't have a home to go to, Rosa said. Not that Marcelinho's mother had seemed to mind, fiddling with the girl's hair, tying it in ribbons, plaiting it in braids. Margarida hadn't seemed to much mind either. It wasn't as if Antonio had a lot of friends. Any besides Margarida, come to that. Not that he was disliked, but he couldn't play hide-and-seek, or kick a ball, or ride Ferreira's donkey backwards. Besides, he was smart. Smarter than everyone.

Even before the books. But Marcelinho preferred not to think about the books.

Even when Antonio did bring someone home, it was mostly to do their homework together. Not that they got a lot of peace, Rosa popping her head around the door every five minutes to ask if they were hungry, thirsty, wanted to stay for supper. Stuffing them with bread, cakes, oranges. Margarida never went home without a ribbon, fig, comb of honey in hand. As if she were a waif. When the Machados had so many houses, vineyards, cows, they might have given half away and barely noticed.

The Key

When Fredo sweet-talked Ana into revealing the secret hiding place of the key to the House of Palms, Marcelinho was first to borrow it. He hadn't forgotten the cloud bed. Or the promise he'd made himself to one day fall asleep in it. Sink into that cloud mattress and let sleep take him. He hadn't planned to lie, for what seemed like hours, staring up at a plaster bird on the ceiling with long legs and a slender neck. A Margarida bird. At wit's end, he finally allowed himself to think about her, but only from the neck up. Which immediately made him think of her breasts, his hand sliding under the cool silky coverlet and into his pants. He had to use one of Ana's dusters, afterwards, to clean himself up. Mere minutes later he started thinking about Margarida's ankles. Which led to her legs. He wouldn't have slept a wink but that he was thoroughly worn out.

The moment he opened his eyes, she was there, gazing down at him, wings outstretched. Margarida.

He asked Fredo, no slouch with girls, for advice.

'Ask if she wants to see the house. They're all desperate to see it. Trust me. You can stay as long as you like. All night if you want.' He winked.

*

Marcelinho went to the house a little early, to prepare things. Fredo had suggested a simple supper: bread, cheese, wine, a few candles. Marcelinho set one end of the big dining-room table for two, placed two candles on the table, before, inspired, placing a few small white flowers found growing near the front door between them. Flowers or weeds? Decided against it. Too obvious. As if he were trying to seduce her. Which he wasn't. Or was he? The only thing he knew for sure was that he was sweating badly. It wasn't as if he had a lot of experience. He'd only done it twice, most recently with a friend of Fredo's second cousin, visiting from São Jorge. Lara? Laura?

Margarida had jumped at the chance.

'I've always wanted to see inside,' she said on arrival. 'My parents used to come here all the time. They used to hold dances, balls here. Plays, even. My mother said the murdered woman sometimes used to act in them. That she was like a little doll, fair, with china-blue eyes. No wonder her husband's friend couldn't keep his hands off her.'

'Some friend,' Marcelinho said witheringly.

'You'd trust Fredo with your wife?' She gathered up some loose strands of hair, tucked them into her topknot. He felt himself colour, suddenly remembering her pushing Antonio down the hill, her hair streaming out behind her, utterly fearless.

He pulled out a chair for her.

She sat, chin propped on a hand, studying him.

'Wine?' he asked.

She nodded.

'You look different,' she said, watching him pour. He had some trouble keeping his hand steady. 'Your hair's different. Curlier.'

He ran his hand through it, shrugged. Then, realising something was required, 'Yours is ...'

'Still a mess,' she supplied. 'At least I can put it up now.'

She noticed the muscles in his arms. He never used to have muscles. Or a dusting of black hair on his forearms. Or chest, peeping out from his white shirt.

'You look fit,' she said.

'All the rowing,' he said diffidently, but pleased.

'Not to say harpooning,' she said darkly. 'Poor creatures.'

'Brutes,' he corrected.

'Because they fight? Because they want to live?'

'You don't know what they're like.'

She cast a sceptical glance over her glass.

'Antonio and I used to try to think up spells,' she said. 'So you wouldn't catch one.'

'Obviously didn't work,' he said, a little sourly. They were both silent then. She'd never liked him, he thought. Only his brother. 'It's not just the hunt,' he tried. 'It's afterwards. All of us together at the table. The stories.'

'My father used to tell me some.'

'Dom Ricardo went whaling?'

'When he was young. I don't imagine he ever caught one.'

Marcelinho grinned.

She'd always liked his smile. He'd always had beautiful teeth. Rosa's teeth. He and Antonio were both quick to smile; you could tell they were brothers. She remembered seeing them together in the street once when Antonio had fallen over. Or been tripped; he was an easy target. Marcelinho had helped him to his feet, dusted him off, smoothed back his hair. Like Rosa. Most boys would have laughed.

She supposed Antonio would have changed too. She missed him after he went to Lisbon. Missed? Her heart actually hurt. Just as when she'd sprained her thumb and hadn't been able to sleep for it throbbing. Her father had sat with her one night, she remembered, crooned some song he used to sing when she was little. Then made one up, about a thumb that ached because it had lost its other thumb. She'd loved her father for that. It had seemed a whole lot easier to overlook his lame jokes and the way he never stood up to her mother. At least Antonio hadn't gone to America like his Uncle Luis. What if he never came back? If she never got the chance to tell him what she thought of his stupid letters? He hadn't mentioned Chuchu once. He knew how much she meant to her.

*

After supper they danced, without music, by candlelight. At her suggestion. Everyone, in the old days, she assured him, used to dance after supper. Then suddenly she thought of Antonio. Of how, with his foot, he would never dance, not with her, not with anyone. Some faint consolation, she supposed, that women weren't dancing with him in Lisbon right now.

After a while, Marcelinho began to hum under his breath, to fill the silence. Then, remembering an old love song João sometimes sang to his mother, tried out a few lines on her, words muffled in her hair. She pulled away momentarily to look up and smile.

He pulled her back. So close, he could feel the ribs under her dress.

He had some trouble getting the pressure right: too hard, too soft, too low, too high, too close to the nape of her neck with the faint down of dark gold hair. She kept trying to lead. She took his hand, fitting it more closely to her waist. He pulled away, feeling a stirring in his pants. She pulled him back. Not a clue, he thought, about men. Never having had a brother, but for Antonio. As good as a brother, wasn't he? Brother? Who was he kidding? Sweetheart. Made for each other, Rosa said. Peas from the same pod, grapes from the same vine. He'd been mad to ask her here tonight. To ask Fredo for advice.

He kissed her. He didn't mean to, didn't even really want to. He just couldn't bear the tension. Their teeth met with a little clatter. She pulled away sharply. He started to apologise, but she shook her head, hand to her mouth.

'I've bitten my tongue.'

He examined it, as if about to pull teeth, by the light of a candle. Romantic? He peered into her mouth like a horse doctor. There was a little drop of blood on her bottom lip. He didn't know what possessed him, but he licked it. She pulled away in shock, then laughed.

'You're going to eat me now?'

He looked at her, bewildered, then pulled her to him, and kissed her again, parting her lips with his tongue. 'Ouch,' she said, but softly. There was something musky and dream-like in her mouth, and with his eyes closed he felt like he was on the boat at night, with the water black all around him and the thrill of being far from land, nothing but sea.

*

He showed her the house.

Mounting the stairs, she paused to examine the velvety wallpaper, running a finger over it. 'Like Chuchu,' she murmured.

She walked from room to room, gazing at paintings, tracing

a finger over carved gilt frames, ignoring beds. In the main bedroom she abruptly sat down at the dressing table, taking a penetrating critical look at herself in the glass. He walked over and stood behind her. Their eyes met in the mirror. She reached up, touched his image, traced the hair where it fell into his eyes. Taking his hand, she smoothed it over the thick plaited mass of her own piled-up hair, then drew it down to the nape of her neck. He bent, laid his lips there. Strange that he knew what to do. Like being in the boat the first time. As soon as he'd felt the smoothness of the wood, stroked it, felt the boat stir beneath him, whispering to him at every stroke, he'd been possessed by someone other than himself. Not clumsy. Not wordless.

Nothing more happened. Not that first time. Or the next. Or the one after. A few kisses, another dance, more kisses, then home. Home to bed, savouring every detail. Like watching a play unfold, Margarida thought. Hardly able to wait for the next act.

*

The fourth occasion, it was late afternoon: sun slanting through a crack in the curtains, picking up coloured threads in the carpet. He unpinned her hair, placing the pins on the dressing table, as precisely as harpoons in the rack. Then, picking up a handful of hair, wondering at its unruly softness, bunched it in his fist, kissed it.

She walked over to the bed, sat down on the edge. She began to tease out the knotted strands of her hair as he watched, leaned closer to her. Then bent and ran his tongue from the base of her throat to her chin. Smoothed a hand over the bodice of her dress, moulding it, taking his time. Like running a hand over the boat, silky, not a nick of a splinter.

The sun went behind a cloud. She remembered a sudden plunge into gloom. And that she helped with buttons, eased folds of material aside, petticoats, pulling the bunched material from beneath her, not to crush it. He remembered their lying side by side, gazing into each other's eyes. And that when she closed hers the lids were traced with faint, achingly blue veins, so delicate he could have broken them.

Stroking her breasts, he heard her breath catch. They were hardly bigger than a man's, dark-nippled, muscled. He could see the webbing between her ribs. Like the spars of the boat. The length of her thighs hardly less than his own, oddly boyish, oddly arousing.

She was impenetrable, however he tried to push inside her. Gently at first, then determinedly, then grimly. With the momentary thought of a tale Antonio had once told him of a wooden horse, used to breach the defences of a great city. She did what she could to help, frowning, applying herself to the task. She tried to open herself wider, to let her thighs loll. Then flinched when he ran the tip of his tongue over an eyebrow, as if he'd crossed some invisible line. Moments later, she felt something warm spurt inside her. Then he was still. So still, her heart turned right over. Could he have died? Was she to be found, crushed beneath him, thighs lolling like a frog's? With all her strength, she pushed him from her. He rolled away, looking hurt. She smiled then, in faint apology, pulling down petticoats, buttoning up buttons, wondering if the murdered woman had also immediately regretted her actions. If, caught on the stairs by her husband, knife at her heart, she'd wished with every fibre of her being that she could undo what she had done. And he? Covered in her blood? She flushed, seeing the little smudge of pinkish stain on the coverlet.

Truth

There was no-one to tell. She and Antonio used to tell each other everything. It's how she knew that Marcelinho used to sob himself to sleep, some nights, because João was cross with him. That when his brother had suddenly got fat, Antonio had dreamed the same dream, over and over, that Marcelinho was turning into a whale. (And now look at him, she thought, like a picture Antonio once showed her in one of Palmira's books, of David). She'd been privy to Rosa's secret stash of rosary beads, to the knowledge that João only went next door to borrow a tool so he could drink with Gonçalves, that on the rare occasions Rosa and João were out together, Marcelinho asked to see his brother's foot, even gave him a coin, sometimes, to touch it.

Antonio was never afraid of the truth. Asked to read the Lord's Prayer to the whole school, he told her it was only because the teachers felt sorry for him, though perhaps some thought he must have done something terrible to offend God. In another century, he said, he'd probably have been burned at the stake, or had his throat slit like some sacrificial goat. Then he showed her illustrations in one of Palmira's books of people with no arms, six toes, two heads, not that she could have sworn to it, eyes scrinched half-shut.

She used to run all the way home, some days, she felt so bad about his foot. Not that he complained, or felt sorry for himself; unlike her, blubbering if she so much as stubbed a toe. When she told him about the bullfight on Terceira, which her father had taken her to as a surprise birthday treat, she cried so much she threw up.

*

There was hardly a minute that she didn't fret about falling pregnant. Couldn't seem to torment herself enough, imagining herself with a big, fat, ugly belly, waddling like a duck. Reminded herself, daily, that one of her friends had unhappily had to leave school to get married; that when one of the maids had turned up for work with her belly straining against her dress, Angelina had fired her on the spot.

Even when she skipped a bleeding, and another, when her breasts hurt, pressed against her dress, when she threw up almost the second she opened her eyes, she refused to countenance the truth. Then sat bolt upright in bed one morning and knew. Everything. The when, how, why, where. The day Marcelinho, arriving at the house straight from work, traces of whale blood still under his fingernails, took her from behind. And, unable to see his face, she imagined it was Antonio inside her, his hands on her breasts, his breath on her neck, hardly able to keep her feet for lust.

*

She waited until her father was away in Faial to tell her mother.

'Pregnant?' Angelina repeated dully. 'Dear God, child. How? Who?'

'Marcelinho.'

'The Carvalho boy?'

The late bloomer. The whale tamer. The handsome white-toothed one.

'Dear God! How could you be so stupid? You, of all people.'

She'd probably have fallen for him herself, that same age, Angelina thought. They were a breed apart, harpooneers. Honed by the elements, rippling with muscle, with the death-defying stare of the toreador.

'I'm not having it,' Margarida said. 'I'd rather kill myself. It will ruin my life!'

'Don't be so melodramatic,' Angelina snapped. 'How far gone, exactly?'

'Six, seven weeks? I've never been regular.'

'A least you're not showing. Neither was I,' Angelina added grimly, 'on my wedding day.'

Some actress am I, Margarida bitterly berated herself that night. Some astute observer of human nature. Why, she was hardly better than half the nincompoops she'd gone to school with, fretting over which frock to wear to afternoon tea with the Dabneys. She'd barely given a thought that whole year to anything but Carvalhos. As if it weren't enough, she told herself scornfully, tying herself into knots over one brother. Imbecile.

Very early the next morning, she saw Angelina leave in the carriage, returning some while later with a package under her arm. She came to her room shortly afterwards, with what seemed to be a glass of squid ink.

'Drink. Every last drop. Mind you don't gag.'

Margarida's gorge rose, first sip. Then she thought of the thing growing inside her and swallowed it down. She barely made the closet before she threw up.

Angelina's next potion was as gelatinous as seaweed. Margarida obediently drained the glass. And another. A third. She spent the day on the pot, but nothing else budged. And no amount of near-boiling baths, cod-liver oil or running on the spot could make it.

Angelina was forced to concede defeat.

'We're going to have to tell your father.'

*

Margarida and Marcelinho were married in the same church as both sets of parents. Far from reluctant, he seemed perfectly happy to marry her. Tickled pink at the prospect of becoming a father. He kept asking to see her belly. Just as he'd once asked to see Antonio's foot. So even with her intended husband's ear to her rapidly increasing bump, though hardly able to bear the thought of him receiving the news in Lisbon, her thoughts turned to his brother.

The day of the wedding, she barely managed to hold out for the duration of the service before, with a fleeting kiss for her new husband, racing back down the aisle. Marcelinho followed at a trot, steadied her by an elbow as she threw up between graves. Angelina, elbowed out of the way, recalled his blinking back tears as he said his vows. That his Adam's apple had worked as he slipped the ring onto her daughter's finger. Like Dom Ricardo, she thought scornfully, on their wedding day. Weak, mawkish, sentimental men. The curse of the Machado women.

In the marital bed that night, Marcelinho snuffling beside her in his sleep, Margarida contemplated the day. In truth, it was hard to fault the man, she thought. One last chaste kiss when she'd begged off sex, one last adoring look at her bilious, bloated face, then sleep. He was beautiful, asleep. Almost more beautiful than when awake. Lips chiselled and richly pink, broad brow untroubled, though the long lashes fluttered now and again and the fingers of one hand, tucked beneath his cheek, flexed and curled. Such adept fingers. Strange, now that it was sanctioned, how little she wanted it. She laid both hands on her stomach, held her breath, listening. Surely it must know she didn't want it? Had done everything she could to be rid of it. Was it plotting revenge? Was she to be fated, like so many in life, and on stage, to die in childbirth?

At least, she thought gloomily, she'd be spared the next forty years. The house she would daily have to live in, the man she would have to nightly make love to, the children she would have to yearly bear.

*

Her father had given them a house for a wedding present. Handing her a handkerchief in the graveyard, one of the fine monogrammed linen ones of which he was so fond, he'd glanced miserably away from the spectacle. Poor Papa. She'd shattered his dream of her, just as Angelina had. At least he'd spared her life with her in-laws. Not that she would have much minded, she thought, living with Rosa. She just about had, as a child. At the modest reception, at her parents' house, Rosa had gushed over Angelina's dress. Then frozen the smile on her mother's face, reminding her they were soon to be grandmothers. João, tipsy on her father's wine, had slapped him encouragingly on the back. Poor Papa. She knew exactly what it must have meant to him to have to toast her union with a whale fisherman with the first of the new vintage.

Angelina had kitted out the new house, formerly home to her father's late eldest sister, Dorotea, with rugs, chairs, crockery. Margarida's sole contribution the little rug, embroidered with birds, retrieved from beside her childhood bed. She set it in front of the window-seat in the front room, where you could see the waves breaking and the real birds flitting free in distant trees.

Marcelinho vowed her father need only see his new grandson to come round. As if, Margarida thought, he was about to forget any time soon that Marcelinho Carvalho had deflowered his sole beloved daughter and heir.

The Fall

'I must be in love,' Fredo observed gloomily, helping Marcelinho ready the boat one morning.

Marcelinho grinned. It wasn't the first time.

'I can't sleep. Or eat. Not a crumb.'

'You didn't seem to be doing too badly at the table last night. Who is the fortunate young woman?'

'Ana.'

On closer inspection Fredo did look a bit pale, his freckles more pronounced.

'You're sure you're not sickening for something?'

'I'm in love, I told you,' Fredo said a little testily.

'And she?'

'Thinks I should go to America.'

'America?'

'It's Ana Silveira Soares.'

Marcelinho abruptly put down an oar. 'Christ, Fredo. You didn't say she was José's daughter.'

'A disgrace,' Rosa had said to João, home from José's wife's funeral some months earlier. 'A pauper's grave. Hardly a flower for the coffin, biscuit for the wake. Just him, blubbering. Threatening to throw himself in with her. As if she hadn't enough of him in life. We were friends at school. A lovely girl. Kind. Generous. Devout. Until he got his hands on her.'

'A thug,' João pronounced. 'Even at school, he was known for a temper. Even before the drink.'

'He'll kill you,' Marcelinho said now.

'Shoot me.' Fredo nodded. 'The same way he does rabbits. One leg at a time. So Ana tells me.'

'What are you going to do?'

Fredo shrugged.

'Elope?' Marcelinho pressed.

'To Brazil? The upper reaches of the Amazon? You know she prays for him. Every night. Without fail. A real softie.'

*

Marcelinho was helping ready the boat a few days later when the youngest of Fredo's five sisters ran up.

'Fredo's sick,' she panted. 'He says he can't work today.'

'Hangover,' they muttered to a man.

Marcelinho hardly gave it another thought until late that night when there was a violent pounding on the front door.

Opening the window a crack, he looked down to find Fredo gazing up at him.

'What?' he hissed. 'If you've been drinking, I'll kill you.'

'Oh, please!' Margarida abruptly sat up in bed. 'Allow me. It'd be my pleasure.'

'I need your help. It's an emergency,' Fredo pleaded.

'Emergency? What emergency? Never mind. Wait.' Marcelinho pulled on his trousers as Margarida burrowed back under the bedclothes with a snort.

Even by the light of the candle, he could see Fredo was ashen. 'Ana's had a bad fall. I need to borrow João's cart.'

'She fell downstairs?'

Fredo shook his head. 'On Mount Pico.'

'Mount Pico? What the hell were you doing up there? It's the middle of the night.'

'It was hours ago. We started this morning. I'll explain later. I left her my coat, but she'll fucking freeze to death if we don't put a move on.'

Marcelinho grabbed the blanket from the spare bed on his way out.

'We'd best take Ferreira's donkey,' he said. 'Bonita's not up to it. Besides, the poor beast could do with an outing.'

Donkey collected from an obliging if bemused Ferreira, they went to wake João. Though Marcelinho tried to cast the best possible light on things, his father was grim-faced, harnessing the donkey to the cart. They were about to set off when João climbed out, returning some minutes later with the old door of the shed, heaving it into the tray of the cart. Struggling to restrain the eager animal, they set off at a clip.

'So, what happened?' Marcelinho asked Fredo.

'She slipped,' he said simply. 'Reaching to pick a flower. I'd just fallen behind to take a leak, else I might have been able to stop her. Fucking idiot!' He smacked his forehead violently.

'Language,' João growled.

'You went up there to pick flowers?' Marcelinho was incredulous.

Fredo shook his head, impatient. 'She wanted to climb it,' he said. 'For her mother's sake, she said. Seems she never got the chance. Besides, she's hardly been let out since her mother passed away, but to clean,' he added. 'And that's only because her old man wants the money for drink.'

He'd want more than money, João thought, after tonight's caper. He'd want a lynch mob.

Fredo sighed heavily.

'We'll get her down,' Marcelinho soothed him. 'Don't you worry. It's probably not as bad as you think.'

'Worse,' Fredo muttered. 'Trust me.'

Both glanced up at the mountain, stars standing proud against its crooked peak.

'We could see right past São Jorge. Almost all the way to Graciosa,' Fredo said. 'We saw your boat come in. Did you chase one?'

Marcelinho shook his head. 'Didn't come within a mile of it.'

'Have you been up, João?' Fredo nodded at the peak.

'Once,' João said shortly.

'To the top?'

'On my hands and knees, the last bit.'

*

It was well after midnight by the time they reached her. It was slow going, the door carried awkwardly between them. They talked desultorily as they scrambled their way up. Marcelinho had never been so high. He kept glancing back as the darkness spread out around them. He thought he saw the light of a passing ship. Then a star, peeping out from behind the peak. Then a whole rash of stars. The air grew colder, the higher they climbed. Marcelinho tried not to shiver, for Fredo's sake. His friend was uncharacteristically quiet. It was everyone's dream, Marcelinho thought, to climb Mount Pico. Old people said they wished they had. Claimed they almost had. Had come within an inch of it. Dreamed about it, still. It was strange being on its flank; he'd been aware of the mountain since the day he first opened his eyes. Probably looked at it a dozen times a day and hardly noticed. Used it for compass, chart, timepiece. Forgot, until feeling its volcanic grumbling, that it was as much enemy as friend. Better than a lighthouse for steering home in the dark. Unless the clouds came down, and it vanished.

*

They heard her teeth chattering before they saw her. João enfolded her in the blanket as Fredo gently chafed her frozen limbs. He hadn't overstated the case, Marcelinho thought; she was more than usually pretty. Brave too, given the inch of bone protruding above the rim of her right boot. He wondered if life with a drunk made you stoic. Perhaps why Fredo never mentioned those scars. João bound up the break as best he could with the cloth Rosa had thought to push into his hand as he was leaving, then all three lifted her onto the door. She flinched almost every step of the way down, but no word of complaint.

Even managing a faint smile when she saw the waiting cart.

It was dawn by the time Marcelinho dropped the donkey off at Ferreira's. The beast so pleased with itself, it immediately trod on its owner's foot. It'd be a month of Sundays, Marcelinho thought, before it was let out again. Ten minutes later, he was home.

Only to be stopped in his tracks, on opening the front door, by a spray of blood on the bottom tread of the stairs. Even befuddled with exhaustion, he knew it for blood. Just not how it had got there. He stood some moments, trying to work it out. He must have brought it home on his boots after work, he reasoned. When he hadn't been to work for over twelve hours, and it was fresh. A frightening thought hit him as he nudged it with the toe of his boot, before taking the stairs, two at a time.

Angelina was in the chair beside the bed, leaning over Margarida, so all he saw of his wife, at first glance, was an arm, dangling limply over the edge of the mattress. Angelina span round at his gasp.

'Shhhh!' she hissed. 'You'll wake her.'

He was so relieved that she was alive, he began to tremble. There were splatters of blood on the floor, sheets, on Angelina's hands, though she appeared not to notice.

'The baby?' he mouthed.

She shook her head. 'Gone. She started to bleed almost right after you left.' She took his arm none too gently and led him out, leaving the door ajar.

'She fell?'

'Fell?' She shook her head, puzzled, impatient. 'Miscarried. It can happen with the first.' And second, third, fourth, she thought.

'Will she be all right?'

His mother-in-law avoided the question. 'The doctor's given her something to help make it come away fully. It's not over yet. Not by a long shot.'

'Dear God.'

'Where were you?'

He began to explain, but she cut him off.

'Later. Go boil some water. And we'll need rags. Clean ones. As many as you can lay your hands on.' Then, almost to herself, 'Thank the Virgin Mary her father's away in Horta.'

'We could try to get a message to him.'

Angelina looked at him, incredulous. 'Water. Quick now.'

*

Though he'd helped deliver the odd calf, Marcelinho had never experienced a human birthing. Or such a feeling of helplessness. He would have exchanged places with Margarida in a moment. Would have cried out loud enough to be heard in Faial, he knew; bitten his hands to bloody nubs. He'd never witnessed such pain, wave after wave racking her. Every spasm contorting her face. So white, she might have been freshly bled. But barely a murmur escaped her. Though she almost broke his hand in her grip.

Angelina, who'd lost three sons, knew the bloody remnants of a boy child. And one nearer three months than two.

When a tear rolled down Margarida's cheek, Marcelinho wiped it gently away. 'For the baby,' he murmured, with a mournful glance at Angelina. She opened her mouth to speak, closed it again.

The Fight

Almost everywhere Fredo went after the night of Ana's fall, sooner or later José Silveira Soares would make an appearance. Soon, he couldn't take a shave at the barber shop without José's eyes following every stroke of the cut-throat razor. He became part of Fredo's neighbourhood. Part of his life. Leaning against a wall, smoking, when Fredo came home from work at night. Standing beside the slipway, hours on end, following every move of the flensing knife as Fredo carved up blubber, seemingly oblivious to the stench. Marcelinho encouraged Fredo to ignore him. Fredo'd heard that Ana had been sent away to Corvo, to relatives. That she would never walk straight again. That he was to blame. Secretly, every part and fibre of his being agreed.

*

They were washing down the boat one evening, when Fredo looked up to find José weaving up from the dock, headed straight for them. One of his old drinking buddies, Pires Moreira, was tugging at his arm, as if to dissuade him from his course.

There'd been a fierce wind all day, only just abated. They'd half pulled their arms out of their sockets to get home, and no whale for their efforts.

'Trouble,' Fredo said, straightening up.

'Ignore him,' Marcelinho muttered. 'He's spoiling for a fight.'

'Better out in the open, than skulking,' Fredo said, with a wash of relief.

'It's hardly going to help things,' Marcelinho pointed out. 'You getting your head stove in.'

They took their hats off at his approach. As Ana's father neared, Fredo found his hands were slippery with sweat. His heart pounded almost as much as when rowing home across the wind-tossed sea. José stopped inches from him, breathing hard. They were much the same height, but the older man was powerfully built, neck corded with muscle, which stood out now, as if the blood had set.

He stared at Fredo some moments with bloodshot eyes, then aimed a gob of phlegm at his boot, saying, 'I know why you took her up there, you cunt.'

'Sir.' Fredo astonished Marcelinho with his reasonable, even penitent tone. The words that followed seemed to come straight from the heart, as if he had said them to himself a hundred times. 'It was a truly stupid idea, I agree. I bitterly regret what happened to Ana. I'd turn back the clock in a moment, if I could. I would never—'

'Have raped her?' José brutally cut him off.

For a moment, Fredo appeared stunned. 'Raped?' he finally managed. 'I'd never force myself on Ana. On any girl, sir. I love your daughter,' he added earnestly. 'With all my heart. More than my own life. I'll marry her tomorrow, with your permission.'

'I'll kill you first.'

'It was she who wanted to climb it,' Fredo went on, in hurried explanation. 'We both did. Ana told me—' Then abruptly stopped. It would be madness, he realised, to mention her mother.

'She fell, trying to fend you off.'

'No,' Fredo said. 'She slipped. I swear she did. It was an accident.'

'*You* swear?' José barked laughter. 'You lured her up there, you cunt. I know how you scum work. I knew your father.'

'Best leave him out of this,' Fredo muttered, with the first hint of real anger.

'I knew your mother too,' José added silkily. 'Better even than your old man. He thought he was the first, but I had her many times before he did. She was good too. Better than most whores.'

Though knowing full well he was being provoked, Fredo aimed a fist square at José's face with all his strength. Marcelinho heard the man's nose break a moment before an arc of blood drenched his shirt. José staggered, momentarily thrown off balance. Then, almost instantly recovering, returned the blow, sending Fredo sprawling. He began to scramble to his feet, but Marcelinho grabbed him by the shirt-front and swung him round.

'Stop! For God's sake! Enough!'

'I'll kill him. I swear it. The man's a fucking lunatic. You don't know the half of it. No woman's safe anywhere near him. Not even his own flesh and blood.'

Marcelinho clasped his friend in a bear hug and bodily levered him away.

'He's her father,' he hissed in his ear. 'You're not going to change that. Or help her. Not like this.' He glanced back to where Pires was now in loud and earnest conversation with José.

'Here.' Repeatedly, Pires pushed a handkerchief at his drinking companion. 'Come on, old mate,' he urged. 'You're bleeding.

Time to go, hey? He's got the message. He won't be going near any girl any time soon. Time for a drink, hey? My shout. A double. What do you say, old friend?'

Perhaps it was the thought of a drink that swayed José, or maybe the pain had finally broken through. Spurning the proffered handkerchief, he wiped away the blood with his shirt sleeve, glared menacingly at Fredo, but there was some distance now between the two brawlers. Marcelinho suddenly felt the fight go out of Fredo. His friend began to shiver. Shock, or the wind turning icy cold, subduing the whitecaps into long sweeping troughs. Marcelinho was surprised to find that it had grown dark. Somewhere close by a dog was barking in a frenzy. He watched warily as José and Pires turned into one of the houses of their cronies.

*

That same week, Fredo took ship for America. He and Marcelinho rowed out one moonless night to a whaleship waiting off Horta to sail with the dawn tide for New Bedford. Their every stroke in perfect unison, oars barely troubling the placid surface of the water. The sole sound, a goat braying in the distant hills. Marcelinho hardly slept that night. Very early, as soon as he judged the ship safely over the horizon, he went round to Fredo's house with a letter for his mother, along with a small wad of notes and the assurance that she would live to see her only son's return.

Margarida doubted it. Lying in bed, Chuchuzina in her arms, she thought of how Marcelinho would miss him. And that Fredo, for all his protestations of undying affection for friend, homeland, mother, sisters, sweetheart, whom he'd sworn to return for, would soon forget them.

She thought, as often, of the lost baby. Lost? Could you lose something you didn't want? Marcelinho had barely left the house, she recalled, before she began to bleed. A few spots of watery blood, a few cramps, no worse than her monthly pains. So eager was she to help the thing along, she'd strained on the pot. Every pain had seemed to bring her a moment closer to freedom. But it hadn't wanted to be free. Had clung to her, cleaved to her, come away piece by bloody piece. She could hardly bear to think of the pain. Yet found it hard to think of anything else.

*

Losses came thick and fast that year. Only days after Fredo's departure, Chuchuzina went missing. Too weak, still, to venture out, Margarida leaned out of the bedroom window plaintively calling to her as the dusk came down. When she didn't return for her supper, Marcelinho went to look for her. He found her within sight of the house, in the gutter. Grateful for the rapidly closing dark, he wrapped her in his jacket, walked down to the churchyard where he knew the earth to be still soft from a recent burial and buried her there. Deep, so that the dogs wouldn't be able to uncover her. Using the toe of his boot to spoon dirt over the initials José had carved into her belly.

'She'll come back,' he told Margarida, steeling himself to meet her gaze. 'Probably found herself a suitor,' he said with a grin. 'She'll be back, tail between her legs. Just you wait.' He was only glad Fredo was beyond the man's reach.

Feeling Margarida's hand fruitlessly searching the counterpane for her that night, he pulled her to him, stroking her hair, as she sobbed.

*

After that night, she often let him hold her in the dark. Something had shifted deep inside her. Sometimes she'd put on the voices of the characters she'd played on stage, or imitate friends and neighbours, to make Marcelinho laugh. In turn, he confided how he'd found a whole new family in whaling; discovered, in other men's eyes, the respect he'd always longed to see in his father's. He told her of the laughter and boastful banter, rowing home with a whale in tow; how the sail caught the last of the sun, turning it to gold. How he sometimes thought of a tale Antonio had told him of a man who spent half a lifetime crossing oceans in pursuit not of a whale, but of a golden fleece.

*

Chuchu was too old and weak, Margarida knew, to have ever strayed. She knew that Marcelinho must have found her. But she never asked. Her courage failed her. But she thought of her often, and of the baby. She liked to think of them together, in the dark, as Marcelinho slept. He held her so close, she could hear every beat of his heart. And the baby's heart? And Chuchu's? How fast that had beaten, a flutter against her own. After a time, she couldn't fall asleep unless he held her. And in the morning, playing her fingers on his muscled belly, would pretend blindness, glancing at the ceiling with a little frown as her fingers crept lower until they bumped the tip of his erection.

'Well, who's this? Do I know you? Have we been introduced?' And though she teased, she knew that this was no plaything. That it was lethal as any sword.

*

Some weeks after Chuchu's disappearance, wittingly taking his life into his own hands, Marcelinho brought home a stray kitten, found that day on the dock. Tiny, whimpering, dwarfed on his open palm.

He held it out to Margarida.

Though her every instinct was to snatch it to safety, she let her arms drop.

'You think you can replace her?' she said stonily. 'Would you replace your mother if she died? Me?'

But within the hour he'd been sent off for fresh milk. Warm, straight from the udder. She spent the night dipping a cloth into a saucer, dripping milk into the tiny mewling mouth. When Marcelinho chucked it clumsily under the chin, it turned and licked his hand. He was oddly moved. They'd never had pets, as kids, Rosa not being overly fond of dogs or cats. Margarida fell asleep with it in her arms, and Marcelinho, rolling over, felt its fur brush his skin, and snuggling into the eiderdown, grinned: Alfredo, a tiny wiry ginger tom.

Farewell

Antonio's Lisbon sojourn, which, for any number of reasonable reasons, had stretched to some five years, ended abruptly one morning with the news that João had suffered a stroke and was gravely ill.

Within the hour, Palmira had booked him passage on the first boat to Pico.

Though more than half expecting to one day receive some sort of summons from home, never had Palmira envisioned such a dire one. She was instantly racked with guilt. She'd kept him from them. Though not exactly encouraging him to stay, she had hardly urged him to return. She had let things drift: and seen him flourish, his mental and physical capabilities growing by the day. As had her hopes, only lately beginning to crystallise, that he might stay on, continue to the university, study the natural sciences as Tomás had. Selfish, deluded ambitions, she now saw. As with the operation, delays had been readily accepted: violent winter storms, bouts of influenza, chess titles, final exams. Now, knowing how he chafed to go home, she did everything in her power to speed him on his way.

*

Those five years away, Antonio had often thought of his father. Of all his family, each attached to some vivid memory. Margarida doubled over, laughing at something he'd shown her in a book; his brother grinning as he straightened at his flensing work to ease his aching back; his mother at the kitchen table, looking up and smiling at him as he came through the door. Now he remembered João as he truly was: impatiently clearing his throat, gazing thoughtfully out to sea, frowning over some tricky calculation, grinning like a madman at one of Gonçalves's many lame jokes.

*

Rosa had been first to write and break the news of his brother's marriage to Margarida. Those first weeks and months, he recalled, he'd found himself almost overwhelmed by wildly conflicting emotions: bewilderment, disbelief, rage, jealousy, regret, grief, guilt (he'd stayed away too long; hadn't written often enough; had become absorbed in another life, another world). Even felt a strange relief: his whole life, she'd occupied almost every waking thought, and now he'd been forced free of her. He'd blamed his brother, Margarida, his foot, Palmira, his parents, himself. Nothing helped. Nothing altered the fact that two of the people he loved best in the world now loved each other. It was some time before the worst of the shock wore off. Before he felt able to write with any sincerity to give the union his blessing. Even as he fretted that it might not be needed, wanted, its absence even noted.

*

Almost every week, his mother had kept him up to date with news of the family's doings. Aware that his own letters were read aloud, he'd mostly kept to a general account of life in Lisbon. Unable to say what he knew his parents most wanted to hear, that he was coming home, he'd avoided mention of the future. Now it had arrived.

Palmira helped him pack. She steeled herself to the task by thinking of all the mothers, in the endless history of loss, who'd sent sons off to war. Who knew what the future held in store for him? For any man? Tomás had danced around a room one moment, been unable to walk the next. All she could say for sure, Palmira thought, smoothing and neatening clothes, concealing small treats inside shoes, socks, hats, was that he left with far more than he'd arrived with—not just books, Tomás's chess set, a supply of his best handkerchiefs, but knowledge. A whole head bulging with it. She had played her small part, she knew. And Tomás, too.

She waved him off at the dock with one of her late husband's voluminous handkerchiefs. Like a white flag, Antonio thought, waving a facsimile in return. Signalling mutual defeat? Strange that only days before, anything and everything in the world had seemed possible; as if a man could live on books, feed a wife and family on words. Overnight, an abyss seemed to have opened between his dreams and reality. Grown wider with every passing minute. Like the expanse of water rapidly opening between himself and Palmira, as the great ship, engines churning, steamed past the Tower of Belém, the flags of the many surrounding ships snapping in a high wind. Not that he didn't want to go home to his family, to Pico, he thought, in rising panic, but what would he do without this world of books? Without dreams, visions, others' voices in his head? Stare at the sea, as he had before on Pico, without thought or knowledge of what lay beneath? Nothing in his life but fish and grapes. For he knew that even if João recovered, it would be his duty to remain to help support his family.

By evening they were already well off the coast of mainland Portugal, heading due west. Emerging queasily on deck, Antonio found his spirits lifted by a large pod of dolphins swimming alongside, dipping playfully in and out of sight. Mile after mile they kept up, threading a path through the churning froth, seeming to revel in the ship's company. Even in the cabin he could glimpse them, flashes in the corner of his eye.

*

That first night aboard, there was talk of the return of the plague. Antonio learned that, only days before, a child had died on Flores. And when the ship reached São Miguel, the largest, most populous of the islands, a week later, there was news of further deaths: two more on Flores and, closer to home, one on São Jorge. He thought of the precious whalebone, snug in its many layers of paper, safely stowed, below decks, in the chest. The Aunt had insisted that he have it, though more than precious to her, for luck.

Homecoming

Perhaps it was the threat of plague that made the cliffs of Pico seem so forbidding the day he came home. Perhaps it was that, unlike his dreams of homecoming, when the sun always shone, the day was dull and threatening rain. Perhaps it was just that the first sight of his family, huddled together in deep mourning, João absent, saw his worst fears realised. Tears flooded his eyes and were impatiently wiped away at the sight of Rosa, supported on either side by Marcelinho and Margarida. His mother become almost as frail and shrunken as Margarida had grown tall and womanly: both hardly recognisable. Unlike his brother, still a head taller than any man in the crowd.

Rosa clung to him, her tears falling unchecked. As if, Margarida thought, she'd awaited his arrival to fully give way to her grief. Antonio mopped them up with one of the Uncle's handkerchiefs. Told of its provenance, she proffered a first, faint, watery smile. Clasped in his brother's embrace, Antonio could only think of his father's; how, coming to his room at night and believing him asleep, he used to stand and gaze down at him, face suffused with love.

Unlike Margarida's grim countenance. She barely grazed his cheek with a kiss, pale and stiff as the little ruff of white lace around her neck.

All the way to the dock, she'd rehearsed what she would say to him, what he would say to her. The conversation had taken any number of twists and turns, burdened, like the worst of melodramas, with an overabundance of smiles, tears, sighs, leaden silences, haughty looks. She hadn't needed the sight of him, grown almost as tall and handsome as his brother, to know she'd married the wrong man.

Whereas, handing him into the cart, as so often, Marcelinho patted him encouragingly on the back. Glancing back at the ship below as they slowly ascended the hill, Antonio was filled with a sudden piercing certainty that he was never again to see Lisbon. That whatever his future held, it lay here, on Pico. Perhaps it was the absence of his father that truly brought home to him what the years away had cost. Perhaps it was the way Margarida's eyes slid over his, to seek out his brother's. It seemed he'd lost more than a father. He remembered the day the whale stranded; Marcelinho had gone on his way, whistling, with no idea of what that whale's death had meant to his little brother. But perhaps, after all, he had known. And that there was little to be said, little to be done, in the face of death.

'Just look at you!' His mother turned in her seat to face him. 'Your father would hardly know you, you've grown so tall and straight. We always knew it was for the best, you going to Lisbon. We were always of a mind, João and I.'

Antonio opened his mouth to speak, closed it again with a faint, rueful smile. It seemed that his father, like Uncle Tomás, like all the dead, was already well on his way to becoming someone else.

*

Over the coming days, Antonio pieced together the stories of his father's fatal illness. How, when he failed to appear for the midday meal, Marcelinho had gone in search of him, only to discover him sprawled unmoving in the vineyard. Utterly still, he said, but for his eyes, which blinked furiously, as if with some urgent message. Though what it might be they would never know, João not only having lost the power of speech but of movement too, the whole of the right side of his body paralysed, his face contorted. Marcelinho carried him home, helped Rosa put him to bed, never for a moment imagining he would never again leave it. Three long days and nights they sat beside him, watching his struggle for every breath. On the fourth, despite her fervent prayers, Rosa said, his heart began to falter and Marcelinho was sent to fetch the priest. Neighbours, friends, old mates from the boat arrived in a steady stream to pay their respects. But João continued to lie unmoving and they all went home. Just before dawn on the fifth day, Rosa said, she sensed a slight returning pressure on her hand, and leaned over to feel João's final faint breath on her face.

Gonçalves, she said, sobbed inconsolably at the news. Ferreira, arriving at the house to offer his condolences, volunteered his cart and donkey for the funeral, himself at the reins. On the day, the beast was almost as slow and sedate as old Bonita, Rosa said, her voice trembling between tears and laughter; it paced out the funeral route as if it were leading some grand procession, not the humble cortège that wound its way through the narrow streets to the graveyard.

'I knew you'd come.' She gripped his arm, as if unwilling to be parted from him a moment. 'I didn't doubt it, ever. He was so proud of you. You were just like his own father, he said. Eager to know how the world worked.'

*

Marcelinho found himself swamped with work after João's death. Astonished to think of how his father must have laboured: in the vineyard, tending goats, cows, mending the innumerable things in need of mending. Often, he recalled, he used to glance back from the whaleboat at the vines walled in their individual lava shelters, safe from the icy blast off the sea. Never for a moment thinking of the work involved. Or that his father might have preferred to be headed out in a boat, rather than labouring in a vineyard. For what had he truly known of his father?

Only that he'd sometimes imagined him dead. And Rosa with him. And only himself to look after Antonio. But he'd never really believed his father would die. What was the point, he thought gloomily, of all those whales he'd laid at his father's feet, as Manoel's old dog did birds? João was never going to look at him the way he did Antonio, reading aloud to him at night, hardly able to take his eyes from his face. He was never going to win his father over now. He remembered the day he'd harpooned his first whale, when João had rushed down to the dock to shake his hand. And afterwards, at the long table, was first to raise a glass to him. He drank himself under the table that night, he recalled, revelling in the pride in his father's eyes.

Coming in early from the vineyard one afternoon, he slipped into João's shed, which until then he'd done his best to avoid. Leaned against the door as light streamed through the gaps in the planks, dancing with motes of dust. Seeing his father's whittling knife still on the bench, he rummaged in the wood-box for a likely off-cut and began to chip away at a nub of wood, as he'd so often seen his father do. He'd hardly known João's hands still. The knife felt strangely at home in his hand; the silent arching and fall of wood shavings soothing. Increasingly absorbed in the task, he tried to reckon up all that João had made over the years. All the tools, plates, vessels for carting water. Walking sticks for Antonio. The old cart, still in its place in the corner. Spindles and pegs for his mother. The odd doll for Margarida. And for him? He'd never wanted anything, been in need of anything. With a glance down at his handiwork, he was surprised to find that he had the passable beginnings of a top. His father had never let him near the shed, or his tools. Or himself. Tossing the almost-top into the basket and slipping the knife into his pocket, he went out, closing the door behind him as carefully as if João were watching.

Antonio also visited João's shed. It was hard to believe, surrounded by his father's things, that he was gone. He imagined him out in the vineyard, soon to return. Everything was in its rightful place. The familiar list of things to be mended, acquired, borrowed, paid for on the bench-top; the boxes, neatly labelled; every tool on its hook; chisels and planes lined up, handles worn smooth. Everything but his father. He saw, right away, that his father's knife was missing; knew, that same instant, that Marcelinho had taken it. Felt a pang of jealousy and rage. Then one of foolishness. He only need open a drawer to find another such knife. It was the principle of the thing, he assured himself. No-one should take what didn't rightfully belong to them. Knives. Wives. He gave his head a shake, wondered if João had also come there to work things out. It was unthinkable that he would never see him again, that he had vanished. With nothing to be done about it. When it was almost an article of faith, with João, that given sufficient time and patience, just about anything might be fixed.

Not that anything was in need of fixing, in the beginning. Having temporarily moved to the family home after João's stroke so as to be closer to Rosa, Marcelinho and Margarida, at her urging, decided to remain. Without fuss or fanfare, Marcelinho assumed his rightful role as head of the family, his rightful place at the head of the table. Gathered around it, they made plans: Antonio offering to keep the books; Marcelinho to tend the vines; Margarida, in the general spirit of the thing, to help Rosa with the goats and the kitchen. Eliciting rare smiles all round. Her own perhaps broadest, remembering, as often in those first months, the many hours she'd spent under the Carvalhos' roof, as a child. Still surprised, daily, to find João absent. And two boys become men, flushed with their father's wine, talking, as men everywhere on Pico, of crops, weather, tides.

Marcelinho counted his blessings daily. Counted them again. A beautiful wife, a solid roof over his head, vineyards, a good living. Did he miss the hunt? Miss the endless hours spent carving up blubber, the terror and tedium of waiting for a whale to surface? Miss puking over the side of the boat, staring into the depths, half convinced it was just the swell rocking and tapping at the boards? Miss it? To the very bone.

Returned to his family, Antonio wondered how he could have stayed away so long. Within a month, Lisbon seemed a dream. In two, he couldn't recall opening a book that wasn't a ledger. Small wonder, he thought, João had acquired the habit of totting things up. And if he did sometimes miss the great city and the Aunt and the life she had so generously provided for him, it was as nothing to how he missed *her*. Barely a hand's span, a footfall away from him, from dawn to dusk. As unattainable as if still a thousand miles away, across the vast, treacherous Atlantic.

Reconciliation

Shortly after Antonio's return, a letter from Palmira arrived for Rosa.

Their correspondence had languished those last few years, not just because Antonio had assumed the role of Lisbon chronicler, but because Rosa had found herself increasingly reluctant to enquire after an absent son from an even longer absent sister. Palmira's letter, full as it was of sisterly affection and what seemed genuine regret for Rosa's loss of João, prompted her to attempt a kindred response.

She spent hours labouring over it at the kitchen table. Hours staring off into space, getting up only to sit down again, wondering whether it was time to milk the goats, or give the table a good scrubbing. Thinking that she should perhaps leave her reply for another day and instead make a start on the evening meal. She could almost see, from where she sat, João with those long, fine fingers of his, fossicking in the little box he kept on the kitchen dresser for useful things, things sometimes hard to fathom but never thrown out.

My dearest Palmira, she finally began, only to immediately pause.

Dearest? In truth she probably would never have spoken or written another word to her sister if Antonio hadn't been returned to her. If Palmira had tried to concoct yet another scheme to detain him in Lisbon. Only to suddenly recall, not having thought of it in years, her little boat, crushed under her mother's boot and the argument between the sisters which had led to their mother's wrath. Palmira had only wanted the trinket because it was Rosa's, she was sure. Just as she had wanted Antonio, Rosa now thought, without a child of her own. The thought, accompanied by a spasm of anger and resentment, caused tears to fill her eyes. Fumbling in the pocket of her apron for a handkerchief, she wiped them away and after some moments continued.

'I think only the loss of João has truly brought home to me what you suffered, losing Tomás. Not just the constant hurt, but the terrible longing and loneliness that seem never for a moment to diminish ...'

Suffered? Palmira had mourned Tomás deeply after he passed away. And doubtless still did, Rosa thought, for they had enjoyed a more than usually happy union. Much like herself and João, she thought; they'd exchanged smiles, so she'd been assured, while still babes in their mothers' arms. She and João had been in the same class all the way through school, often only rows apart. She had played an angel in the Nativity to his wise man, the chief requirement of his role being to point, unspeaking, at the guiding star.

'João and I talked often of your generosity, that lacking it Ton might very well have been unable to walk. But I confess it was only on seeing him, so upright and moving almost as freely as his brother, that the full extent of your gift was brought home to me. I only wish João had been here to see it.'

Gift? That first winter he was in Lisbon, Rosa recalled, she'd knitted him a scarf made of wool spun with her own hands. A pair of stout socks against the cold, though hardly a pair, with feet so sorely mismatched. His second winter away, she'd baked him a *bolo rei* for Dia de Reis—no match, of course, for the cakes of the Confeitaria Nacional which he'd so warmly praised, but made with nuts from the old almond tree and their own raisins steeped in sweet wine. João had made a box for it, delivering it to the dock himself, to assure her, he'd said, that it was safely aboard the ship. She'd found it hard to sleep, she recalled, thinking of it in the hold, in the crush of luggage, possibly flattened, misshapen. Had he eaten it, she wondered now, that cake fit for a king? She had certainly enjoyed the making of it. Even the careful wrapping of it in cheesecloth. Had thought of him at her side, as a child, leaning against this self-same kitchen table, helping stir the batter, dipping his finger into it the moment her back was turned. She'd tickled him to make him confess, but gently. Unlike his big brother, forever slapping him on the back, so full of life and vigour he seemed to find it hard to comprehend a brother so unlike himself.

'I remember the day the chest arrived, the look on Ton's face when he saw the books. I'm sure he must have told you what it meant to him, the best present in the world for a boy such as himself.'

And herself with little to give him but prayers, Rosa thought, a touch mournfully. Even when it was in the oven, filling the house with its sweet aroma, she'd suspected that cake wouldn't ever be eaten. That sometimes a thing just had to be made. Or written.

'I was very grateful for your kind words on my loss, Palmira. I confess I still find it hard to believe João is gone. Every day, come sundown, I look to see him coming towards me down the lane. It seems, without him, I have no-one to remember with. I can't tell you how grateful to God I am, my dear and only sister, to have you still. Only today I thought of Father, how kind he was, always telling us stories to make us laugh when we were sad or downcast. I often think of them all together *in God's house, Father and João and Tomás, and perhaps Luis, too, patiently waiting for us. Or perhaps, in my dear João's case, a little impatiently, as was his way.'*

It was late afternoon by the time she finished the letter. Enclosing it in an envelope, she went next door to ask Gonçalves to take it to the dock for despatch on the Lisbon steamer. And if she felt a little queasy at the evasions and half truths it contained, Rosa was overall more than glad to have written it.

The Scourge

Marcelinho was first to succumb. In late from the vineyard one afternoon, he scooped a bucket of water from the well, only to find himself hauling up two. He rubbed his eyes, blinking hard. Abandoning the bucket, he made his way unsteadily indoors. Reaching for a cup from the kitchen dresser, he was surprised to find himself hardly able to lift it. A cup. He stood some moments swaying, frowning in puzzlement. Before slowly hauling himself, hand over hand, up the stairs and falling bodily onto the bed, feebly tugging the covers over his head against the light stabbing at his eyeballs.

He was burning up with fever, an ugly flush covering his face, livid as a birthmark, by the time Margarida discovered him there. Rosa and Antonio came in response to her anguished cry. Rosa, whose late father, a large, vigorous man, had been reduced by the plague to a fretting, bawling infant, knew, at first glance.

Within hours the fierce red tide had spread down Marcelinho's chest, back, belly. They stripped him of his clothes, bundled them up for burning, assigned themselves tasks: boil water, make gruel, prepare bandages. Rosa hunted out every sheet she possessed, sent to neighbours to borrow more. Within the hour, their puny resources had been marshalled. Even as they knew that however he was bled, fed, tended, his fate was already sealed.

By nightfall, his whole body had begun to spasm, the bed moving inches across the floor. He cried out, eyes wide, as if at some unseen horror, and fought to quit his bed, only to fall back as suddenly onto the pillows, spent. Violent shivering racked him, setting his teeth chattering. He lashed out at Margarida, holding a cup to his lips; flung up an arm, striking Antonio in the face. They tied his hands to the bed frame with bandages, securing his legs by the ankles. It took all their combined strength to hold him down. He began to quieten as the night wore on. By midnight, all to be heard was an ugly rattling sound issuing from deep within his chest. Within the hour, he had broken out in sores: chest, back, throat, eyes, ears, lips, nose. And in the groin, a monstrous, evil-looking swelling. Night-long, Rosa sat beside him, wiping sweat from his brow, as Margarida and Antonio padded to and fro, boiling water, tearing up sheets for bandages, turning him on the hour.

All the while, making promises to God.

Never again.

Not one wrongful thought of her.

Not one lustful thought of him.

Not one futile wish.

In the small hours, hand to his forehead, Rosa cried out in alarm. 'He's burning up! If we don't cool him, he'll fit.' Herculean the task of lifting him from the bed, submerging him in the copper, but somehow they managed it.

Soon, though, faint tracings of blood began to appear in his eyes; an hour later a watery bloody fluid was seeping from his ears, nose, anus. Like a dying whale, Antonio thought. Fire in the chimney, they said of a whale mortally wounded and spouting blood, heart pierced by a barb.

Just before first light Rosa insisted Margarida fetch the priest. 'Hurry,' she urged. 'He can't last much longer.'

'Wait,' Margarida begged. 'Wait until dawn. I'll go then. I promise.'

Almost the very instant the sun roared into the sky, a blood red ball, bringing with it a strange, unnaturally warm wind, the fever broke. Within the hour, Marcelinho was sleeping, brow cool to the touch.

*

All day, the wind gathered strength. By evening, the passage between Pico and Faial was already impassable. The roar of the sea such that across the bay, in Horta, people fervently crossed themselves. The churches filled, everyone praying and lighting candles for neighbours, friends, relatives, temporarily lost to them across the narrow strait—but for who knew how long? The channel boiled and churned, throwing up great clouds of spume, along with haplessly flapping birds. The whaleboats were tied, re-tied, checked on the hour by the men huddled together in the port, playing cards to while away the anxious hours.

Rosa prayed herself hoarse, crossed herself until her fingers ached. She knew better than to blame Him. He could always take more. From the way His hand smacked the water into ever more towering waves and turned the wind gale-force, she knew that He was angry. With her? Because she'd wished, once too often, to have been taken with João? Because she'd been envious of Palmira, going to Lisbon? Surely a letter must count for something? Feverish, hardly able to stand, now perversely wanting only to live, by nightfall Rosa, too, had succumbed. Night-long, Antonio and Margarida hurried from one to the other, soothing, coaxing, chiding, encouraging, half delirious with terror and fatigue.

Just before dawn, it occurred to Antonio that he had brought the plague with him from the ship, in Uncle Tomás's old chest, on the whalebone. On himself.

He was the plague.

'Bed,' Margarida barked, when he broke the news. 'Not another word.' She pushed him from the room. Only going in some while later to find him still fully clothed, on the covers.

'Bed, I said,' she chided. 'Clothes off.'

He smiled, white with exhaustion. 'I used to dream you'd say that,' he murmured.

She wearily placed a hand on his forehead, relieved to find it cool. He sat up, began taking off his shirt.

'Shall I help with your leg-iron?'

'That too,' he said, with the trace of a smile.

And not alone, she thought, going out.

*

There was no sense to it, no reason: the old lived, the young died. Halfway through the second day, Rosa's fever broke, and she recovered quickly. A cousin, just turned twenty, was taken in the space of a few hours. Marcelinho began to show improvement, but it was some weeks before he was able to handle cup and plate, months before he was able to think clearly or walk without the aid of a stick. He remembered little of his illness. But for the heat, which returned intermittently, leaving him flushed and throwing off blankets. Odd chills came and went, setting his teeth chattering. When he took his first step, Antonio and Margarida were there to support him. Only when his appetite fully returned did they truly breathe easy. Antonio set the bench from the shed beside the front door. And there Marcelinho spent almost every waking hour in desultory conversation with Gonçalves, or whomever chanced to pass, his face tilted to the sun, a rug tucked over his knees. Turned, overnight, into an old man.

*

The night Marcelinho's fever broke, they'd gone outside for air, propping themselves against the wall, staring in blank exhaustion at the stars.

'The Archer.' Margarida had nodded at the constellation. 'You used to see it from your room in Lisbon. It made you homesick, you said.'

'So you did get my letters.'

'All three.' She shot him a glance.

'You were right,' he said. 'About Lisbon.'

'I knew you wouldn't come back,' she said. 'You wouldn't have, either, but for João.'

'Yes, I would,' he protested mildly. 'For you, I would. In fact, I almost said something before I left.'

A grim little laugh. 'What? Don't marry my brother?'

'Wait.'

'Wait?' She was quiet for some moments. Then sniffed. 'Like Fredo's mother? Or yours, with that long-lost brother of hers? Wait for how long, exactly? A lifetime?' A shiver suddenly went through her. She wrapped her arms around herself, chilled through.

'I love you,' he said, almost conversationally. 'You know I do. I always did. I always will.'

'Puppy love,' she said scornfully.

He was silent for some moments. 'Remember that doll you had, before Chuchu?' He held her glance. 'The one with the hair like yours, stuck up in clumps? You used to take it everywhere with you. Wouldn't leave home without it. God, I used to envy that thing.'

'Poor dolly,' she murmured, almost undone by the tenderness in his voice. 'I could never get the knots out.' Feeling herself incline towards him, she abruptly straightened. 'I was pregnant,' she said harshly. 'We had to get married.'

He was silent so long, she thought he hadn't heard.

'Almost three months pregnant.' And when he shot a curious glance at her belly, 'I lost it. Almost right after the wedding. A boy, so Mama said. Though I don't know how she could tell.'

He was quiet for some moments.

'I'm sorry.' He met her eyes. 'I had no idea.'

'Sorry?' She too was quiet some moments, then shrugged. 'I didn't want it.'

Or your brother. Or this stupid life, she thought fiercely. She made to push away from the wall then, but he grabbed her hand, holding her in place. For a long moment their eyes locked.

'I should never have gone,' he said.

'Don't be so stupid,' she said brutally. 'You wouldn't be able to walk if you'd stayed. You ought to be grateful. Grateful to your aunt.'

'I am. You know I am. I only meant—'

'I know what you meant,' she cut him off.

Only the thought of Marcelinho, now sleeping peacefully, could prevent her returning the pressure of his fingers on her own.

'It's too late,' she said. 'You know it is.' And extricating her hand none too gently from his, went back inside.

The Vines

Gonçalves was one of the first in Lajes to discover a dull bloom on his vines. He declared it a form of blight. Much as he'd diagnosed lice on the stranded whale. Whereas Marcelinho, as aware as most of the dread disease which, some twenty years before, had devastated many of Pico's prized verdelho vineyards, immediately suspected the return of phylloxera.

Within a week, whole rows were affected. Within a month, almost every vine in every vineyard on Pico showed symptoms. Within months, vineyards which had survived hurricanes, droughts, tropical storms, lava spouts, were unrecognisable. Row upon row of shrivelled vines, tangled thickets of brown stalks, barely a leaf between them, and those so paper thin they turned to dust between the fingers, blew away in the wind. Vine dust. The sun caught it, a little miasmic cloud of pulverised gold, suspended above the vineyards. Beautiful in the late afternoon sun.

Men prayed. Begged. Cursed. God came in for more than His fair share of blame and vilification. Men made promises they couldn't keep. Everyone had a remedy. Nothing worked. Men tended their vines as priests tend the dying: day and night, without respite. Full moons, the fields were full of babbling men on their knees, praying to ancient gods dragged from oblivion. If they could have, the islanders would have bled the vines. Some of the finest wines to have ever graced the tables of popes and kings had come from them, wines never to be seen again. Vanished overnight.

But in the beginning they had hope.

Like everyone else, Marcelinho sent specimens off to Lisbon. Wished desperately that João was still alive. Almost as desperately glad that he wasn't. He waited some months for a reply. When it came, it was little consolation to find his hunch confirmed. With no help for it. Nor cure. Nor even need of one, with no vines left.

They'd barely begun to comprehend the loss when it was the turn of the orange groves. A different affliction, but equally virulent.

The mountain only need belch, after that, to stop people in their tracks. Was that mist billowing from its crooked cone? Smoke? Sulphur? It began to rain. It rained for a month. The peak vanished, the mountain, the sea, all the other islands. They wallowed, alone, in a sea of mud. People talked of Job's afflictions. Rosa went for an extended visit to Madalena, on the tip of the island, to offer what comfort she could to her sister-in-law, Serafina, inconsolable at the loss of Filipe: an innocent, taken in a matter of hours.

Plague was still sweeping through every island, taking mothers, fathers, brothers, old and young. Smaller communities had been decimated; not enough men left to tend a dying vineyard. Old women with bad knees crouched among the rampant weeds. Mount Pico grumbled. The earth moved in small vindictive jabs and jolts. The supply boats stopped coming from Lisbon.

Despite all, Margarida started to slip out of bed at night. Through slitted eyes, Marcelinho would see her pause on the threshold, glance over her shoulder at the bed. At him. He would try to steady his breathing. How did a man breathe in his sleep? She'd seem satisfied, tiptoe out, freeze for a moment when the door creaked, closing it in slow motion. He'd flip onto his back the second she was gone. He could feel the urge in her, stronger every day. Every night. Like a pustule, readying to burst. He thought frequently of pustules. Blood. Mucus. The ugly things she had inevitably witnessed, nursing him. He could feel it between them. His body. Brutish. Weak. She could hardly wait to tell him she didn't love him, but his brother. He'd rather have his legs shot off, like José's rabbits, one by one, than hear that.

João had got his number. Selfish. Inadequate. On all fronts. Taking furtive peeks at the other boys at school, later at fellow whalers, it had occurred to him more than once that he might be a little less well-endowed than some. A cripple could probably manage the job as well. Probably better. Cripple. Crippled. Some of the kids used to call out after them, walking home from school. Ignore them, he'd urged Antonio. Pretend you don't hear. Wise counsel. Head pillowed on his arm, he'd try, without success, not to imagine what they were up to. She always came back. Just before dawn, slipping into bed beside him with icy feet. Even though he always swore not to, he'd turn over in his pretend sleep to put a warming foot over hers. He fancied he could smell him on her. Sometimes she'd come home with bruises. Small, but enough to make Marcelinho wonder. She became almost preternaturally inventive with excuses. Seemed the world was full of violent buckets, scissors, ladders, doors.

The Vigia

Ferreira was the one to suggest that Antonio work as a whale spotter in the local *vigia*. His oldest boy, Dante, he told him, was after someone to replace him for a couple of months so he could help out in the vineyard.

'Not a lot of money,' he said. 'But easy work.'

Antonio, acutely aware of their diminishing funds and of the need to employ a labourer to help the still weakened Marcelinho in the vineyard, he himself unequal to the task, resolved to accept Ferreira's offer.

*

It was a wooden box, perched high on a hill overlooking the bay, solidly built, like all *vigias*, to withstand the winter gales. There was a stool on which to sit, a ledge on which to steady a spyglass or place a compass or book, a viewing slit through which to scour the ocean for whales. A handy flare, to be lit whenever a whale was sighted.

There were long tormented days before he could bring himself to light one. Seemingly overnight, he'd developed an aversion to boats headed out to sea. He let a couple of the great beasts through, but there were other lookouts, and the Picoan wasn't born who couldn't spot a whale at sea. The second week, he brought along his journal, drew up columns with pseudo-scientific headings: Date, Time, Sex, General Characteristics, Unusual Markings. He showed Margarida when she brought him his lunch, left behind one morning on the kitchen table. The day's tally: one bull, old, weakened by age or injury, harpooned an hour after sunrise. Two calves, one cow, all taken. And very nearly a boat and crew with them. The cow had put up a real fight. Twins? Was it possible?

'You'll go mad,' she said.

'We need the money.'

'I've got money.'

He shook his head.

'It's a real hike up here,' she fretted. 'How will you manage when it rains?'

'Slowly.'

They exchanged wry smiles; his stock reply, when asked how he'd manage anything.

'You need your old cart, that's what. There, look!'

Reluctantly, he followed her pointing finger.

'Why are they splashing?'

'Feeding. Probably a run of fish. Take a look.' He directed the spyglass, hand on hers. 'Scooping up whole shoals.'

She returned the next week, with freshly baked bread.

'Hungry?'

'Ravenous.'

Taking the spyglass from him, she trained it on Lajes. 'Oi! I can see something big and grey. Gonçalves's underpants! Flapping in the breeze.'

He laughed.

'No!' she said, when he tried to take them from her. 'I have to take notes, on my neighbours.'

How had he grown so handsome? With his brother's curls? And his bony, clever face, bonier and cleverer than ever?

'Here,' she handed him the spyglass. 'I'd better be off. Mending duty. Not half so grim, but still.'

*

Sleepless with thoughts of her, Antonio saw the lamed whale from his bedroom window that night. Lit by the full moon, swimming across the bay, veering to one side with every stroke of its fluke. A large calf: confirmed when the mother surfaced beside it. They swam on for a time, forging a crooked course across the silvery water, before she once more sounded, leaving the calf to its wayward course. Injured? Lamed? She wouldn't have any choice, the youngster suckling all the time, but to leave it, and go in search of food.

There'd be a race, at first light, to get the boats out. They'd take her first. No-one wanted an enraged cow on their hands. Then the calf. It wouldn't leave her. No matter how many harpoons whizzed about. It would stay, bellowing, moaning, trying to nudge her back to life, to the end. There was a flash of lightning, low on the horizon. It had been threatening rain all week. He went back to bed.

*

After the first few weeks, she didn't bother with a reason. Afterwards, neither could remember what they'd talked of. She helped with the journal, sketched the odd whale. Had some difficulty in grasping the size. Fell off the stool, laughing, when he drew the male's member.

It took two whales for them to become lovers.

They were watching a male and female frolicking in the bay. Spouting, flippering, tail slapping. The male throwing itself in the air, breach after breach.

'Showing off,' she said. 'You're all the same.'

Within minutes the first boat appeared, from Ribeiras, a tiny dot, hard to pick in the stretch of blue. Antonio picked up the flare, put it down as another appeared from the direction of Lajes. There'd be a fight to be first. There was a good-natured rivalry between the crews. Sometimes not so good-natured. There'd be some wine drunk tonight. Some stories told. Barely a year ago, he thought, Marcelinho would have been among them. Rowing his heart out. Lungs fit to burst. The Ribeiras crew was first to put up sail. The Lajes boat quickly followed suit, both closing rapidly.

It ended almost before it had begun. The male charged the Ribeiras boat, head-on. In minutes, it was quivering with harpoons, spouting blood. Mortally wounded, it stood upright on its tail, then fell back with a volcanic splash. The female was swimming towards it when the Lajes boat put the first harpoon into her.

One whale each.

Margarida grabbed Antonio's hand. Then him. Eyes brimming, she enveloped him in her arms. 'I don't understand,' she moaned. 'Why didn't she swim away? Why didn't she try to escape?'

*

'Remember the whale that stranded?' he said afterwards, in her arms.

'The one that blinked at you?' she said.

'When I knew we were the same.'

'Except they're fish,' she said drily.

'Mammals,' he corrected her gently. 'They blink. And eat. And sing. And live where everyone knows everyone else's business. Like us.'

She pushed the hair from his forehead. 'You won't survive.'

'I can document everything,' he said with a shrug. 'Who knows, it might come in handy.'

'Stubborn,' she sighed.

'Me?' He seemed amused.

They were quiet some moments.

'I used to dream about kissing you,' he said.

'Like this?'

'Nothing like as good.'

Fingers in his hair, she sifted curls. 'Why did he charge?'

He shrugged. 'To protect the female? Because he'd had enough?'

Lifting her head from his shoulder, she caught a glimpse of the sea. 'They've tempers?'

'Perhaps. We've a deal in common. Curious. Restless. Wanderers.'

'Like your Uncle Luis,' she said. 'Rosa always said you were just the same. Don't you dare go to America,' she added, with a sharp glance.

'America?' He shook his head. 'Look at the time. You'd better be off.'

'Don't try to wriggle out of it.'

'What?' He gazed at her quizzically, grinning. 'What would I do in America?'

'Promise,' she said fiercely.

'Promise.'

Knowledge

Marcelinho knew, the moment he saw them together.

Anyone would have, after they became lovers. What was he to do? Throw her out in the street? Challenge him to a duel? Forbid them to see one another? Hadn't he stolen her in the first place? Hadn't his brother merely stolen her back? He tried not to think about it, but it gnawed. He found it hard to eat, sleep, breathe. He told her it was a return bout of the fever. Surely it was better, he reasoned, to know. Lance the boil, get the thing out in the open, make a clean breast of things. Not that he'd ever found a lot to be gained, he reminded himself gloomily, from admitting to anything, lost hats included.

He set out for the *vigia* late one morning, astonished at the strength he'd lost. He'd thought himself his old self. The self they'd snatched from the jaws of death, the self they'd tended tirelessly, selflessly, day and night, muttering incantations, prayers of intercession, when they'd thought him asleep.

He pushed himself. Just as he had in the boat. Rowing until his arms screamed. Coming home happy, bloody, drenched in sweat and salt. He walked to the end of the vineyard, where it gave way to the fields. And then along the track beside the sea, through the long grass. It was utterly still. Not a whisper of wind. He suddenly remembered the House of Palms. João standing at the gates, looking up. Perhaps he was standing at the gates of heaven now, he thought. Wanting to know how much things cost. He kept trudging to the base of the hill, then began the climb. He had to stop a couple of times. It was no real hardship, no more than in the boat, to consider the sea, the sky, a few puffs of cloud on the horizon.

There wasn't a sound, his ear pressed to the door. The place was deserted. He felt a great wash of relief. Then one of doubt. So where did she go, all those hours she was missing? Visiting? She didn't have anyone to visit, aside from her parents. She was stand-offish, people said. Brought up to think she was better than everyone else. Brought up by Angelina, so you could hardly blame her for being selfish, impulsive, headstrong. Perhaps she had another lover. Dozens of lovers.

He pushed open the door, feeling foolish. His brother's leg-iron was standing upright in a corner, unsheathed from his leg. Where was he? He pushed the door wider, took a step inside. Between her legs, that's where. Thrusting. So vigorously, she was holding onto the ledge. Sprawled, half naked, beneath him. Antonio was moving fast, rhythmically, making a strange groaning sound.

No. It was her.

'Yes. Yes. Yes.'

Antonio was first to see him. He almost toppled over, trying to reach for his shirt to cover himself with. She reached up a hand to save him. Then got to her feet, feverishly pulling down her dress, buttoning up buttons. The silence pressed in on Marcelinho. Just as when he'd once fallen overboard and, tangled up in rope, felt his eardrums about to burst.

Antonio's shirt was bunched around his waist. Marcelinho was taken aback by the muscles in his upper arms, across his chest. He tucked himself in, buttoned his trousers, hands trembling.

Marcelinho turned and walked out.

She called after him. He was sure she did. Almost sure. He was breathing hard and crying. He couldn't stop.

Marco. Wait. Please.

At the top of the hill he wiped his eyes, glanced back. But there was no-one, no-one following. He supposed he'd hoped that she would. He hunched down in the long grass, safe from view. But nothing stirred, though he stayed a long time, peering through the grass, thinking how small the *vigia* was compared to the sea. How even his troubles would seem small, given the size of the sea. Himself too. Like an ant. Like the little line of ants struggling through the long grass beside him, battling a towering forest. It was all a matter of perspective. A few blades of grass as good as a jungle. Glancing up, he saw a boat far out in the bay. A Ribeiras boat? He couldn't say. He watched for a while, the *vigia* utterly silent. He didn't know what to do. Stay? Go home?

He made his way back to Lajes, to the dock. He would have given anything to see Fredo. He would have known what to do, what to say. Sorry? Sorry I barged in? Sorry I thought it was a good idea? What had possessed him? Not for a moment had he thought the thing through. Why couldn't he have just put up with it? Did he think, for a moment, she was going to give his brother up? She'd never give him up. Never.

On the dock they were working, flensing a young male. He could see its genitals laid bare. Its skin peeled neatly off, left hanging.

He went into a drinking hole near the dock, one of the ones José frequented. No-one there knew him. They were all old men. He felt right at home. He drank a couple of shots. Then a couple more. He supposed, after a while, he must be drunk. He didn't feel it, just cold. Chilled through. And empty. They would never forgive him. She would never forgive him.

*

Over and over, Antonio relived the scene. Every time swept by a stronger sense of anger and self-disgust. What had they been thinking? They hadn't even locked the door. The whole thing was grotesque. The word stuck. Staring at a list of figures in the accounts book, he found a small nest of pubic hair. Cutting a slice from the loaf, he saw himself sawing away. Grotesque.

*

None of them said a word of what had occurred. All eyes on Rosa at the supper table. If they were more than usually polite— please, thank you, would you mind—she didn't remark upon it. Margarida's eyes slid over both brothers, and away. Rosa's every activity that day was discussed. Every ache and twinge of Serafina's recently confirmed second confinement. Margarida and Marcelinho left the table together, as every night. But the moment Rosa's door closed, he took a blanket and went downstairs.

*

Antonio continued, at the close of every day, to keep the books. With more than usual diligence, double-checking every figure, addition, subtraction. Afterwards, he took to wandering down to the dock. No-one would think to look for him there, he knew. Not that anyone was looking for him. She certainly wasn't. Or

Marcelinho. Even Rosa seemed oddly reluctant to ask where he was off to.

He missed her. Not just her naked self, the one she wrapped around him like a giant squid. Not just the way she stroked his hair, like the Aunt, as if to draw out the pain. He missed every part of her—nose, mouth, ears, fingers, the small gap between the front teeth. The days passed in a blur of trying to remember all the things he had to tell her. Small things, large things, stupid things. All things.

The sea seemed different, down by the dock. From the *vigia* it was cold, remote. Full of the certainty that sooner or later he would have to light that flare. Now it almost felt like a friend, his only friend. Faithful. Persistent. Never for a moment giving up, aiming itself truly at the shore.

Occasionally, he'd see someone he knew, most often one of Marcelinho's old mates from the boat. He wondered where the rest had got to. Married, working for their fathers, put the hunt behind them, become fathers themselves, been taken by the plague, or a whale, or America? He remembered Marcelinho and Fredo hanging around the dock, arm-wrestling, trying to shove each other off the jetty, dredging up anything left half alive in the rock pools.

It seemed he wasn't the only one drawn to the sea. Any number of villagers would wander down to stare at it, taking in the circling gulls, boats, waves, horizon, before, seemingly content, they went away again.

There was always something there to help pass the time. Kids squabbling, throwing stones at the surf; dogs chasing waves, sea nipping at their tails, scrabbling back up the slipway. Often he thought of the whale that blinked. Of Marcelinho, blinking back tears.

*

She missed him. From the moment she woke until the moment she fell asleep, most often just before dawn. But there was a little nugget of resentment. A whole mountain range some days. How could anyone make her so happy, and so unhappy? How could an absence make everything so hollow? What if he hadn't come back? If they'd lived their whole lives apart? What then? She remembered the worms they used to dig up from Rosa's garden and keep in jars, so he could see what happened to them. When what happened was they all curled up and died.

Within days she was at his door. 'Let me in,' she hissed. 'I'm freezing.' Afterwards, they lay naked and entwined, looking at the stars. He'd been first to point them out to her when she was thirteen. She'd barely noticed them before that. Then couldn't venture out at night without trying to figure out which was Antares, which Sirius.

Monsters

They made love in the outhouse when Marcelinho was in the fields. On the kitchen table while he was milking goats. To the sound of him decapitating a chicken, within very sight of the house. In the shed, on the floor, in sawdust and sweet-smelling curls of freshly turned wood. They slipped out to a field newly scythed by him to make love so passionately under the warm sun the stubble was imprinted on their skin.

There were Margaridas he hadn't even dreamed of.

Repentant. Eyes red-raw from tears. 'I can't bear it. I can't bear to see him suffer so. How can we be so cruel, so heartless? Dear God, I remember when you told me about Vasco da Gama cutting people's ears off, burning them alive, even babies. Our hero. I couldn't believe anyone could be so monstrous. And now us, Ton. Us.'

Mournful. Tears seeping, even as they made love, from tight-clenched lids.

Passionate. Breath quickening as she draped her naked body, inch by inch, over his.

Ever hopeful. Fingering a loose lock of his hair, twisting it ring-like around her finger. 'Imagine if we lived in Lisbon, Ton.

Imagine the life we'd have. Full of books and paintings and music and plays. Dinners in the Praça do Rossio and coffee and *pastéis de nata* at those wonderful *pastelarias* you were so fond of.'

Every tryst, they resolved to end the affair. Felt, those first sweet hours of renunciation, the euphoria of the sadhu or saint. Felt, within days, themselves gradually weaken. Felt, after a week, so sick with longing and despair they could barely breathe.

Lost

A small island loomed very large, Antonio discovered, when seen from a small boat. He wondered if Marcelinho felt even half as daunted when he first went out whaling. It wouldn't have seemed as intimidating, he thought, to its Portuguese discoverers in their stout wooden ships. But puzzling. A green iceberg, fringed with black. Not that he'd ever seen an iceberg but in a book. He'd seen very little, now he came to think of it, but on a page. On the ship from Lisbon, he'd fallen asleep to the drone of steam engines. Out here, all to be heard was the splash of oars, the slurp and slap of water against boards, an occasional grunt from one of the men, the cry of a passing gull. Pico began to shrink as they picked up speed. He had no trouble at all in keeping stroke. His last year at school, as promised to himself and encouraged by Palmira, he'd joined the rowing club. Every Sunday morning a small group of them had rowed on the Tagus, a river so vast it might easily be imagined the sea.

He'd overheard them talking on the dock, earlier that day. Though eager to return home to Ribeiras before dark, the skipper was worried a broken tiller, cobbled together that afternoon, might not hold. Besides, they were short a man, one of their fellows down with some belly complaint. Antonio had strolled over after a while, mindful of his gait, and volunteered. Not without thinking, but having thought so much he believed he might go mad.

What would the Aunt have said of a man who stole his brother's wife? How did anyone really know what they were capable of? Believe in their own innocence? Think they wouldn't ever fuck the wrong person, torment a living creature, break a brother's heart. Convince themselves they were made in a different mould.

They'd rowed in pairs on the Tagus. It was something again, six grown men rowing together with purpose, barely skimming the surface. The wind tore away every sound, every breath, not a moment to pause, raise a hand, wipe away the spray.

Almost within sight of Ribeiras, one of the men saw a spouting whale. As one, they stayed their oars, wallowing in the troughs, as the skipper got to his feet. Shading his eyes, he scanned the choppy water, then leaned his full weight against the damaged tiller. And again. A moment later he gave the order to change tack, threw the tiller in the other direction, and they were picking up speed. For the first time, Antonio felt the thrill of pursuit.

'Row, lads, row now, my dear ones. You'll be home before supper, I swear. You'll be eating sweet whalefish all month. Put your backs into it now, my boys. Your very hearts and souls. That's the fucking way, my heroes! That's the fucking ticket! Else I'll have to get your sweethearts to row. I'll have to rope in your grannies and aunties. I'll have to ask the priest to absolve you of your useless fucking ways, if you don't row lively now, lads.'

The boat fast closing on the beast, Rodrigues, the harpooneer, made to rise. Well-muscled, handsome as Marcelinho, with a small bristling moustache. A hissed word from the skipper, he as instantly subsided. Becoming aware of their presence, the whale, with a few pounding strokes of its fluke, surged ahead. The skipper laid a finger to his lips. They rowed in earnest then, unable to suppress the sound of their laboured breathing. Antonio's arms screamed at every stroke. To take his mind off the pain, he studied the neck of the man in front of him. Arturo. How quickly he'd learned their names, their necks, the impressive swelling of their muscles. Each with his own way of tackling the task: this one hunched over like a miser, as if grudging every stroke. Another so open-chested, so eager, he seemed to want to embrace the sea and every whale in it. The waves were larger now, and dark, spilling and slopping over the sides of the boat, drenching them as they skeetered up and down mountainous slopes. The boat dipped prow-deep into waves, before throwing them off. As determined, it seemed, as themselves. The skipper's face impassive, though now and again a nerve tugged at his mouth. Antonio fought a rising panic. Surely they would stop and turn back, surely they couldn't go on much longer. Moments later, they surfed down the flank of a brutish wall of water to find themselves almost on the cow's tail. And beside her a calf.

The skipper immediately hissed for the sail to be put up.

'Cow?' Rodrigues asked in a booming whisper.

'Calf,' the skipper shot back.

The cow surged ahead, calf lagging in her wake. Overshooting it on the crest of a breaking wave, they suddenly found themselves wedged between the two whales. The cow brought her fluke down hard, and again, churning the water to a froth, then suddenly turned. The skipper screamed for the boat to be brought round. Rodrigues, fully aware of the peril they were in, leaped to his feet, braced hard against the kneeboard, harpoon at the ready.

'Throw,' the skipper yelled, all caution gone. 'Throw!'

Antonio heard more than saw the iron pass, sensed it embedding itself deep in the calf. At its roar of anguish, the cow surged past, almost swamping them in her wake. She tried to haul the calf onto her body, but it slid off, thrashing in a sea of blood. Again and again she made the attempt, seemingly unaware of the boat rapidly closing. Rodrigues had all the time in the world to steady his aim. He was a moment off throwing when she turned and charged the boat head-on. It exploded beneath them, wood, metal, men shooting into the air. Antonio had the momentary, not entirely unpleasant, sensation of flying, before he landed on what felt to be a bed of rock. All the air knocked out of him.

He immediately sucked in a lungful of water, dragged down by the iron on his leg. Mouthful after mouthful he gulped, all the while sinking. He might have been attached to an anchor, so rapid was his descent. He desperately tried some moments to free his leg of the brace. Only for it to suddenly jack-knife, hitting him full in the face. Blood gushed from a gash to his forehead, clouding the water all around. He reached frantically for the surface with both hands, only to snatch at the fat gelatinous moon of a jellyfish, reflecting the last of the light. He opened his mouth wide in sudden wonder and felt the sea rush in. Was he going to die, he wondered? Was this dying?

Was this it?
Sinking.
Was this it?
Pain.
Terror.
Falling.
And?
Glimmer.
Light.
Not falling.
But up, up, up.
Flying.

Light.
Dazzling.
Exploding.
And within it?
Someone?
Advancing?
Hand raised?
In greeting?
In salute?
Hailing him?
João?
God?

Antonio was gone. He had left the room and the door had shut. All that remained was his earthly flesh, thrashing the water to a bloody foam, limbs jerking as if attached to strings, convulsing some moments as though he had come back to life.

But he was gone. Eyes wide and staring, he was sinking into the fathomless depths, tumbling over and over, arms outstretched. Parting a cloud of bright fish, brushing the tentacles of an octopus. On and on into the lightless zone. So deep, a whale in close pursuit of a giant squid paused to turn a small unblinking eye on him, before speeding on.

*

It was late morning before the men were found. Clustered together all night, clinging to spars, oars, each other, whatever remained afloat. Long since grown silent. All the cheer and camaraderie they'd encouraged and fostered in one another gone. All the tales of hope, survival, homecomings forgotten. Their chief thought, even as it sapped their lives, of water. Hauled aboard, they told the all-too-familiar tale of a man lost at sea. Tripped on a rope, struck by beast, oar, boat—who could truly say? Only that he was gone. Drowned. Never to return home. Unwilling to mention that bare moments before Rodrigues had steadied to deliver the second barb, the young man had sprung to his feet with an anguished cry. Whether of fear, protest, pain, horror, none could rightly know or say.

Almost everyone in Lajes harboured a theory. Gonçalves thought it grief for a lost father. Hadn't they seen how pale he'd got? How thin? He'd never known a father and son closer. Some, like Ferreira, put the blame fair and square on Lisbon. Everyone knew the city unhinged people. Ate them up, spat them out. Hadn't it consumed countless of their youngest, bravest, finest over five centuries of unjust wars, bloody battles, forced conscription? Lisbon had a lot to answer for. Some few thought he'd felt the need to test himself: just because you had a gammy leg and were smarter than everyone didn't mean you didn't want to be just like them. Hadn't he asked to join them? Pleaded? The skipper, only lately returned from the mainland after a lengthy stint in the army, hadn't even heard of the Carvalhos. No idea the lad was a cripple.

The only thing agreed on: if it had been a Lajes boat, the tragedy would never have occurred.

*

Everyone felt for the Carvalhos. There was hardly a soul in Lajes who hadn't lost someone—father, mother, friend, child, wife, husband—and who didn't understand the pain. There was no shortage of suffering. What was left to a soul but to go on? The sea would continue, as always, to murmur with the voices of those lost. Their faces to form in the clouds above the peak; blown away, only to form again.

SODOMY

Beginnings

Rummaging in the pockets of her husband's suit almost a year to the day of Antonio Carvalho's presumed death, Margarida's mother was surprised to discover a note. It was an unusually warm spring day, and Angelina more than usually out of sorts. Perhaps sensing something amiss. Something more than a suit in need of pressing. Who knew when next it might be needed, she thought gloomily, the way Margarida was carrying on: still picking at her food, sighing, wandering the family home, to which she'd returned, half the night like a wraith. So thin, it seemed the least puff of wind might blow her away. Like the spume off the sea, airborne in the violent wind that had torn through Lajes the day of Antonio Carvalho's funeral. Margarida had looked intently out to sea that day, Angelina recalled, as if she might see him, hear him. As if, had Dom Ricardo lessened his grip a fraction, she would have torn free to hurl herself under the waves. Give her time, Angelina had thought. A couple of weeks, a month. A year, and still she pined. If only she would sob, Angelina fretted. If only she would break her unbearable silence. As when her daughter was an infant, Angelina put an ear to her door each night, to assure herself she still breathed.

The suit reeked of tobacco. Plunging a hand into the inner pocket of the jacket, anticipating the nub of a cigar, she instead discovered a piece of paper, folded suspiciously small. Opening it, smoothing it out on the palm of her hand, she read:

My darling, forgive me, I am unable to see you tonight. Tomorrow? Same time? I long for you. As always. Your Mariana.

Angelina was astonished by the violence of the blow. For some moments she found it hard to breathe. Then began to tremble. Pain gripped her heart. Followed by rage.

The Widow Fortena. A stiff, proud, haughty woman, reputedly cold. Cold? Hardly, it would seem, from the stash of notes quickly discovered in the 'secret' compartment of Dom Ricardo's desk. And if cold, Angelina thought, then cold like the ice that covered the pond in winter, that, brushed against, ripped away the skin, exposing raw, bloody flesh.

The Dom, unfaithful. It hardly seemed possible.

Not just possible. Fated. At least according to the ageing Lothario, confronted that same night. Far from repentant, the Dom revelled in his conquest. He told Angelina that, having called on the widow to discuss some minor financial matter, he'd instead found himself talking of music, of the poetry of Luís de Camões. And, in one brief afternoon, he said, encountered more laughter and passion than in twenty years of marriage. He was in love, he told her, with surprising bluntness. And with no intention of giving the widow up.

She'd been at the funeral, Angelina recalled, when they'd buried the empty casket. A mantilla had covered her face, body shrouded in a widow's cloak. The very picture of modesty. Though he was reputed to have been killed in a hunting accident, it was common knowledge that Colonel Fortena had shot himself. Leaving a young wife amply provided for. A woman of some means. No fortune hunter, scheming maid, importuning hussy, but a woman in want of nothing. Save a husband. Her husband. Angelina could barely remember the last time he'd come to her bed; when she'd wanted him to.

The next morning, at breakfast, she announced that she was to leave within the week, for Lisbon, and Margarida with her. Gratified by the flicker of life in her daughter's eyes. Enraged by the obvious relief in the Lothario's. Chucking Margarida under the chin, Dom Ricardo even went so far as to suggest she might like to buy a new outfit for the trip. Angelina felt the first stirring of doubt. Was it entirely wise to leave the stage to a rival? She continued with her plans: booked first-class passage for them both, arranged for the dressmaker to call, even organised a day trip to Madalena, across the island, to purchase travelling cloaks.

And newly boarded, and still within sight of land, was delighted to find herself vindicated. A handsome, if somewhat portly theatre impresario, who'd been in Faial for the production of a play by the great Almeida Garrett, joined them for lunch at the captain's table. He asked if he might call on them once they were settled in Lisbon. Call on Margarida, Angelina had no doubt, given his smitten glance, her plans beginning to consolidate nicely. She would take a house in the city, a large, expensive one. Spend her days shopping. Her afternoons and evenings at musical soirées and the theatre, Margarida her companion. Absence, she reasoned, could only make the heart grow fonder. Not that she particularly wanted a fond one, merely the old one.

Kept awake throughout the crossing by the relentless drone of steam engines, she often found herself uneasily occupied with thoughts of Dom Ricardo and the Widow Fortena. She wondered if they still talked of poetry, or merely fell upon one another. She wondered if the Dom nibbled at the widow's ear, as he once had hers; if he nestled, all unknowing in his sleep, into her side. Often her cheeks burned hot in the dark. As antidote, she made mental notes to order opera glasses; seek out recommendations for a dressmaker; lay down a generous supply of gloves, fichus, fans. The list went on.

*

It was Margarida who had broken the news to Palmira of Antonio's death, Rosa and Marcelinho overcome with grief only too grateful to be relieved of the cruel task. Besides, Margarida reasoned, only she, his soulmate, truly understood all that his life shared with his aunt in Lisbon had meant to him. Palmira's reply had run to any number of tear-stained pages. She'd written that a shade had seemed to fall from her eyes with his arrival. That with every passing day, she had grown increasingly reluctant to let him go. That, to her abiding shame, she'd begun to dream dreams vouchsafed only to a parent.

Margarida, by return post, absolved her of all guilt. If anyone were to blame for his death, she wrote, it was herself. She confessed their love affair, holding little back. For almost a year, over stormy seas and calm, through wind-blasted days and nights frozen into Arctic stillness, their letters had criss-crossed the Atlantic. Together, they'd worked to keep him alive. Nothing had been deemed too insignificant if it threw light on Antonio: meals eaten, books read, plays seen, childhood games.

On the voyage to Lisbon, Margarida felt the first faint stirrings of hope. For hadn't Palmira, whom she would soon meet, seen her long-lost brother in a Lisbon street? And Marcelinho? Perhaps he would find another, she thought, with a sudden upwelling of grief and remorse. Someone worthy of him, who would love him as he deserved. She had barely been half a wife to him. Then reflecting on an impassioned discussion with the impresario at dinner, thought of the great plays she had longed to perform in, tales of love and loss, treachery and betrayal, passion and joy. Tales, Margarida thought, impatiently wiping away tears, very like her own and Antonio's. And surely such a tale, both surprised and consoled by the thought, might one day find a place for itself in the world? On the stage perhaps—herself in the leading role? Who could tell, Margarida thought, a glimmer in her eye, what the future might hold.

The Bluff

Pausing on the bluff overlooking Lajes, some months after Margarida's abrupt departure from the island, Marcelinho spotted an unfamiliar whaleship in the bay. A thick mist was banked up behind it, as if only the sails staved it off. He called in at the dock on his way home. Leaning against the seawall, he watched for a time as a half-dozen men loaded supplies into a rowboat.

Sizing up the stranger's broad back and muscled arms, one of the band finally strolled over.

'We're short a hand.' The man nodded at the anchored ship. 'If it's a berth you're after.'

Marcelinho shook his head. Then, 'Where headed?' Offhandedly.

'New Bedford. Once we've a full hold, that is.'

'You've no room.' Marcelinho indicated the heavily laden rowboat.

'Room to spare.' The man grinned. 'Room for an army.'

Marcelinho later found it hard to remember the walk home. Only that his thoughts churned almost as much as his gut. It was out of the question, he thought. He had responsibilities: a wife, mother, life. What life, wife, mother? An empty life, a wife in name only, a mother who only need look at him to be cruelly reminded of a lost son, preferring to spend her every waking moment in Madalena with Serafina and her little one. Where was the harm in it? A year or two at sea, good money earned, a chance to see the world. New Bedford. What if Fredo were still there?

*

Gonçalves helped load the sea-chest onto the cart.

Drove him to the dock, too, with the occasional curious sidelong glance. 'Chip off the old block,' he announced, as if the thing were finally settled. 'Your old man couldn't have been more than fourteen when he joined the hunt. It's in the blood.' He turned aside to spit a gob of tobacco into the dust.

Marcelinho had left a note for Rosa, and what money he had.

The crew elbowed space for him, companionably enough. Rowing out, he wondered if beasts ever felt as he did, when they stopped struggling and accepted their fate. Clambering aboard, breathing salt, tar, rope, oil, blood, he felt something inside him stir. A faint breeze tugging at a ship at anchor. Half man, half merman, they said of Azoreans such as he.

Within the hour, they set sail. Not to make land again for six long months. Signed on as a foremost hand, Marcelinho was more than halfway to South America before he was afforded the opportunity to throw a harpoon.

He couldn't have later said all he felt that day, holding back tears as he watched his homeland recede. Relief? Excitement? Grief? The sight of that tiny beloved place, that insignificant dot of land that had kicked, tormented, battered, hurled hot rocks at him and generations like him, had him by the throat. The dying sun turned the cliffs to gold, lighting all the houses of all the people he knew, had always known, as he assured himself, like everyone who'd left before, that he would one day return.

As the ship met the open swell, the rhythmic creak of caulked timbers, the hissing surge of displaced water began. Every day, from now on, he would wake to it, fall asleep to it. Be swept along like the least animal, bird, insect that took as its home the vast undulating wracks of weed, the tides, currents, rhythms of the sea. And to who knew where, or for how long? Hours after the last island had gone from sight, Marcelinho remained on deck, watching the phosphorescent wake of the ship part the black waters, in a brisk following wind, as if his very future was writ on the waves.

The Voyage

The *Lady Stella*, recently out of Nantucket and true to her captain's word, returned to Pico almost three years to the day she'd sailed out of Lajes with Marcelinho Carvalho aboard. Surprisingly little the worse for wear too, given she'd covered almost half the known world in pursuit of leviathans.

That her luck had changed the moment Marcelinho stepped aboard was well remarked. From the start, he was known for a lucky man. Within days of setting sail from Pico, they had caught the elusive trade winds, speeding them to the rich hunting grounds of the Gulf of Mexico where whales, regular as steam packets, arrived each year to calve. Unusually, the ship returned to Pico with—aside from the severed pinkie of one José Lascelles, lost somewhere in the rigging off the Cape Verdes—all hands intact. All, that is, but for Marcelinho. Of him there was no sign. Rosa, venturing to the dock to interrogate the captain personally, could vouch for it, returning home pale and shaken.

Almost as pale and shaken as her errant son that moment, the ship on which he'd only lately been promoted chief harpooneer, the *White Hart*, being so covered in ice and sleet that Max found it hard to tell stern from prow. Or sky from sea, or cloud from flying spume. He was even moved to offer up a rusty prayer. Max? Not the first man, all at sea, to remake himself. Or, as in Marcelinho Carvalho's case, find himself remade, his 'foreign' name mangled in the mouths of strangers.

*

No-one bothered Max Carver when he was carving. Not that his company was exactly sought after. He wasn't known for small talk. Or large. Was, at best, known to occasionally grunt assent, frown displeasure, offer up a sigh, whether of despondency or resignation, none could say. A tall, large-boned, handsome young man, if with some premature strands of white in his beard, he could slice blubber faster than anyone aboard. Then turn his hand from blood to bone, to scrimshaw, as easy as some miscreant might roam from thievery to murder. Max could carve so small, you'd be in need of a magnifying glass to examine the scene; could carve on the tip of a bobbin, or the length and breadth of a whale tooth. Might carve you a set of tiny animals, or dolls for a girl child, if he had a mind to. Not that he had much of a mind to, intent as he was on his totemic works: small boys with crippled legs; men bent, straining, over oars; women clutching to their heaving bosoms holy bibles; girls with streaming hair, in tiny, chiselled strands.

It settled him. Propped against the mast, carving, Max was as close to happy as he got; in fact, he sometimes found it hard to wait for the blubber to be rendered down, the last cask of oil to be lowered into the hold, so eager was he to resume his self-appointed task. Only two things aboard would he have given his life for. His brother's battered old sea-chest. And these scribbled bones.

At Sea

Those first five years at sea, Max spent hardly more than a handful of weeks on dry land. He liked to be always on the move, to find nothing fore or aft but open water. Far from feeling empty in emptiness, he felt at home in it. Far from fearful of the chase, he liked nothing better than to hear the cry *She blows!* When the sight of a whale broke over a ship like a storm, setting boats flying and men's hearts pounding, a man couldn't doubt for a moment that he lived and breathed. And even on whale-less days, or days becalmed, there was consolation to be found in carving.

A further five years and Max found himself headed north. Far north. Further north than he'd ever before ventured, leaving in his wake the familiar grounds of New Bedford and Nantucket for the Gulf of Maine, the Cabot Strait and on, further north still, until it felt as if a magnet had him in its pull.

Long weeks of rain set in, flattening the sea, dampening the already dampened spirits of the crew. An unhappy ship, the *Pied Curlew*, short on whales and with a short-tempered captain. Long days of mist followed rain. They woke one morning to an impenetrable wall of it to one side; on the other, a sky of palest china blue. For days they sailed between the two, one shoulder steeped in warmth, the other in a bone-deep chill. It lifted one night, smooth as a curtain, to reveal a sky so clear, men gathered at the rails to remark upon the unfamiliar constellations, the shooting stars that fell almost as perfectly as if shot from a cannon.

The next morning, they woke to air unnaturally mild, a bloom of green algae stretching as far as the eye could see. Upon it, countless turtles so unfamiliar with man's ways they were scooped up as easy as pease-pudding with a spoon. There was sweet turtle meat for all that night. Except for Max, with some vague, uneasy memory of other such blooms. Borne out when he awoke the next morning to find half the ship wretched and spewing.

*

Daily entering unfamiliar waters, the men grew more unnerved. Confined for long hours as the weather closed; squabbles quickly breaking out. Even Max was surprised to find himself hankering for sight of land, another ship, the chance of a convivial gam with some fellow passing whalers. Long months since they had known any but their own unkempt, quarrelsome society. The captain assigned the more restive to the lookout, a stint in the crow's nest in a freezing blast usually sufficient to take the wind out of most men's sails.

For all that, a violent scuffle occurred one morning, worse only being averted by the prompt intervention of the first mate. The following morning, one of the men involved was found stabbed to death in his hammock. A culprit was soon denounced and seized, manhandled up on deck, protesting his innocence. The captain was summoned, the crew assembled in ranks. Max regretted the death. Though the man's name eluded him, he knew him for no troublemaker, but a willing hand with a ready smile. The accused stood little chance of a fair hearing. There wasn't a captain alive who didn't fear mutiny, who wouldn't hand out a whipping or put a man overboard, lacking a piece of wood to cling to or the chance to say his prayers, to keep a ship free of strife. Max saw one of the assembled men swipe at his eyes with his neckerchief. The dead man's brother? He'd seen them together often enough. Portuguese, like himself. Dark, handsome, slender, lithe; the two were like as twins.

Almost at the thought, the young man stepped forward, breaking ranks. As one, his fellows shrank back.

Grief must have driven the poor lad mad, Max thought. No man in his right mind would willingly make himself known to an irate captain.

'The man's innocent.' He pointed an unwavering finger at the accused. 'He played no part in my brother's death.'

'Hold your tongue, boy,' the captain growled. 'Else I'll have you overboard this minute.'

'It was him.' Seemingly fearless, the lad pointed out another, older man, a known troublemaker. 'He killed my brother.'

'Brother, be damned,' the newly accused spat. 'Sweetheart, more like.'

'Best hold your tongue, you cur,' the captain said, in a voice deathly quiet. 'If you've a mind to keep it.'

The captain studied the young man keenly.

'The knife was hid in his boot,' he volunteered.

'Liar,' the older man snarled.

'Liar, you say?' The captain was dangerously smooth. 'I'll be the judge of that, you ne'er-do-well.' He continued to size up the young man, peering closely at his face.

'You'd swear to it?'

'On my mother's grave.'

'He tried to put hands on me,' the older man shot back. 'Vermin.'

The captain thought some moments, scratching at his beard, then crotch.

'Take him down,' he ordered of the older man. 'Put him in irons. If it's vermin he's afeared of, he'll have no shortage. You, boy,' he said, with a jerk of his bearded chin.

Paulo, Max suddenly recalled. Paulo Sousa de Medeiros.

'Long watch. I'll have no snivelling.'

*

Strange, Max later thought, how Paulo seemed to materialise with his name. Or perhaps it was merely that he had something to raise him above the common herd. Suspicion. Disgust. As if there weren't a man among them, six months without a woman, who hadn't at least countenanced the thought. Hadn't, if but for a moment, noted a gleaming, muscled back, a dimpled cheek, wondered at an arm brushed, seconds longer than seemed warranted, against their own.

Perhaps it was just that, having also lost a brother, Max was moved to take Paulo under his wing. And to find sly amusement in the glances it earned him. The boy was hardly more than Antonio's age when he'd drowned. And with the same endearing good nature, as quickly became apparent, the more Max got to know him.

He'd often think of Paulo standing before the captain, a slight, upright figure, determined to speak the truth. He wondered if he would have done the same. But then Paulo, unlike his fellows, forever talking of conquest, whether of woman or whale, had never been one to boast, but quietly applied himself to whatever task was at hand. Whereas Max had seen any number of those self-proclaimed heroes brought to sobbing exhaustion, reduced to quivering, bawling infants by the immensity, the impossibility, of the whale. In truth, when it took the harpoon and ran, a man had no more control over it than over a breaking storm. Every last man a breath from being swallowed up. Every last man kin to Jonah.

The Friend

The captain now evincing a grim determination, despite the lateness of the season, to try his luck in the fabled grounds off the Grand Banks of Newfoundland, they continued a course north. Only, within a matter of weeks, to find themselves groaning under a mounting cargo of ice. Soon, great glittering sheets of it hung from the mainsail, formed waves along the ship's rail, fine strands along the rigging. Cabin boys were set to work to keep the wheel free of it. The captain rose later every day, stayed more fleetingly at the helm. The first mate was afforded the honour of freezing his fingers to the bone. They were cold, cold beyond belief and unprepared for it, with insufficient clothing and shoes. Emerging from the galley to raise the delicate matter of their dwindling supplies, the unhappy cook stubbed a toe—Max, in passing, heard it snap, like an icicle.

Long days passed, with no whales seen. Unless turned albino, Max thought, like the great bears. There was little enough to do to pass the time. He continued doggedly at his carving, blowing and chafing his fingers into clumsy life. Like everyone, surrounded by endless grey sea and sky, he found himself increasingly beset by melancholy. Seized by a yearning, familiar to the Portuguese, for that which was and never would be again, for that which might have been and never was. *Saudade*, they called it.

The crew grew as sluggish as the ship, its timbers bumping and grinding against pack ice as it made feeble progress. Turn back, Max had a mind to urge the captain. There's nothing here; no good will come of it. One evening a light was spied, port-side, then more, and more: fires, flickering in the distance, so insubstantial as to seem only to illuminate the dismal, barren nature of this northern land. The following morning a string of islands spread out before them, almost filling the horizon. Leaning against the rails, day-long they watched the land slip by. Conjecturing the fires to be those of cannibal tribes, the captain ordered a course steered well clear. The next morning, floes appeared and, with them, penguins, seals, polar bears, launching themselves soundlessly into the icy waters; no time for a man to even reach to powder a gun. Narwhals were among them, unicorns of the sea, clearing a path through the slushy channels with their sword-like tusks.

Late that same day an iceberg was sighted, a speck on the horizon, increasing hourly in size. An icy snow-blasted wind blew up, bearing, Max thought, all the hallmarks of a blizzard. The captain ordered the ship turned south.

*

Blizzard and ice left behind, they continued a course south, without incident and with a mounting cargo of oil, only within months to find themselves becalmed in the dreaded horse latitudes of the Sargasso Sea, the ship unmoving long days, then longer weeks, on waters smooth as glass.

The heat having grown unbearable below, Max and Paulo, along with their fellows, slept on deck. And when the accordion and pipe fell silent, and the last of the ale was drunk, with only some man humming to himself somewhere in the dark or loudly snoring, the two of them would often lie smoking and staring up at the stars, or yarning in quiet, desultory fashion.

Such nights, Max thought, a man couldn't help but be reminded of his youth. When every hot starry night seemed overfull with possibilities. With so much desire and restlessness and tedium that a young man would itch to break free of his very skin, never thinking for a moment of sleep, or of the sun soon to rise, but only the need, on such a night, for something to be broken, smashed, breathed in.

*

One hot night, having imbibed more than his customary quota of ale, Max felt moved to reveal to Paulo how he'd felt on first seeing his brother in his crib. How his mother had rushed to cover up his brother's foot, to spare him the sight. Telling the story, which he had never before shared, he was surprised by a feeling, almost painful in its intensity, of pity for Antonio, and for himself, to think how much he'd once loved his brother, the tenderness he'd felt. Wondering if he perhaps loved him still. If he forgot everything that had happened and only thought of that infant trying to kick free of the covers, while his mother desperately tried to conceal him, could he love his brother again? He wondered how he would have felt if he'd been born like that. If he would have been as cheerful and sanguine as Antonio, and tried to make the best of things, or just felt sorry for himself.

Paulo listened in silence, momentarily laying a hand on his arm when he was finished. Then told him, in turn, of a boy in his village whose leg had been severed by his own father in an accident with an axe. A handsome boy, admired by many. But with only one leg, it seemed the thing had eaten away at him, Paulo said. He began to shun other people, to imagine they talked of nothing but the ugliness of his injury and his uselessness, a boy unable to go to Lisbon to join the army and fight for his country, a boy good for nothing but begging alms in the street.

'Your brother was brave,' he murmured, 'to endure such misfortune.'

More than endure, Max thought, abashed.

On another such night, Max told Paulo the story of Palmira's books; Paulo wanting to know if it was the self-same chest beside Max's bunk, badly worn and scuffed. Max thought the story, as he told it, of two brothers and a chest that appeared out of the blue, from across an ocean, sounded almost like some story Rosa might have read them from the bible. Like the story of Cain and Abel, he thought, the only biblical brothers he could remember. Perhaps they were always at cross purposes, brothers, he thought, always wanting what the other had. Not books, he thought. But a father's love.

*

Shortly after Max confided the story of Antonio, Paulo revealed a story of his own. One, he said, which he'd never before told a living soul. Max was touched that his young friend felt moved to share such a confidence. Even Fredo, whom he'd known his whole life, had never talked of those scars on his back. And even he, in revealing his brother's story, had later felt some not insignificant discomfort, aware of how, once told, a story could never be reclaimed.

Paulo told him the story of his Uncle Eduardo Francisco de Medeiros. The youngest brother of his father, a man loved by one and all, Paulo said. One who only needed to enter a room to have those assembled wreathed in smiles.

They lived on Flores, Paulo told Max: aunts, uncles, cousins, a large, close-knit family. But as he grew, Paulo said, he began to notice something odd about his uncle: that he took every opportunity to seek Paulo out alone. He'd come to the house when his mother was at church, his father out in the fields, and always ask the same things. What was he studying? What was he going to do when he grew up? Work with his father? Follow his brothers to America? Go on the boats? Strangely, Paulo said, he seemed never to register his replies but always asked the same questions, over and over, closely studying his face all the while. On one occasion, Paulo said, he reached over to gently brush a stray hair from his cheek. On another, he took hold of his hand, turning it over in his own to ask if he'd ever had his fortune read. Paulo said that he felt more and more uncomfortable when alone with him. Whereas in company, he said, his uncle was the same as always: joking, teasing, in high good humour. The year he turned fourteen, Paulo said, he'd been in bed with the fever when the uncle arrived unannounced one afternoon. Finding him unwell, he was solicitous in the extreme. Sitting at Paulo's bedside, his uncle placed a hand on his forehead, stroking the sweat from his brow as tenderly as a mother. Only, moments later, and without warning, to push him roughly back onto the pillows and climb in beside him. He stroked Paulo's neck, chest, thighs, buttocks. Already feverish, Paulo broke out in a fresh lather of sweat. The uncle stroked his belly. Mortified to find himself growing hard, Paulo tried, he said, to clamp his thighs together, but the uncle pushed them apart. Taking hold of him, the uncle worked at him until he came. 'I was young,' Paulo said, as if in apology. 'It was only a matter of moments.' Taking hold of his hand, the uncle then placed it on himself. 'And I let him,' Paulo said, seemingly in wonder. 'I didn't even try to stop him. It was like a dream.' He was silent some moments. 'Even now,' he went on, subdued, 'I wonder about it. Whether I might have encouraged him in some way. If he thought I wanted him to do what he did.' The uncle left that day, Paulo said, without a word. Almost as if Paulo had offended him in some way. But the next time Paulo saw him, he was the same as always: laughing, joshing, telling jokes. 'It happened many times after that,' Paulo told Max. 'Whatever I did, I found it impossible to escape him. I even hid in a cupboard once, but he found me. Like a bloodhound. Nothing could stop him.' Paulo's parents, finally aware that something was amiss, asked him what was wrong. Why was he so stand-offish, so cold towards the uncle, who'd always been a hero to him.

'And you couldn't tell them?' Max said.

Paulo shook his head. 'What could I have said? He could do no wrong. Everyone loved him.'

It was too dark to make out his expression, but Max knew what the retelling of the tale must have cost.

'It's why I left home,' Paulo finished. 'Why I went to sea. On the first ship that would have me. A whaleship.'

Aware of the courage required to share such a tale, far more than to recount the story of a crippled brother, Max reached over and laid an encouraging hand on his young friend's arm.

The Storm

Bonded as brothers, together Max and Paulo followed the whale. From Cape Cod's Stellwagen Bank where, gorged on krill, the great fish were soon picked off; to Barbados and the Cape Verdes; then around Cape Horn and north to Kealakekua Bay in Hawai'i; to the Marquesas and the rich Molucca Passage grounds and on to the inhospitable waters of the Okhotsk Sea.

Perhaps it was chance, or mischance more like, that barely two years after first venturing to those far northern zones of the Atlantic, they once more found themselves headed for those self-same desolate regions of snow and ice. In another season, on another vessel, the *Tourmaline*, with an unfamiliar captain and crew. The sole constant, each other.

But where formerly all to be seen were frozen wastes, now all to be found were sea and wind. Wind from dawn to dusk, scouring the waters a deep bruised blue. Within weeks they'd caught more whales than they could accommodate below. The captain, scion of a Boston whaling family, barely into his second voyage and with a new bride aboard to boot, ordered additional barrels to be piled up on deck, wherever space could be found. Already with some reservations about the young man, Max felt increasingly uneasy.

And not alone, it seemed, from the rumblings below deck about the perils of a woman aboard. Silenced, to a degree, when she sewed up a six-inch gash in a man's leg, neat as the ship's surgeon, made insensible at the time by drink. Daughter of a New Bedford sea captain, she reminded Max of Margarida, the way she looked a man straight in the eye.

Perhaps it was the *Tourmaline* itself that lay at the heart of his unease, Max mused: one of the new steam-driven square-riggers, faster than any vessel he'd ever whaled on, its engines churning day and night without reprieve. Perhaps it was just that it never failed to give him pause when he harpooned more whales in a day than he formerly had in a month, thanks to the new explosive harpoons. Perhaps it was merely the absence of the lulling sound of the wind in the sails at day's end, replaced by the perpetual grinding of the steam-driven propellors, that had him turning nightly on a spit. Or, perhaps, more than all this, it was the absence of Paulo, seconded from his customary above-deck duties to assist the ailing ship's cook, that troubled him so.

Off Newfoundland, they passed the same islands as on their previous voyage north, but closer in this time. Sufficiently close for Max to vouch that, far from being uninhabited, or home to uncivilised cannibals, the shores were dotted with brightly painted wooden houses. Almost as vividly coloured as the iridescent green and yellow weed that fringed the jagged shoreline and glittered in the sun. They witnessed no fires this time but their own, burning day and night with a hellish intensity, rendering whale after whale into oil; the stench of blood and putrescence permeating everything they ate, touched, breathed. Max couldn't help but be reminded, seeing the barrels pile up, of the stories he'd heard of Nantucket: half the town, and its inhabitants with it, consumed in one unholy conflagration of whale oil and lumber.

One evening, near sundown, they were surprised to find themselves almost entirely surrounded by a large pod of sperm whales, drawn to a vast run of cod. Max had often heard tell of their freakish numbers, such that, in the season, a man might walk as readily upon cod as on land. The engines were let idle, the better to see the whales feed. Such was their frenzy, some thrust almost upright on their flukes, the better to scoop up great maws of fish. Seemingly oblivious to their mortal enemy, lined up at the rails, to exclaim at the spectacle. They might readily have harpooned a dozen.

When next Max chanced to glance at the horizon, he found in its place an immensity of black cloud. At almost the same moment, an unnaturally warm breeze blew up, swirling and growing so quickly in intensity that within minutes the sea was turned to a seething mass of whitecaps, dazzling in the dying rays of the sun.

Within the hour, they were in the grip of a tempest, the likes of which Max had never before encountered. Hour after hour, they struggled to beat a path clear of it, the increasingly laboured sound of the engines drowned out by the roar of the wind. Rain broke over the ship in icy, needling sheets, blown horizontal by the gale. Wave after wave swept the deck. The night so dark, Max could barely make out his hand, clutched to the rail; the cries of his fellows, shouted orders of the captain, all lost to the roar of the wind. They'd been struggling some hours when Max was knocked violently off his feet; the ship had come to such an abrupt halt his first thought was that the anchor had been dropped. His next: rock? whale? A moment later, he was swept the length of the deck by a breaking wave. Flung hard up against a coil of rope, he grabbed hold of it, hanging on for his life, as wave after wave swept over him. For long moments, the ship bucked violently to free itself from whatever held it in place, weighted down more every moment by the flooding ocean. With a shriek, as of human pain, it finally tore free, tilting violently to port before slowly beginning to right itself, engines screaming. That same moment, Max saw the first mate disappear overboard. With nothing to be done for it, not even a murmured prayer to mark the man's passing. The ship continued, but painfully slowly now, lurching more to port with every wave and the engines straining and groaning—an awful sound. It was only a matter of time, Max knew, before she foundered. Galvanised, he loosened his grip on the rope a fraction; heartened, with a backward glance, to see Paulo grimly hanging on to one of the whaleboats. His clasp, Max was relieved to note, as desperate as the captain's bride's, her cloak flying out like a wing as she held fast to her husband, his hands locked around the wheel.

Reluctantly abandoning his coiled saviour, Max leaned into the gale, elbowing men aside as he forced a path to the companionway, Paulo at his heels. 'Chest,' Max mouthed, by way of explanation, though none, he knew, was needed. Within a minute, they'd manhandled it up the narrow stairway and onto the deck. Only to find, in the short interval below decks, that panic had broken out. Men rushed frantically about, knocking aside everything and everyone in their path. A few clustered together in one last desperate attempt to free a whaleboat. Abruptly loosed of its restraints, it cartwheeled through the air, taking men and barrels of oil with it.

'Leave it!' Max screamed to Paulo, a moment before the chest was torn from their grasp and swept overboard. Themselves following only a second later.

Max was held under so long, he shot to the surface like a breaching whale, maw gaped wide, only to be immediately sucked under again. Endless minutes he was dunked like an apple in a seething barrel, before finally able to snatch a lungful of air. Wallowing momentarily in a trough, he caught sight of Paulo, some distance off, gamely flailing his arms to stay afloat. He immediately struck out for him, eyes never for a moment leaving the dark, waterlogged head. The younger man was barely afloat by the time he reached him. Max held him up as he retched and spewed; the waves now almost human in their malevolence, punching and slapping at them, gathering themselves up like clubs as if enraged to find the men still alive. Swept up on the crest of one, Max could find no sign of the ship or the chest. Only, moments later, to catch sight of the latter, wildly bobbing on the crest of a wave, miraculously still afloat and barely more than two ship lengths off. Held up by a raft of weed thick as a man's thigh, torn free from one of the nearby islands, he would later discover. Not that he paused to wonder at it, at the time, as he struck out with his remaining strength, dragging the flagging Paulo behind him. He was still some feet away when he launched himself at it, only to be pushed under by a monstrous wave. The second attempt, his fingers grazed the strap. They curled so tightly around it the third attempt, it would be days before they fully recovered.

If it had been the depths of winter, they would have frozen to death in moments. But though the water was icy, and their skin soon shrivelled and became corpse-like, and for long blissful moments they were barely conscious, they survived to see the dawn, one of Max's hands still manacled to the chest. The storm had barely begun to abate when a small boat, bravely put out from a nearby island, shot down the side of a wave and almost ran into them, jolting them back to life.

The Island

Max woke some twenty-four hours later, to the sound of heavy breathing, muffled, as if someone were entombed. Himself? The sea. Surging onto a rocky shore, before petering out. Opening his crusted eyes, he was for some moments dazzled. Everything had stopped. Sea. Wind. Ship.

Raising himself cautiously on an elbow, he was profoundly relieved to find Paulo, barely an arm's length off, sprawled on what appeared to be a salting bed half filled with dried cod. Sound asleep, his dark hair plastered over his face. Unthinking, Max reached over and brushed it gently away.

'Ah, so you're awake,' their host and saviour, standing in the doorway, observed with a grin. The local dialect being unfamiliar, not to say incomprehensible to him, Max heard it more as 'Errysoake.'

He smiled, for all that, in gratitude.

Emerging to relieve himself a little while later, expecting what, he couldn't have said—houses? people? a town?—Max found a barren stretch of treacherous-looking water, temporarily subdued and breaking gently against a barricade of rocks. An immense sky soared above, and all around was an immensity of land covered in tall yellow grass, soughing in the wind. Along with one tiny solitary house, the wall of which he now leaned against as he pissed. Almost overcome by the urge, rising out of nowhere, to cross himself.

Perhaps it was the small graveyard, some distance off, surrounded by a tall, forbidding fence. Meant to keep out what, Max wondered uneasily. Bears? Wolves? Going back inside, he stubbed his toe on a half-buried rock, lacking shoes. Lost at sea like everything except the trunk. And Paulo.

They'd be in need of shoes, their host and saviour, Seamus Foley, assured them, rummaging out some old boots of his own. It was a half day's walk, he explained, to the town where he lived: Tilting. A cluster of brightly painted houses, reached, they were soon to discover, through a daunting maze of bog and stunted growth.

Tilting. Max never heard the name without thinking of the ship, listing at an impossible angle. Of the captain's bride, barely out of her teens or her father's house, sliding across the deck. Of how too many barrels of oil could destroy a man's life. That a man might do well to always leave a little leeway.

Awakening

Of their ship and fellow mariners there was no sign. No bodies half submerged in the undulating beds of weed. No corpses drifting ashore, piece by piece, on a rising tide. Solely themselves and the chest. Along with a few splintered barrels, blown landward days later, leaking oil.

With little hope, so late in the season, of securing a berth on some passing whaler, they resigned themselves to wintering on the island.

Foley, ever helpful and in exchange for a promise of their assistance in building a new fishing stage, found them a place to live. A small saltbox on the edge of an inlet locally termed 'the Pond', belonging to one of the many locals away sealing in Labrador. A doll's house, pea green with a trim of white, the ceilings so low they had to almost bend double to climb the stairs.

Having presumed him something of a solitary character, they were surprised to discover Foley happily married with four small energetic daughters. Which went partway to explain, Max thought, the Foley residence being hardly more capacious than their own, why the man seemed always so eager to quit the place, to tend his sheep, or undertake overzealous maintenance of his boat or fishing stage or share with them his seemingly inexhaustible supply of local knowledge. A soft-faced, sturdy man of middle years, his pale blue eyes seemed to reflect a general amusement with life and, in particular, with the antics and irregularities of his 'harem', as he fondly termed his all-female household.

They learned from Foley that their countrymen had been the first Europeans to discover the island. Perhaps, Max thought, that was why he'd felt such a strange and immediate affinity for the place. Originally labelled Y del Fogo, or Ilha de Fogo, Island of Fire, after the many fires of the native Beothuk, seen by the Portuguese explorers on approach, it had long since become known as Fogo Island.

A long, curved beach lay close by the house: Sandy Bay, dotted with smooth boulders which, submerged on the rising tide, reminded Max of the giant turtles he'd seen, and eaten too, in the Galapagos. Tall yellow grass grew to the water's edge, moving constantly in the wind. As did the surface of the brackish pools and bogs, sunk deep in the stunted vegetation, relentlessly agitated by the salt breeze.

Those first days they spent convalescing, sprawled on the rocks below the house, smoking, talking, idly watching the tides come and go and the local gulls gorging themselves on snow-crabs. Max studied their technique. How they bashed the crabs senseless on the rocks, before, mindful of the claws, flipping them over to drill into the soft underbelly for the sweetest meat. Then tore off the claws, one by one. Like José's rabbits. There were little drifts of empty claws in all the rock pools.

*

Max had seldom seen an island so barren, yet so rich in beauty.

As aboard ship, the weather might change in an instant. The second morning in the house, they woke to a black sea fog, pressed hard against the windows, advancing and retreating all day, as if in some macabre dance, only to be replaced, at dusk, by an ethereal mist, billowing up out of the sea, bubbling like the hot springs at Furnas. Almost daily, violent squalls blew up, only to subside, leaving in their wake great cliffs of cloud, rising in vast, towering steps heavenward.

Though they hardly stirred from the settlement those first weeks, they finally ventured inland in search of meat. Foley told them that caribou had appeared on the island some years back, thought to have swum from another island, in search of food. They would come right in, he said, when the snow set in, to the settlement itself.

Setting out shortly after dawn, following the now familiar rocky shoreline, they entered strangely disquieting territory. Dense thickets of vegetation abruptly closed over their heads, while, underfoot, masses of tangled roots were mounded over with bright moss. Eerie green chambers, bereft of all sound. Lacking even the murmur of the sea, which seemed then to roar as they emerged, as if in welcome.

They followed the track to higher ground, the earth increasingly hollow and spongy under their feet. Wherever they looked were bogs, rocky ponds, barrens, water so black it was impossible to gauge the depth.

'Best watch your step,' Max cautioned Paulo.

Foley had told him that more than one unfortunate, stumbling home alone in the dark, had found himself consigned to a watery grave.

They climbed the crest of a rocky pinnacle to find an expanse of empty ocean to one side; on the other, high meadows, dotted with caribou.

They set their sights on a young female, a little apart from the rest, Paulo asking to take the rifle, borrowed from Foley. Max handed it over with some misgiving, only to see the caribou fall, first shot.

'I used to shoot rabbits with my father.' Paulo grinned. 'Smaller. Quicker, too.'

That same week, a male humpback appeared in the Pond. To Max's astonishment it was let swim, unhindered. All day it swam from side to side of the placid stretch of water, as if in search of something. Its mate, Foley told him, harpooned some years back. As itself, he added. Despite that, every year it returned. People would have no sooner thought to harpoon it, he said, than hang the same man twice. Other whales, Max discovered, were despatched readily enough—two taken barely a stone's throw from their front door.

*

Winter arrived overnight, without warning, accompanied by bitter winds. Only, a week later, for summer to return. An Indian summer, growing fiercer by the day, the familiar scant vegetation shrivelling hourly to reveal the very bones of the island. Wild berries suddenly sprouting in every cleft and fissure. Daily they picked their fill, an inexhaustible supply. They worked much of the day, then swam in the brackish bogs, floating among rafts and islands of reed. And in the cool of the evening, rowed out as far as their arms would take them, to fish for cod. Max relished the opportunity to study the island from afar. Its low rocky shoreline as unlike Pico's black cliffs and lush slopes as a shore could be.

Wind-blasted. Nothing but rock, water, cloud. Hardly more than an anchor for passing ships. Yet people had been drawn to it: stayed, built, bred, flourished. Whatever had brought them there, he felt it in his bones. The closest thing on earth, he thought, to a ship.

They swam in nearby Sandy Bay one afternoon, throwing off clothes, charging into the shallows. Max surprised, as always, by the nest of black curls on Paulo's chest, the boy he'd befriended long since become a man. He still whooped like a boy, splashing and beating up the water, drenching them both. Max threw back his head and laughed. When had he last played with water? Thrown himself blindly backwards, and felt it close over his head?

Moments later he heard Paulo give a shout of pain. He swam over to where his friend stood in the shallows, peering over his shoulder at his back.

'Jellyfish.' Max examined the sting, already radiating across the small of Paulo's back in ugly crimson streaks. It had come in on the tide, a lion's mane jellyfish, almost indistinguishable from the rocks at their feet. Scooping up a handful of sand, he made to rub it into the sting, but Paulo pulled away sharply.

'Hold still,' Max ordered, in his father's voice. Then recalled the gentle ministrations of the captain's young wife. 'This will help the pain.'

Paulo's skin was already raised in livid welts.

Max rubbed salve into it that night, Paulo flinching at every stroke. Back in his room, Max heard him groan. Then found himself listening for it. What if he grew worse? What if he were in need of a doctor? Then wondered if João had ever lain sleepless, worrying about him.

He found it hard to sleep, for the creaking of Paulo's bedsprings. Staring at the ceiling, he suddenly remembered the Margarida bird, on the ceiling above the cloud bed in the House of Palms. Surprised to recall that he was married, still. He hadn't thought of Margarida in years. Had learned, early on, not to think of her. Then fretted that Paulo might be scarred for life, like Fredo. He thought of the softness of Paulo's skin, as he'd applied the salve. Thinking he heard Paulo cry out, he swung his legs over the side of the bed, his ears straining, heart beating hard. He finally got up, put on his breeches and knocked at his friend's door.

Paulo was on his side, facing away from him and naked, the sting shocking against the paleness of his buttocks.

'I heard you groaning,' Max said gruffly. 'I'll get you some brandy. It'll help you sleep.'

'No,' Paulo turned over to say. 'I'm fine. Go back to bed.' Max glanced away from the sight of his member, nestled in dark curls.

'I wasn't asleep,' he said, dry as João. Walking over to examine the sting, he stopped, suddenly aware he had an erection.

'I'll go see about that brandy,' he said, flushed dark.

Paulo, at full stretch, reached and grabbed his hand. He tugged. Tugged again. Max stared blankly down at him, unable to move for shock. He'd been stung by a small manta ray once, thrown off his feet. It wasn't too dissimilar: the burning, the weakness in his legs. Paulo tugged, almost playfully now, at his fingers. His eyes never for a moment leaving Max's. Max stood some moments longer, then sank onto the bed. Gratefully, he closed his eyes, felt Paulo's fingers on his face, stroking one side then the other, as if to fix the shape in his mind. Then his mouth, soft, nuzzling on his neck. His ears. He had a sudden memory of the young caribou, falling, as he lay down beside him. Collapsing gracefully onto the grass. Paulo kissed him, beard rough against his own. Max felt his cock straining against his breeches, as Paulo reached to unbutton him. He drew a strangled breath, grabbed hold of Paulo's hand, pushed it down hard on himself, surprised to find his tongue in Paulo's mouth, no memory of how it came there. Thrusting, deep, deeper still. Unaware he was about to come before he spurted over them both. He lay frozen in place. Taking hold of his hand, Paulo laid it on himself, laid his own over it. Worked bare seconds before he, too, came. Max pulled away then. Opening his eyes to an unfamiliar room, dark, small, cramped, reeking. Without a word, he got up, pulled up his breeches and left.

*

Just like the uncle. The despised uncle. Sleepless in the dark, Max went over and over the day, searching for some reason, some sign or portent. He recalled that as they'd arrived at Sandy Bay, three crows had taken off, filling the bay with their mournful cries. The same bay, Foley had told him, in which a settler, Turpin, pursued by Beothuk, had swum out to an anchored ship for aid, only to find it deserted. His head, Foley recounted, was later found, far away, near the Exploits River. He'd surely lost his tonight, Max thought, with a grimace. If to somewhat less permanent and painful effect. The people of Tilting still talked of Turpin: one of their own, Irish. Max wondered if the bay were ill-fated. If Paulo thought he'd seen something in his eyes. Or seen what was there.

*

Neither said a word, at breakfast, of what had occurred. But talked, as often, of a long-proposed trip to Little Fogo Island, some miles to the north. Max of the oft-repeated opinion that, given the unpredictable nature of the weather, it was best postponed. Foley had told him, he said, that any day now winter would truly arrive. Max didn't ask after the sting. He didn't want to remark on anything to do with Paulo's body, having thought of nothing else all night. Clearing the table, Paulo volunteered that the sting was much improved. That the salve had been of help, with perhaps the merest glimmer in his dark eyes.

They talked of the proposed trip again that night, at supper. Paulo still in favour; Max now more than ever against it.

'Let's see what tomorrow's weather holds,' he finally said, in compromise.

'We'd do well to take snowshoes,' Paulo said.

Perhaps he should make some, Max thought. Like João, making a new bookcase. Was any word, thought or deed a man's own? Was everyone possessed by others? Did Paulo's uncle still whisper in his ear? He had no intention of venturing to Little Fogo Island with Paulo. Of being marooned on an even smaller, more remote island, with some young man he evidently found it hard to keep his hands off.

They turned in, as on so many nights, directly after supper. Max blowing out his candle to signal imminent sleep. Only to lie wakeful, endless hours. Straining at every sound, thinking he heard him at the door, saw the handle turning. Willed it to. Calculated just how long he could last before bursting through Paulo's door, grabbing him in a headlock and forcing those soft, velvety lips onto his aching cock. He almost whimpered, at his knock. Lay, for a good second, as the door opened, a sliver of light flooding the darkness, before turning over to leave a Paulo-sized space at his side.

The Struggle

As soon as it grew dark, each night, they fell upon one another. Wrestling. Grappling. Floundering. On the bed, floor, up against walls. In silence, but for the occasional grunt, groan, slap of flesh on flesh. Only to fall asleep, tangled in each other. Max, waking to find Paulo's leg hooked around his waist, his head almost buried in Paulo's armpit, quick to disentangle himself and return to his room.

He woke just before dawn, one morning, to find himself pinned in place: Paulo's arm a dead weight across his chest. His face bare inches from his own: thinner, darkly coloured from wind and sun, the cheekbones pronounced. Even in sleep, he seemed, from the upturn of his mouth, to find some amusement. At him? The faint streaks of silver in his hair and in his beard, which, since the shipwreck, were more than ever evident. He could feel the rise and fall of Paulo's chest against his own, the steady beat of his heart, as the room slowly began to lighten and he struggled with the urge, growing stronger by the moment, to remain. To just give in to the thing. For hadn't he longed, his whole life, for this? To be loved, heart, body and soul? It was almost full light before he finally found the strength to extricate himself and return to his room.

In the kitchen that same day, perhaps sensing some alteration, Paulo suddenly put his arms around him and pulled him close. Max instantly froze. 'Take your fucking hands off me,' he growled, with a panicked glance at the window, as if half of Tilting were lined up to watch. Paulo let fall his arms, looked away. Max banged the door hard, going out. He strode along the path beside the sea, then sat for a time on the rocks, wondering how you could love someone in the dark, revile them in the light. He found it hard to swallow for the lump in his throat. An ugly sound escaped him. He bit it down, wiped his eyes on his sleeve.

Returning, he found Paulo at the kitchen table, chopping onions, wiping away tears. In bed that night, Paulo rubbed his face so hard against Max's beard, his cheeks were reddened in the morning.

In the trading store for supplies, the next day, Max furtively searched the other men's faces. Surely they must know, he thought, surely have guessed. They seemed much the same: mild-mannered, slow to talk—unless of cod, the prospects or otherwise of a good season, the rising or falling of the price of fish. Tom Flanagan, who'd helped lathe the boards for the punt. The young blacksmith, Kennedy, who'd exchanged a bag of flour for some help in the forge. Colm O'Shea, who'd supplied them with shot for a borrowed gun in exchange for a brace of ducks. Good men all. With good wives and good sons and good daughters.

Using a borrowed knife and somewhat rusty skills, it being some time since he'd put them to use, Max had carved handles for fishing knives for those self-same men; boards for bread for those self-same wives; doll's houses and soldiers for those self-same sons and daughters.

Paulo had tended and cleaned and cooked anything that crowed, cooed or swam, to the amusement of not a few of those self-same matrons. He'd scoured the rocky shoreline daily for oysters and whelks, and even once, in desperation and lacking a gun, had wrestled a wayward wild goose to the death.

Hadn't he once wanted a wife? Max tormented himself with the thought in bed that night. Someone to talk to when he came home at night; someone to make love to; someone who'd cook and clean for him, share confidences with him in bed?

The following evening, directly after supper, Max made his way to the outskirts of town, to a house Kennedy had told him of that sold home brew. He drank there for a time, idly chatting to a small group of fellow drinkers, before leaving to make his way to another house, close by, where, the unmarried Kennedy had told him, an accommodating young widow dwelled.

Max remembered little of their fucking that night, only that seldom in his life had he felt such relief, or emptiness, lying afterwards in the reek of their bodies. He lay with her almost the whole night, to drive home the point, before making his way back to the saltbox cabin. Driving home the point, he thought, with about as much finesse as he'd used to drive in the harpoon, those first hollow years after Antonio's death.

Arriving at the cabin just before dawn, he made something of a show of it, clumping down the hallway in booted feet, closing his bedroom door with force enough to shake the boards. Then waited. But there was no response.

*

Day and night he struggled with it. How could it have happened? When had it begun? When had things altered between them, shifted inside him? On some long-ago hot starry night, becalmed at sea? The day Paulo shot the caribou? The animal's death had moved him strangely. Unlike the whales, forever thrashing and fighting, desperate to live, it had sunk without protest into the grass. It might have been asleep, but for the pool of blood. He recalled, walking back to the house, that even the sky had seemed altered. The boggy pools less forbidding. The eyes of the dead caribou, carried effortlessly between them, oddly forgiving.

He went to see the woman again some nights later. And, returned home, thought he heard Paulo at his door, but it was only the wind, a loose shutter banging loud as his heart.

*

A few weeks later, he brought her home. She walked in all unaware, colour on her lips, cheeks, hair a bright false yellow. She was a fair-looking woman all the same, and good natured. They all three sat in the kitchen, drinking. After a time, Max drummed his fingers on the table, as if impatient to take her. With a pointed glance at the staircase, he got to his feet. She smiled. 'And your handsome young friend?' she said. 'Wouldn't he also like a little something?' Paulo smiled faintly, shook his head.

Max took her for a long time, the longest time he'd ever taken a woman. She was patient, if puzzled, aware that something was amiss. It was unnatural fucking: shrieking bedsprings, the pig-like squeal of iron against iron, harder than drilling rock. She made a gratifying amount of noise when he finally managed it. Would have woken the dead, if Paulo had not been lying rigidly awake. Max would have bet his lay and life on it. He hurried her out, paid her almost double the sum agreed.

He made a pact with himself. He could fuck him, but only when truly desperate. He was strict. Unyielding. It was for the good of both their souls. So he assured himself. Over and over, hand aching as he worked at himself. Like a canker, he reasoned, the thing needed to be starved of food.

*

Not long after the woman's visit, the weather finally closed in. They woke one morning to snow. It fell for a week without pause: slow meandering drifts then swirling white-outs, blown horizontal by icy winds. Accumulating in inches, then feet. For long sleepless hours Max lay abed, imagining Paulo or the ship moving beneath him. Wondering if he might pretend to sleepwalk into Paulo's room. Woke to snow still falling. The second it let up, grabbing the snowshoes he'd made, he rushed out.

He spent much of the time, when the weather allowed, out of doors. Every morning men gathered on the shore of the Pond: chatting, smoking, repairing boats and nets for the far-off spring. It was the fallow season, no whales or seals, just the occasional polar bear strayed or stranded on the frozen sea—everyone grateful for the meat. As they were for the berries—pigeonberries, blueberries, raspberries—preserved against the endless winter. There was only so much salted cod, potatoes, turnips, cabbage, laid down in a root cellar, a man could happily stomach. A permanent haze of wood-smoke hung over the houses. A pretty scene, Max thought, red saltboxes, snow falling, children skating on a frozen pond.

*

Keenly aware of their continuing good fortune, they offered a hand wherever one was needed.

He and Paulo ventured inland, along with the other men, into the frozen marshes and bogs, to fell trees for firewood, hauling them home on sleds.

Max helped Foley fashion a new fence for his sheep. Not that a fence ever gave them pause, Foley told him. A wild, stubborn bunch, only the knife could still them, he said. The pen lay beside the sea, the sheep dirtier than week-old snow. Max had seen them pristine, burrowing into grassy caverns against the heat; now they stood staring in puzzlement at the frozen wastes. Foley told him the story of a whaler with a broken ankle, also obliged to over-winter in Tilting. He'd been down at Sandy Bay one day, Foley said, when he struck something with his stick. Hollow, too small for a root cellar. Kneeling, he put an ear to the earth, then, prodding and wiggling, uncovered a canvas sack. Within it a pistol, fully loaded; a ring, glittering with stones; a handkerchief, so heavy with coin he was hardly able to lift it. The man gave up whaling on the spot, bought a boat, spent his days fishing cod. Still did. Foley grinned. He was that man. Never a day, he said, he didn't thank God for that broken ankle.

With the other men, Max and Paulo moved a house, belonging to Colm O'Shea, across to the other side of the Pond. The ice now being thick enough, so Colm assured them, to bear it. They'd never lost one yet, he added in a slightly nervous aside, but for one sunk up to the eaves, coming ashore, piece by piece, the following spring.

Day-long they laboured, along with a team of horses, to lever the small saltbox, perched on a slide, across to the other side. While the women came and went, bringing food and drink and encouragement, and the children, in the spirit of the thing, slid anything that could be slid across the ice. By nightfall, the house was safe in its new location. Its former site, occupied for over a hundred years, half obliterated by a fall of snow.

The Sisters

Kennedy introduced Max to his next-door-neighbour, Edith Bockerty, the middling-young dark-haired widow of a sealer, at one of the island's many kitchen parties. Lively gatherings, in company with friends and neighbours, with much music and dancing and general high spirits. Though he hardly imagined himself much of a catch, Max was surprised to find Edith keen. Perhaps it was because she'd spent a deal of her married life on her own, her late husband being away much of the time, sealing, in Labrador.

He called on her some weeks, before bedding her. Some weeks later, he asked her to supper, grimly amused to find Paulo, seemingly resigned to his humiliation, presiding over the meal with his customary good humour, even joining them in a hand of cards. The following week, Edith arrived with her younger sister, Sarah: so as to make up a fourth, she said, with a pointed glance at Paulo.

Making love to her that night, Max heard Paulo and the sister talking animatedly at the kitchen table. Then heard Paulo laugh. Thought how he'd hardly heard the sound in months. Then found it hard to come, thinking how he'd made his life a misery, both their lives. The younger sister was slender, dark-haired, with a fine swan-like neck. Given the choice, he suspected he might well have preferred her over Edith. Then wondered if Edith had purposefully kept her from him. Ashamed of the thought. It was unworthy of her, of himself.

After that first occasion, the sisters always arrived together. Once the supper dishes were cleared, they, all four, played cards, Paulo and Sarah, the young sister, talking nineteen to the dozen, laughing and joshing, Max and Edith about as animated as a couple wedded twenty years.

One morning, he almost collided with Sarah as she was coming out of Paulo's room. She smiled shyly. Or was it slyly? He wondered if Paulo had slept with her to pay him back, to make him jealous. Or had merely wanted her; he knew he'd had both men and women in the past.

The routine had been in place some time when, waiting for the sisters to arrive one evening, Paulo revealed, to Max's astonishment, that he'd asked Sarah to marry him. He'd quickly grown fond of her, he said; she reminded him of his own sister to whom he'd been much attached. She hadn't hesitated, he said, to accept. Unsurprisingly, Max thought, grim. Not just that he had a lot to offer any woman—he was handsome, lively, animated in eye and speech, with an ability to turn his hand to almost any task—but that, given the island's general paucity of men—drowned, lost to the sea, or to the mainland, or to the provinces in the west, or the sealing grounds of Labrador—any one of a dozen women would have snapped him up.

'I've grown tired of whaling,' Paulo said. 'I thought I might try my hand at fishing. I've grown to like the place. I've a mind to settle down here.' Importuning Max, all the while, with his eyes. 'Perhaps start a family.'

Have a son, Max thought, studying the floor. A son. He could think of nothing else.

'Well, good luck to you,' he finally managed. 'She's a fine young woman. Pretty, too.'

You don't marry your fucking sister, he wanted to shout. It's fucking madness. You'll bring her nothing but misery. And yourself, with it. You'll soon revert to your old ways.

He felt heartsick whenever he saw them together. The girl seemed relieved, grateful even, when he offered his congratulations. She'd always deferred to him, as to an older brother, or father. With no idea of what had gone before. It'd probably be a kindness, Max thought sourly, to tell her.

Some days later, Paulo revealed that he had. The first time they'd slept together. Max had seldom felt such pain as at the revelation. Not just that he'd been made to look a fool, his base nature revealed, but that Paulo had spoken to her of what they had so privately shared.

*

They were married in the Catholic church in Tilting. The event hastily arranged so that Max might attend. He'd secured passage to New Bedford on a Norwegian whaler, stopped at the island to reprovision after a winter trapped in the Greenland ice fields.

He sat in the front pew, with a disappointed Edith and the rest of the Bockertys, clueless as to what he might represent, unless the sole person to have known Paulo more than a few months. Paulo had spent almost every waking hour, the preceding week, preparing a wedding feast. Attempting to make up for other lacks, Max had thought. But seeing them exchange vows, he wondered if there were any lacks. Just because he'd never managed to make a woman happy, he thought, why begrudge Paulo the chance?

*

The *Kristiansand* left Fogo Island the day after the wedding, so burdened with oil after her extended trick that passing whales could disport themselves with impunity. There was barely room aboard for men. Relieved to be back at sea, Max took up whale tooth and knife, flexed his fingers, waited. Nothing came. Not for a long time. The thing had settled in him like a stone. It was some time before he realised that he was, in some way, changed. That he had learned, perhaps, what few men do: that a man's seldom what he believes himself to be. He'd no more left Paulo behind than the rest. They were all aboard with him, his full complement of the lost and the dead.

Rowing out to the waiting whaleship, he'd passed a solitary eider duck, sculling the crystal-clear waters. It had uttered such a cry you might have thought that it had lost everything it ever had. Newly boarded, he'd looked back to find Paulo and his wife on the shore, come to farewell him. With the most perfunctory of waves, he'd gone below.

*

Not for the first time, on that voyage, did he feel lonely. Heartsore. But perhaps, for the first time, he knew there would be no cure. That he'd do well, unless a complete imbecile, to count whatever blessings he had.

Eventually, in New Bedford, he visited the Seamen's Bethel, where, Paulo had told him, he'd first learned to speak and write some words of English. And attended religious services in that tongue, he'd said. Had it borne fruit? Max knew that most, aware of what had passed between them, would have said no. Whereas he had no doubt. Few people he'd ever known had proved as fair and faithful and true, and so much a part of him, as Paulo Sousa de Medeiros.

MURDER

The Cut

Max remained in New Bedford some weeks before taking ship south. He was not just badly in want of distraction, but whales were rumoured to have grown increasingly shy and elusive in the northern grounds. It seemed fresh riches were to be had in the south. A truth borne out, in a matter of weeks, when off Walvis Bay in South West Africa he secured a large sperm whale, brimming with ambergris. His share sold to an agent in Cape Town, Max found himself with an enormous windfall.

Harpooning another sperm whale off New Zealand's Bay of Islands a year later, though the load of ambergris was smaller, Max found his wealth again increased. The further south he ventured, it seemed, the more he prospered. After a three-year trick that saw him twice rounding the Horn, he had accumulated a small fortune, built on whale shit. Ambergris, more elusive, more strenuously won, more valuable than gold.

It was off the coast of Western Australia, on the *Bathsheba*, a handsome, if antiquated, square-rigger, that Max cut his hand while incising a pattern into a whale's tooth. Barely a nick. But from good habit, he washed and cleaned the wound thoroughly and bound it up. By late afternoon, it had sealed right over.

Late that same day, they gave chase to a female humpback. Though the light was poor, and the chances of securing her slim, the captain ordered the boats lowered. Only when they closed on the cow did Max see that she was on the verge of giving birth and would be readily harpooned. There was some uneasiness when the calf emerged from its wounded mother, fully formed and alive. The young harpooneer hesitating to despatch it, Max stepped in to deliver the barb. Securing the calf to the ship afterwards, he found the nick on his hand had become a half-inch gash, awash with blood. His own? The calf's? The thought, if fleeting, made him uneasy. It had been a mercy, as much as duty, he rationalised, to despatch the beast; gulls had already begun to swoop on the afterbirth, alerting every shark for miles around, white pointers, some bigger than the calf itself.

He hardly slept that night for the throbbing. By morning, the wound was livid, hot to the touch, as solid as if a stone had lodged inside his skin. By noon, it had begun to seep a thick yellow pus. By late afternoon Max was dizzy, unable to focus, his head pounding as if his heart had moved into his skull. By nightfall, he could barely make sense of his surroundings. Everything was fragmented: blinding sea, sky, ship sliding across glass, and over all a vast blue dome, ceaselessly throbbing. By the time they dropped anchor off the small whaling port of Albany the following morning, he was delirious, burning up with fever, unable to lift head from hammock. Unaware of being manhandled onto a rowboat and thence conveyed ashore to the town's small hospital.

He was treated by the resident physician, Joseph Finneman, a heftily built man of middle years, more than capable of restraining him when he fought to quit his bed.

'Home! Let me go home!' he pleaded, in delirium. Even dosed with laudanum, his sleep was fitful. In the morning he was cupped and bled, the nurse remarking on the dark viscosity of his blood. When she tried to feed him broth, Max struck the cup from her hand, imagining the squelch of leeches going down. Sharks circled. Someone held a knife to his throat. Over and over, Paulo sank beneath the waves. 'Home, home,' he cried, pleaded, mumbled. Waking or sleeping. His sole refrain.

It was two weeks before he was able to quit the hospital, with the aid of a stick, for a nearby boarding house. He'd got to know quite a few of his fellow patients: sailors, whalers, more than a few wood-choppers—the bush, Finneman told him, being cleared of the mighty karri trees, their ruler-straight trunks destined for shipbuilding and telegraph poles.

As a young man, Finneman had been a surgeon in the American Civil War; his speciality, he told Max, amputations. Max said he was glad not to have to call on this particular expertise. Though would have entrusted the doctor with his life—and had. Finneman told him that, weary of war and seduced by the prospect of fresh adventures, he'd left Boston on a whaleship, bound for the Cape of Good Hope. Only to discover, he said, that he'd merely exchanged one bloody battlefield for another.

Max was glad of his company. A reserved, unsentimental man of few words. They passed many an amiable evening, drinking and playing cards. Occasionally, on Finneman's rare days off, they ventured out into the surrounding lands, following the rugged coastline on horseback; the good medic reminded by the stunted wind-blasted vegetation of the wide-open sky and fynbos of the Cape, whereas Max, observing the way the cliffs plunged precipitously into the sea, thought of Pico. But then the place didn't seem to exist, he thought, that didn't in some way remind a man of home.

Intent on regaining his strength, he began a regimen of daily walks along the town beach. Only pausing to watch the troopers, garrisoned at the fort in Frenchman's Bay, exercise their horses in the late afternoons, urging them at full gallop across the strand, clearing the drifts of flotsam and seaweed in bounding leaps, King George's Sound a glittering backdrop. Max was watching one afternoon when one of the troop took a nasty spill. The rider, thrown clear, scrambled to his feet, unharmed. Unlike his mount, desperately struggling to rise, its cries of pain, Max thought, almost worse than a dying whale's. The young horseman went down on a knee in the sand, gentling the creature, as he examined its hind leg, now bloody and brutally misshapen. With a glance up at his fellows, dismounted and gathered around him, he slowly shook his head. Max had barely turned away before he heard the shot ring out.

Perhaps it was the wind, the sky, the sea, so deeply blue, the land leached of all colour. Perhaps it was the trees, that might have been trees of stone. The sharks that he saw sliding through the shallows, during his increasingly far-ranging walks, trailing lumps of bloody flesh torn from the whales waiting to be flensed at the whaling station. Perhaps it was just the fever that so fretted Max's nerves. It was a year before it began to burn itself out. Two, and still he wondered if he would ever be cool or temperate again. And worse than the fever, the smell. On the wind, in his clothes, skin, hair. Clotting his nostrils, his throat, clenching his gut until everything inside him was expelled. Blood. What whaler puked at the smell of it? At the very sight of it, spread out under the water like a spill of ink?

He remembered Antonio stumbling against the kitchen table, sending an inkpot flying over the family bible. The calamitous hush.

It was over time, he knew, to move on.

But to where?

And if not by sea, then how?

The Mountain

Max went inland. Far inland, as far from sea and ship as he could get.

He set off north, early one morning, in company with a bullock train charged with hauling logs for the Great Southern Railway's new line from Albany to Beverley, a small settlement east of Perth. The sea-chest and its contents, Antonio's whale journal among them, entrusted to the care of Dr Finneman. He would send word, Max told his friend, as soon as his destination was known to him.

He spent the best part of a year in travelling. He journeyed by any means he encountered and in the company of whomever he chanced to meet: gold prospectors, sheep shearers, stock agents, government surveyors, explorers and any number of lost souls, much like himself. He travelled on carts and on camels, on foot and on horseback, following newly charted telegraph and stock routes and ancient paths worn smooth by naked feet.

He headed north from Beverley to Geraldton where, aware he could travel no further, he turned and retraced his steps then headed east, travelling across the uninhabited reaches of the Nullarbor Plain, in thrall to the parched heart of the Great Southern Land. He ventured to Eucla, and on to Port Augusta, where, after some weeks of rest, he once more set off, sights now firmly set on the northernmost settlement of Palmerston. His days soon as monotonous as the road ahead, his every footstep dogged by clouds of red dust. Hardly daring to open his mouth for fear of swallowing flies. No glimmer of water—not a billabong, cattle-dip or puddled rut in the red-dirt road. Only vast glittering night skies that found him, most evenings, wrapped in his swag, beset by thoughts of the past. Of Fredo, of Paulo, of Margarida, of Pico. Of all the many times, in dreams and waking reveries, he'd finally returned home: clambered off ships, thrown open front doors, hallooed through familiar rooms, only to find them empty, everyone gone.

Max spent some days in the small settlement of Stuart, half-minded to make a detour to see for himself the famed red rock, said to tower above the desert like the Pyramids of Egypt, only to press on once more.

He was nearing Tennant Creek when, seemingly overnight, he found himself intensely wearied by the heat and his itinerant life. He abruptly changed tack, heading east through the shimmering grasslands of the Barkly Tableland. Then south through Diamantina Crossing, Leigh's Creek, Port Augusta once more and, finally, Adelaide and the coast. Where, exchanging a lump of ambergris for a wad of cash, he determined to remain. Only, on the day he'd planned to send word to Finneman, to wake convinced that he was yet to reach his destination. And though lacking any foreknowledge of what it might be, was once more compelled to set out. He crossed the Grampians and travelled on to Bendigo, then trekked over the Great Dividing Range to Omeo, traversing the breadth of the colony of Victoria before reaching New South Wales and the coast, intent now on taking ship for the great city of Sydney.

Which he might well have reached, but for Mount Imlay.

The sun was barely risen when Max first spied it. Stopped in his tracks by the sight of it silhouetted against a dawn sky. Its thickly wooded slopes wreathed in early morning mist; its crooked peak seeming to float, disembodied, above the surrounding bush. The Pacific Ocean glittering palely in the near distance. The very spit of Mount Pico. If on a minor scale.

Consulting a fellow traveller, he was surprised to discover that the nearest town was the whaling port of Eden. For all his recent aversion to blood, the word sent a little shiver through him. Eden. Surely the sign he'd been looking for?

Within the week, he'd exchanged a further two lumps of ambergris for forty acres on the outskirts of town. Virgin acres, billowing in blue-grey waves down to a blue-grey sea, it being overcast the day he paced out the land. Standing on a rocky promontory overlooking Twofold Bay, it came to him, like some biblical revelation, that he ought to build a house on that spot. Nothing but sea before him, and behind a sea of bush, pierced by the tinkling bell-like call of unseen birds. He hadn't thought himself in need of a home. Now, day and night, the thought possessed him.

Comfortably ensconced in the Great Southern Hotel in Imlay Street, Eden's main thoroughfare, he immediately set to. He secured himself a builder, a carpenter—and a local drunk and former whaler, Paddy Trehearne, who was to be general factotum and handyman. He'd happened across the man in the public bar one night, so taciturn and morose that Max, with some vague remembrance of Kennedy in Tilting, had felt moved to offer him a job.

Within weeks, the footings for the house were in place; bearers, walls, beams, roof following in quick succession. Seeing the construction rise above the surrounding bush, the locals laid bets. Ship? House? A real bitser, the chief consensus. Much like its owner, a large, swarthy, foreign-looking cove. Though to give the man his due, he kept himself to himself, paid his bills on time and in cash.

Seeing the house, at year's end, near completion, Max was surprised by a near-overwhelming sense of relief. A home. A place to call his own. His hand visible in every part of it. Built of overlapping cedar plank, it bore more than a passing resemblance to a ship. The approach, through dense bush, over stony ground, culminated in a narrow walkway, akin to a ship's gangway. Max's study, modelled on an octagonal room where he'd once spent the night in Nantucket, boasted two large circular windows, very like oversized portholes. The bullnose verandah faced bravely into the prevailing wind, a nor'-easter, and was the equal, at least to Max's fancy, of any but the finest of ship's figureheads.

He called it Broadside. His first act, upon moving in: to erect a telescope, especially ordered from Sydney, such that he'd be able to track a whale halfway to New Zealand through the circular windows of his study. His second: to send word to Finneman. Within the month he'd found homes for his few possessions. The scrimshaw in a glass cabinet, purpose-built. The ambergris, locked away in a chest of drawers. The newly reclaimed sea-chest in the hallway. Then in the dining room. Then all four of the four bedrooms. Before, conceding defeat, he finally set it down in his study, beside his desk. Where it remained, to daily rebuke him.

But not at first. So occupied was Max those first weeks and months in swivelling in his study chair between views of Mount Imlay and Calle Calle Bay, and exploring on foot and on horseback every inch of his new domain, all the while overseeing Trehearne's attempts to build a path of crushed shell and bush rock down the incline to the beach, he barely gave it a thought. And no more did he at night, snug in a bunk built into one of the study walls. Lulled by the murmur of gently breaking waves into the soundest, most untroubled sleep he'd had in years.

The Imposter

Alice Binney's first night under Max's roof was anything but tranquil. Every other minute, it seemed, she was plumping or flattening pillows, climbing in or out of bed to stare at the expanse of sea beneath her window, or at the ceiling above her head, rippling with little waves of sea light. So slight, she barely formed a lump under the bedclothes. So restless, she finally sent them all sliding, in a heap, onto the floor. She tried counting sheep, but it made her think of her late father; she pushed away thoughts of her late mother, of her sister, too, reflecting instead on how she'd lost her last position.

A childhood friend of her employer, visiting from Sydney, had recognised her over the soup tureen.

'Anna!' her unusually good-tempered employer had remonstrated mildly, when she'd splattered pea soup all over the cloth.

'Anna?' The friend had raised an eyebrow. 'Alicja, I think you mean, my dear. Alicja Bra ...'

They could never quite manage it. Originally Alicja Brajkoviç. Subsequently Amelia Brown. Latterly Anna Barker. Currently Alice Binney. But for who knew how long? She preferred to stick to As and Bs. Keep it simple. She'd dyed her hair, in the beginning.

Worn a wig. Almost scratched holes in her skull that first, endless, terrible summer without Katya. Don't forget who you really are, she admonished herself sternly. Not yet.

Not ever.

*

She'd spotted the advertisement in the *Monaro Mercury, and Cooma and Bombala Advertiser*. Small, short on detail. Cook–housekeeper. Immediate start. Terms on application. Eden. Perfect, Amelia-Anna-soon-to-be-Alice thought. A port. By the sea. Handy, if ever in need of a quick exit. Besides, she thought, all that land for sale in the *Advertiser*, those large advertisements for large acreages, it was surely safe to assume people might be a bit thin on the ground. Assume nothing, A-B, she told herself. Hadn't there been a snake in Eden? But the sea … She'd hardly slept, taken the first carriage she could get a seat on. It had barely set out when a kangaroo hopped onto, then off, the track. Katya had a joey for a pet, as a child. A sign, surely?

The interview was almost as bad as being interrogated by the police. The same hard chair, blank face, probing questions.

Name? Age? Last employer? Reason for leaving? References?

She'd taken in Mr Max Carver. He'd done the same, from under heavy lids. Silver streaks in his hair, a badger, gone to fat, badly in need of a haircut. A once-handsome badger. Her father—a dab hand at shearing, tall, a real streak, boundless energy and optimism, dead of a broken heart—would have done a job on him.

It was almost painful, waiting for him to speak. Not that she was exactly chatty herself; eyes lowered, hands laid in her lap. English didn't appear to be his native tongue. But then neither was it her parents'. Or perhaps he'd just had enough of talking. You couldn't blame someone, Alice thought, for tiring of words. Smothering you with pity, eviscerating you with venom. More bark than bite, she'd finally decided.

Max? Maxwell? Maximilian?

She'd copied out an old reference, en route, word for word but for the name change. There'd been a girl in her class at school called Binney. He read the reference thoroughly, folded it thoughtfully. She'd been about to get to her feet to leave when he suddenly looked at her directly. She'd felt sick to the very pit of her stomach. It was like looking in the mirror. A person bereft gazing back at her.

'You can start directly,' he said. Then followed it up with an earnest, halting, oddly endearing little lecture on how she'd need to take especial care with the scrimshaw. She kept on nodding. She'd work it out, she thought. She had most things.

'Trehearne,' he'd told his man, 'take Miss Binney's bags to her room.' Bag, just the one. Katya's old carpet bag, which Trehearne dumped, none too gently, just inside the door. Was it rum? Brandy? She had to fling open a window after he snapped the door shut behind him. Mouthfuls of sea air rushed in, billowing the curtains. She stood there, grinning. Sea, sea! And almost right below her very window, a little beach of white sand.

Fallen on her feet, all right.

Smoke

Max Carver called him Trehearne, so Alice followed suit. The scullery maid, Mary Kathleen O'Brien, called him Patrick. Sometimes Paddy. When he was in her good books, more or less sober, or she was after him to chop wood. Not exactly misshapen, he was sorely lacking in height, flesh, bones, teeth. Small eyes, set close together; hardly a chin to speak of; oversized Adam's apple—a trial to watch him swallow.

'Suffers from the smoke,' Mary Kathleen confided to Alice, of Trehearne. 'Can hardly bear to hear bacon sizzling in the pan. Just the whiff of a bonfire enough to get him reaching for the bottle. Burning autumn leaves an annual torment.'

*

He'd fallen on hard times, he told Max in the bar of the Great Southern. Had a home, once. And a wife.

He hadn't named her. Enid O'Malloran. Four months pregnant, well past her prime when they tied the knot. A bawd with more than usual powers of acceptance, of taking a thing as it came. Hard to fault, in truth. Hardly flinched when he bawled her out. Ducked every backhander. Feisty little thing.

Even when he pronounced, of their squawking, scrunch-faced infant, 'Ugly little bastard', all she had to offer was 'Hush, Paddy. The bairn's hungry, is all. He's after a good feeding.' Pulling out a tit. His tit.

The house had burned down, Enid and infant within. House? Hut, the judge had pronounced, like a sodding building inspector. Highly combustible.

By the time he'd reached it, the flames had turned colourless. All the same, he swore he heard her cry 'Patrick!' Though, in truth, he might have mistaken it in the conflagration of wood seasoned by three years of drought; the stove, iron roof, iron bed, all exploding and crashing down. Nothing but ash, some few shards of bone.

He'd taken his time, worked the whole thing out. When his old man always said he had the attention span of a gnat. He'd tracked the incendiary bastard down, out the back of Dubbo, bailed him up outside a pub one night. He hadn't planned on there being a plank of wood to hand. The thing had just unravelled after that. He kept seeing her face, peering from the flames. Holding up with outstretched arms, the burning bloody infant. As if making some bloody sacrificial offering. Wouldn't have built a bloody house, he thought, if he hadn't a bloody wife. Hadn't need of a bloody wife, only he'd got her bloody pregnant. Bundle of bloody joy, all right.

An accident, the judge decided. The man had merely been clearing a patch of scrub when the wind had changed. No reason for Trehearne to wreak vengeance, take the law into his own hands, the judge said, handing down the sentence. Six months, for unlawful killing.

He'd started drinking in earnest the day he got out. His hands had healed. Scar tissue, the doc had said of his eyes, though he could swear some days they were still full of cinders.

In the Balance

Like new-minted silver, Alice thought, depositing two plumply poached eggs beside the glistening piece of haddock on Max's plate. His beard, catching the early morning light. Still badly in need of a trim.

'Stay,' Max said.

She was halfway to the door. Had barely been there two weeks. She turned, planting feet in the carpet, fighting the urge to bolt. Remembered standing in a corner at school, punished for speaking her mother's tongue. She'd wet her drawers. Now fought the rising urge to pee.

'All well, Alice? Settled in?' He cleared his throat, wiped his whiskers on a napkin, a smear of butter on his beard. She had to fight the urge to dab at it.

She nodded. More seemed to be required. 'I don't look well?'

'Thin,' he said brutally. Or perhaps—she gave him the benefit of the doubt—unthinkingly.

'I'm sorry, sir,' she said faintly.

'Mr Carver,' he said.

*

There was hardly a moment those first weeks when Alice's future didn't hang in the balance. On the one hand, there was frightened rabbit Alice; on the other, a chicken consommé like a little temple pool Max had once seen in Batavia, so clear he'd been able to trim his beard in its reflection. On the one hand, a stuffed leg of lamb so tender he barely needed to chew; on the other, a troublesome barking at night. On one side of the equation, a stick insect hardly fitted for the title cook–housekeeper; on the other a silken bowl of custard, fluffy clouds of chocolate meringue floating within. A Yorkshire pudding more flummery than stodgy pud. Pork crackling that snapped like a Christmas fancy. A rack of lamb that brought a tear to his eye, reminding him of the high meadows of Pico, the sheep fat as clouds.

The second week, Max scrutinised the accounts. Nothing out of the ordinary. No special ingredients, undue expense. Just the usual provisions, delivered weekly from the grocery store in town.

Her mother taught her to cook, Alice said, when asked.

As *her* mother had taught her, she added surprisingly, off her own bat. Then grew almost voluble on the matter of salt. How a pinch, or lack thereof, could ruin a dish. How it behooved a person to taste, taste again. And finally fell silent, ashen, biting on her lip.

Returning to the kitchen, Alice stuffed a fist in her mouth, crossed her eyes, surprised she hadn't mentioned that pastry needed a cool hand; custards patience; that eclairs and cream horns were best reserved for the cooler months. Then whacked her head none too gently with a wooden spoon.

*

Max heard the dog that same night. Barking. Once, twice, thrice, before abruptly falling silent. Stopping mid-stride outside Alice's door on his way to bed, he'd tiptoed on, inching shut the door to his study–bedroom, wincing when it clicked. Mrs Murphy, last but one of the long line of his cook–housekeepers, those past two years, hadn't tiptoed. She'd borne down on him like a man o'war, filling every door with her girth, every silence with her opinion. She'd lasted but three months. Emily Gillies, her replacement, had been the quiet sort. With a defeated air. Bent, as if awaiting the lash. Her food utterly without savour. Her sighs had filled every corner of the house. Her asthmatic breathing whistled like wind in the rigging. She'd managed a year. Too quiet, she'd said, a quiet triumph in her voice. He'd cast the net wider, wider still. With still unquantifiable results.

The Dog

'You mustn't hesitate,' Max said to Alice when a month had passed, 'to ask. If you're in want of something. A new saucepan, perhaps?' he ventured, at a loss as to what ailed her.

'Oh, no. Thank you. I've everything,' she said in a rush, 'I need. I'll fetch the gravy,' she added, hastily backing out of the dining room.

Leaning against the kitchen table, she stared sightlessly at the gravy boat. A Pandora's box, the mouth. Best kept shut.

She kept her eyes on the carpet, going back in. In silence, he watched her put down the gravy, then retreat. But she could hear him thinking. Of how her ankles were like sticks, chest flatter than the plate she was carrying, face scooped out better than any eclair.

She rushed her prayers that night. Fetched the pot from its appointed shelf in the wardrobe, put first one, then, face screwed up in brief deliberation, two fingers down her throat. Tickled them about, the way her father used to tickle trout, acid bile flooding her mouth. She retched, retched again, swallowed it down, pain doubling her up, then vomited into the pot. Fireworks under her lids. She coughed, a loud, barking cough. Wiped her mouth with a handkerchief, closely examining the results. Blood. A neat little spray of polka dots. Folding the handkerchief and returning it, and the pot, to the shelf, she made a mental note not to empty the pot onto the geraniums under the window. The leaves had begun to yellow around the edges. In bed, she lay for a time wondering, as so often, how it might feel to know that any moment the ground under your feet would drop. Praying your neck would snap. That the rope would hold. That they wouldn't bungle the task. Then, expertly banishing the thoughts, she turned over, asleep in moments.

*

A possum, Max wondered, ear to the door. Barking owl? Dog? Perhaps they ought to get one. Trehearne was always complaining of rats: that they swam in from passing ships, swarmed in at night from the bush. Antonio sometimes used to cry out in his sleep. Nightmares? Cramps? Too many books? In bed, his head pillowed on an arm, 'Marcelinho' Max murmured, out of practice. Tongue darting for a remnant crumb of a cream horn, the lingering sweetness of strawberry jam. Finding a trace on a tooth, he sucked. Asleep in moments.

A Solitary Figure

Every morning, on the dot of nine, Alice, at the kitchen window, saw him open the front door. Pause some moments to take in the day's wind, chop, tide, before making his faintly rolling way down the path to the beach. She could have set a clock by him, so unvarying was his routine. A solitary figure. An old whaler, Mary Kathleen had told her, that first day. An odd fish. No family, friends, visitors. Hardly ventured out, she said, but to town, to have his hair and beard trimmed.

Alice was fond of routine. As a child, she'd liked nothing better than to help her mother in the kitchen, baking. All the ingredients lined up, at the ready, before the stately measuring and weighing, the careful sifting and spooning, the delicate folding and oft-times frenzied beating. The shutting of the oven door on something pale and unpromising only to open it to something risen and golden and sweet-smelling. If God were a woman, Alice sometimes thought, surely She would bake. And far from resting on the Sabbath, would whip up Her finest, most magnificent creations, as her mother had.

On tiptoe, Alice saw him down on the beach, one particularly fine spring morning. Examining the rowboat. Running a hand over the boards, before giving it a little pat. Like a man with a dog, she thought, amused. Then saw him abruptly straighten, staring out to sea. At a whale. Spouting. Sending up telltale puffs of white water. Dragging the boat to the water's edge, he climbed in and began to row.

She only need glance up, some days, from rolling a pie crust, to find one of the great creatures waving a flipper at her, catapulting itself skyward only to fall back with a mighty splash. Her chest never failed to swell at the sight. Even though she'd be glad of a peg on her nose, Mary Kathleen had warned her that first day, what with the stink from the Davidsons' whaling station when the wind was from the south.

*

Max was glad of the boat, which had come with the parcel of land. Though he might not miss the reek of blood, he did the movement of a ship. Everything seemed strangely static on land: trees, rocks, house, horizon. The sea-chest, rooted in his study. Some days, it nagged worse than his rotting molar.

No-one even knew it existed, he now thought, as he rowed. Wouldn't be a whit the wiser if he were to row out, very early one morning, and heave it overboard. Somewhere off Boyd's Tower, say. It was deep out there, fathoms deep. It would sink.

But would it? The ever-niggling doubt. Didn't he owe his life to its particular propensity to float? Hadn't it saved them both, him and Paulo? Resting momentarily on the oars, he thought of Alice at the kitchen window. She'd miss it, he thought. For all she kept her eyes down, she didn't miss a trick.

The Thaw

The thaw began with a Chicken Curry.

Waiting in line in the post office, Alice had been surprised to learn that Max was a kind of Spaniard. Portuguese, Alfred, who worked behind the counter, had contrarily insisted. It seemed he'd once known a Portuguese, in Sydney. An animated discussion had ensued. To which Alice, with scant knowledge of Portuguese or Spaniards, hadn't felt moved to contribute.

Alice did, however, it now being confirmed Max was from foreign parts and doubtless fond of spice, unearth a recipe for a Chicken Curry in *Mrs Beeton's Cookery Book* (acquired, as Mary Kathleen had it, by Mr Carver in a doomed attempt to improve the culinary skills of the unlamented Emily Gillies). She made a stab at it that same night. The first mouthful, an unfamiliar look crossed his face. Pleasure? Pain? Indigestion? The second, she thought of her mother, taking the wafer in church. As she retrieved his plate, he held her gaze, then gravely dipped his head. In acknowledgement? In thanks? Feeling the beginnings of a gloat, Alice returned to the kitchen. Hands plunged into near-boiling water to drive home the point, she reminded herself that pride most often came before a fall.

'Bacalhau,' he murmured at lunch, barely a week later, dabbing at his beard with a serviette.

Salt cod stew, so Alice discovered. Mrs Beeton again. The woman was a marvel. And herself with nothing but sea bass. And little to guide her, but three lines in a book. Flying without wings. Close your eyes, Alice, she told herself. Don't. Think. Just. Let. Salt. Fish. There. Done.

*

Portuguese?

From the Azores, it seemed. An archipelago set down in the middle of the Atlantic, almost equidistant between Portugal and Cape Cod. Imagine the winds, Alice thought, in high delight. The seas. The whales. It had taken some searching to find Pico on the globe in his study. Small as an ant. She couldn't imagine him living on it.

Even when she began cooking for him, he'd been on the large side. And now look at him, she thought, a little guiltily. The food he loved, he ate more of.

Despite the beginnings of a head cold, he'd taken the boat out that morning. Passing his room, she'd heard him sneeze. It would do him good, she assured herself; sea air could bring colour to the palest cheek. Look at her own. Then made a mental note to check for liniment in the first aid tin.

Just as well, Alice thought, and not for the first time, that they had Dr Culligan to call upon. Tall, thin, upright, severe. Though he looked to be as easily bowled over as a skittle, he never failed to come when called. Had doubtless saved Trehearne's hand, sliced through with a fishing knife. Sewing it up as neat as one of Katya's seams.

She'd heard Max whistling on his way down to the beach. You couldn't protect people, she thought, keep them safe from harm. Stop them from going out in boats and catching pneumonia. Such tiny islands! Even the largest, São Miguel, easily obscured by the tip of a pinkie. The whole lot less than a hand's breadth from the Dalmatian coast. Their parents as good as neighbours!

*

For the first weeks, she recalled, hardly a word had passed between them. She, achingly careful to place each foot securely on the carpet, delivering plates to the table like a diligent altar boy. He, staring out of the window, or down at the salt cellar.

She remembered his first proper 'thank you'. How his eyes had searched out her own, before fixing on the lamb slices she'd laid on his plate. She'd suddenly felt a lump in her throat, had to swallow it down, serving gravy and mint sauce with what she'd hoped was aplomb. Then, back in the kitchen, had leaned against the table, knees turned to jelly. Thank you. She'd said the same to a fellow visitor, in Bathurst Gaol, who'd offered her half a sandwich. And to the prison guard, who'd momentarily stepped outside, so she and Katya could say goodbye.

*

Kept in solitary confinement, Katya had quickly grown thin, though she'd always been the sturdier, chubbier, stronger, more fearless one. They'd wanted her apart from the other prisoners. Kept her safe, Alice thought. And for what? It had grown harder, every visit, to leave. Not just the sound of the door clanging shut, her sister's stricken face through the bars, but the little padded cell across the way, for recalcitrant prisoners, with all the scratching from all the fingernails.

Her likeness had been in all the newspapers. Days, weeks, months, right up until the end, and after. Taken the day she was charged. Eyes half starting out of her head, hair fallen down. Mad, they'd called her. Ugly. When dreamy-eyed with sleep, sun glinting on her golden locks, surely there was nothing on God's Earth more beautiful than Katya. Surely, Alice had thought, as the weeks had ground to months, surely they'd find someone else. Some other monster to write about. Surely, Katya couldn't be the only one.

Chatting

They got into the habit of having little chats. Most often at lunch or supper time when she served at table. She could hardly get a word out of him at breakfast. Not that she much minded, occupied with planning the day's menu, mentally restocking the larder, counting up all the many things left undone by Mary Kathleen.

It seemed no time at all before they were happily swapping baking yarns for whale lore. Lard versus blubber, Alice privately termed it, with glee. She did her best not to flinch, told of the hunt; she had no reason to think him cruel, no more than she had her father, when he'd had to kill one of the sheep for mutton.

*

Trehearne was surprised to find himself usurped. His morning chats with Max at the kitchen door given over to her tête-à-têtes at the dining-room table. His plans to plant cabbages overruled by a desire for petunias. She took over the kitchen, the scullery, a good half of the verandah, where she sat, on her half day off, book in lap, staring at the sea. And Max. Him, most of all.

*

Max was more than happy to cede Alice the domestic realm, freed up, as he was, to spend his days at the telescope or out rowing in the bay. It wasn't long before he wouldn't have thought to venture into her domain without her subtle say-so. A little smile of encouragement, peeling her way through a mound of windfall apples, as he hovered in the kitchen doorway. An almost imperceptible frown, up to her elbows in flour, at work on some particularly delicate pastry.

Seldom did she overstep the mark.

'I was wondering,' she began one morning, unusually tentative, 'if you mightn't like me to air the chest in your study, Mr Carver. It's been such a summer for mould.'

'Air it?' he said, surprisingly sharp. 'Why, there's hardly anything in it.'

Was she crestfallen?

'Just some old books.' More level now.

'Books?' Newly alarmed.

'Old scientific tomes.' With a shrug. 'Belonging to my late brother.'

He'd never mentioned a brother.

'He was fond of reading?' Alice suggested, being, herself, very fond of the pursuit.

Max considered the question. 'He had a general interest in the natural world.' Loftily. 'Earthworms and such, as a lad. And later whales. Cetaceans.'

'Cetaceans.' The word slithered off Alice's tongue. 'Such marvellous creatures,' she said, all in a rush. 'So majestic. Like mountains. I always love to see them out in the bay.'

Then flushed, very pink.

Max was silent some moments. 'There's no need to trouble yourself with the thing, Alice. I keep a close eye on it.' Stiffly.

He hadn't opened it in months.

Drifting

It was quite some time, out rowing, before Max's fingers failed to curl round invisible harpoons, his muscles to tense, for him to leap to his feet at the sight of a whale. Almost every day he spied them, bobbing like giant kegs as they basked in the balmy waters of Twofold Bay, readying for the long haul south to Antarctica.

He soon got used to them. Many a summer afternoon found him sprawled in the boat, arm heedlessly dangled over the gunwale, the sound of their breathing as good as the sea for lulling him to sleep. Not that he didn't wake with a start. Or feel relieved to find himself still of a piece. Not that they seemed particularly vicious. Or even particularly curious, barely taking the trouble to raise their great heads above the water to keep an eye on him. Strange, but he never felt queasy in their presence. When even a whiff of blood, blown across the bay from the Davidsons' whaling station, could still get his belly clenching.

Confined to his study by a raging westerly or stiff nor'-easter, he'd sometimes catch sight of them through the telescope, soaring clear of the waves as they breached, always with an echoing leap in his gut. If there were calves, or they came right in, he'd sometimes summon Alice to come and look; she'd always arrive at a trot.

In truth, he found it hard to fill the hours. For a time, he again tried his hand at carving, but without success; whatever had impelled him to it was gone. For a couple of months he took up ropemaking. Splicing and plaiting and weaving the stuff into ever more tormented shapes—with no purpose but to adorn the verandah rafters. Then thought he might try his hand at building a boat, but he already had a perfectly good one. He considered growing grapes, perhaps establishing a vineyard; he had the land, but he'd never really been one for imbibing. For some weeks he gave serious thought to acquiring a sheep or goat: useful for cheese, and easily consumed if things didn't go to plan. Even, perhaps, a cow or pig, and some geese. Only to wryly conclude that he might as well be his father, forever tied to the land, with never a moment spare for mucking about in boats. The truth was, he only knew the sea.

He made sure, every now and again, to open the chest. Diligently checked the books for mould. Unwrapped the whalebone, still with no idea of its significance, but that his brother had bound it in enough cloth for a mummy. Before, with a familiar queasy feeling, taking out the little bundle of letters, written and never sent—to Rosa, Margarida, Paulo, Fredo. Antonio's whale journal he always kept for last. And never once, unwrapping the oilcloth in which he'd bound it after the shipwreck, and flicking through the unread pages to look for damage, did he fail to recall the books piled up on the kitchen table; João reaching to tousle Antonio's hair; his brother's hand laid over its cover, even in his sleep.

As for the whales, he couldn't help, over time, but recognise a few. One with a badly torn fluke; another almost weighted down with barnacles; a third's fluke so black it might have been dipped in ink. Every day, aboard ship, they'd kept a faithful record of the catch, along with a rough pictorial of the beasts. He began to imitate the task in a book, very like his brother's journal, especially acquired for the purpose—a rough sketch when a whale was sighted, a brief remark if anything was out of the ordinary. It certainly helped fill the hours.

The Pig

Three years being fed by Alice, and Max grew as fat as a Pico pig. So weighed down by heaviness and the past, he some days found it hard to bestir himself. He might never have emerged at all that winter, but that, suffering a rotting molar, he was seen by Alice picking currants out of a spotted dick. She made an appointment for him with the dentist.

It was a squeeze, getting out of the front door. Emerging into wintry sunshine, pale as a beluga, he wondered if he should enlarge the entrance. Trehearne could probably manage it, he thought. Distracted by a sudden, fresh, pleasantly ticklish breeze on his face, he took an unsteady step, might well have stumbled, if Alice hadn't reached to steady him.

Where would he be without her?

A thought, unwelcome, emerged to tease him in the still hours of the night. Tease? Torment. Nearing his sixth decade, what had he done with his life? Where had it all gone? How had he come to be here, at the far-flung end of the world? No-one to know him, or listen to his stories, his tales of life at sea. No-one to care. But for Alice. He swore, in midnight earnest, to live tomorrow a different life. Take coffee instead of tea. One spoon of sugar instead of three. Eggs poached instead of fried. Be the sort of man he recognised.

Then fell asleep, only to dream of a pig. A brute of a beast, squealing, about to have its throat slit. Only to realise that he was the pig. He woke, heart pounding. It had been his task, every year, after grape harvest, to hold the pig down while João slit its throat. Antonio desperately tugging, all the while, at his father's arm, begging him to spare it. Antonio used to give them names. Pedro. Carmelo. Branco. Max remembered dangling Rosa's crackling under his brother's nose trying to tempt him, but nothing would make Antonio eat pig. Or whale. Not after the books. Whereas before, still with the power to cut him to the quick, Max had been as good as a hero to his brother.

The Cliff

So contented was Alice, after three years in Max's employ, she'd almost begun to think herself free of her past. Only, with the first faint stirrings of spring that year, and all within the space of weeks, for a dead whale to be stolen from Calle Calle Bay; Joe Givins to suddenly, and unaccountably, appear; and for Alice to meet Jean.

That changed just about everything.

*

Alice was standing on the very edge of a cliff when Jean first saw her.

About to jump. Or so Jean surmised.

Not, as was the case, that Alice was merely in silent, loving communion with a lost sister, inspired by the sight on her morning's walk of a spray of early spring jasmine, a flower much loved by Katya. She had once stitched a little purse for Alice's birthday, with just such a spray as motif. Alice had reserved the purse for Sunday best. Even the most turgid of sermons was ameliorated by the sight of it nestled in her lap. Just as, she thought, staring at the untrammelled vista before her, her every loss seemed to find some reprieve in the contemplation of His handiwork.

Jean, seeing only a young woman in peril, immediately snatched up her skirts and ran. She knew, from her daily walks, of the drop at that point, the tangle of rocks far below.

'Don't!' Jean cried, as she neared. 'Don't jump! Please don't!'

If anything, the woman seemed to tilt forward a little in response. Putting on a last desperate spurt, Jean made a lunge for her, grabbing her by the arm and yanking her back from the edge. From almost certain death, she realised, shaken to the core.

The woman stared at her some moments, then blinked. Mad, Jean decided on the spot. Mad as a bolting horse. Doubtless escaped from the local sanatorium. Probably why she was so very pale, she thought, never exposed to the sun. And so thin, Jean could feel all the bones in her arm.

'Dear God,' Jean heard herself quaver. 'How could you jump? And in broad daylight.' Which even to her own ears sounded faintly absurd.

'Jump?' The woman's eyes widened in apparent amazement. 'I wasn't going to jump,' she protested. And, with sudden inspiration. 'I was watching a whale.'

'Whale? What whale?' Jean demanded harshly.

'A humpback. I thought it was a rock. Until I saw its tail. Fluke.' She instantly, and surprisingly to Jean's mind, corrected herself. 'It's probably long gone,' she added, as Jean cast a sceptical glance at the churning waters below.

They stood, some moments, at an impasse, before Jean abruptly released her.

'My dear young woman,' she said, in tones usually reserved for only the most recalcitrant of her young charges, 'even if you didn't mean to jump, you might very easily have slipped.'

'I'm sorry,' the woman said, with what seemed genuine contrition. 'I obviously gave you a terrible fright.'

'That's hardly the point,' Jean said shortly. 'It was an utterly foolhardy thing to do. Particularly with all the rain we've had.'

'Torrential,' the young woman agreed, rubbing at her arm. Then suddenly flushed. She looked far better for it, Jean thought. 'It was very good of you to try to save me,' she said, grown surprisingly meek. 'Brave. As you say, I might have slipped. Pulled you over with me.'

Jean hadn't thought of that.

The woman frowned at her feet, as if they were somehow to blame.

'Well, no harm done, I suppose,' Jean conceded, if grudgingly. Her heart had only just begun to settle. She wiped her hands surreptitiously on her dress.

'A misunderstanding,' the woman said. 'You weren't to know about the whale.'

Jean's smile was strained.

'Alice.' The young woman suddenly extended a bony hand. 'Alice Binney. And thank you. Truly. I'm very much in your debt.'

Almost despite herself, Jean softened a little.

'Jean.' She proffered her own. 'Tennyson,' she added, with a familiar, small, private smack of satisfaction. She was very fond of Tennyson's verse.

The woman's hand was icy in her own. Shock?

Jean took the opportunity, retrieving her pocket watch, to take some further steps back from the edge. 'Goodness!' She gave the timepiece a little shake. 'I'll be late for school, at this rate.'

'You're a teacher?' Alice Binney seemed impressed.

Jean nodded.

'I would have loved to teach,' Alice said, a little wistfully.

'Well, then you should have,' Jean said crisply.

'I'm afraid I'm not particularly good with children.'

'Nor I,' Jean said. 'I can assure you it's just practice,' she added. 'Though it seems I did start rather young. My mother said I was always lining my dolls up, ordering them to do my bidding. Scolding them if they didn't.'

'A regular tyrant,' Alice said, with a faint smile.

'As you'd no doubt guessed,' Jean said. 'Well,' she added, 'I suppose I'd better be off. I don't want a riot on my hands. I must say, dolls were a lot easier.'

Walking away, Jean had to fight an urge to turn and look back. Alice Binney, she thought, seemed to encourage wayward gestures. She still wasn't entirely sure she'd forgiven her. She felt distinctly light-headed.

*

Watching Jean turn the corner, Alice thought that she wasn't anything like any teacher she'd ever had. Immaculately turned out, every strand of glossy dark hair in place, gloves neatly pressed. More headmistressy, she thought, gingerly fingering her arm. Then winced. She'd have a nasty bruise, come tomorrow.

The Jolt

The whole of the rest of the day she met Alice, Jean felt out of sorts. Shock, she diagnosed. Or the dampness of the early morning air. Even, perhaps, an incipient touch of bronchitis, to which she was prone. For all that, putting away the last stick of chalk, closing the last childishly copied letter-book, she decided to clear her head with a walk along Asling's Beach. Striding along the familiar shoreline, she went over her encounter with the strange young woman, as she had, on and off, all day. And if the woman had jumped? No-one would have even known, except for Jean. But perhaps, she posited, there would have been no tragedy. Perhaps Alice was a more than usually accomplished swimmer and would have miraculously survived the fall, and made her own way safely back to shore. But no. She would, almost instantly, have been swept out to sea. Or dashed violently against the rocks. Jean would never have forgotten it, she knew. Her whole life, she would have remembered it. The violent death of a stranger. What a cross for someone to have to bear, she thought, feeling distinctly put out all over again.

She found it surprisingly hard to shake the feeling. In fact, she only need think of Alice Binney to experience a disconcerting little jolt.

As when she bumped into her on Asling's Beach, some weeks after what she'd privately come to term the 'Cliff Incident'. Not that it was in any way unusual to encounter someone one knew on Asling's. It was that sort of beach. A sunny Sunday afternoon, and the two-mile stretch of fine white sand was well dotted with walkers, shell collectors, ball throwers, fishermen, paddlers, sandcastle builders.

Jean recognised her at once. She'd caught the sun; her nose was pink. It was hard not to notice it against the paleness of her face. She was carrying a basket, swinging it, along with her straw hat, its little bunch of strawberries attached to a red ribbon. The scene was unexpectedly jaunty. They exchanged awkward pleasantries before, almost without realising, falling into step. Alice stopped, after a time, to pick up a feather, then a little necklace of weed. Jean found a stick that so resembled a wishbone, Alice urged her to make a wish. But for what, Jean thought, at a loss. An end to days and nights of regret? They stopped to watch a boy launch a kite, the wind having picked up, but almost immediately it fell back to earth. 'Like Icarus,' Jean murmured, surprised when Alice remarked, 'Too close to the sun. I think I've had a touch too much myself.' Putting on the strawberry bonnet, tying the ribbon firmly under her chin.

They sat for a time at the far end of the beach, watching, in amusement, the antics of a small spotted terrier, tirelessly retrieving a stick; then a group of children splashing one another, climbing onto each other's shoulders, only to topple over with shrieks of delight.

'Lemonade?' Reaching into her basket, Alice produced a stoppered bottle, and a cup, neatly wrapped.

'But you've only the one,' Jean pointed out.

Delving deeper, Alice produced another.

'Like a rabbit out of a hat,' Jean said, amused.

'Always have something in reserve,' Alice said. 'Cook's motto. And shortbreads,' she added. 'Baked fresh this morning.'

'You're a cook?'

'Cook–housekeeper,' Alice said. 'Who likes to bake,' she offered after a moment.

Far more than she did killing and plucking chickens, she thought, sipping lemonade, the breeze barely ruffling Jean's shiny, immaculately arranged hair. She'd had to wring the neck of one that morning for the Sunday roast, unable to rouse Trehearne, whose snoring sounded loudly through the rickety door to his room.

She always tried to do it quickly.

'I wish I could swim,' she said, as one of the older boys waded out to breast the larger waves.

'I could teach you, if you'd like,' Jean surprisingly offered.

'I can't even float,' Alice said, doubtful.

'You probably could, with practice.'

'Like teaching?' Alice suggested, with a smile.

'Precisely.' Jean smiled in response.

'Utterly fearless,' Alice now remarked of the boy, flinging himself over and over at the waves.

Perhaps it was the chicken, or that the boy seemed brave to the point of idiocy, that set her wondering, as she hadn't for a good couple of hours, how you managed the business of dying. With grace. Without fear. When there was no-one to call upon.

'Penny for your thoughts,' Jean said, over the rim of her cup.

'Actually, I was thinking about dying,' Alice murmured, off her guard.

'You did look a bit grim,' Jean said lightly. Then, 'I think it must be the hardest thing in the world.'

'For everyone?'

'Well, there's no map. No blueprint. Unless, that is, you happen to believe in God. Heaven, hell, damnation. That sort of thing. Which I happen not to.'

'You don't?'

Jean shook her head. 'Most certainly not. I had more than enough of rules and regulations with my own father to embrace any others.'

'Isn't it a bit tricky, as a teacher?' Alice said.

'I don't tell everyone,' Jean said breezily. 'Anyone, come to that. I probably shouldn't have told you.'

'I'm so glad that you did,' Alice said, so fervently that she blushed. They were silent some moments. Alice got to her feet, brushing off sand. 'I really should be getting back,' she said. 'I'm sure it's grown cooler.' She turned to sniff the air.

'Afternoon nor'-easter,' Jean said, struck, suddenly, by the fineness of Alice's profile. 'Better watch out for bluebottles,' she cautioned, as they started back along the water's edge.

But there were none. Only a cuttlefish, which Jean pocketed, reminded, by its pale bony perfection, of Alice.

The Detective

Alice, pleasantly preoccupied with thoughts of Jean and their chance encounter on the beach, was reaching for a jar of preserved peaches in the grocery store when she looked up to find Joe Givins staring at her. She froze. Almost instantly recovering, she picked up the jar and examined the contents. All the while thinking how he looked just the same, but for a little less hair, a little more afternoon shadow to his jaw, a little more paunch straining the buttons of his jacket. Returning the jar to the shelf, she deliberately picked up another, of plums. Scrutinising it some moments, she returned it with a little shrug, before turning and walking out. Purposefully. As if with some just-remembered errand to attend to. She walked the length of Imlay Street and took the last turn left. And only then glanced back. There was no-one following. The street was empty. She walked on, wondering if he'd known she was in Eden. Had he come looking for her? But why? Why now, after all this time?

He was probably on his way to the house, that very minute, she thought. She'd probably get home to find her bag packed and waiting on the doorstep. Home? Tears pricked her eyes. She blinked them back. It was her own fault, she thought bleakly.

Hankering after the sea. Mooning over pet joeys; undone by memories of that last idyllic family holiday at the seaside when she'd buried Katya up to her neck in sand and made her promise to give her the doll, Mildred. Just teasing, she'd said, when Katya wailed. Only she wasn't. Cruel, cruel. Justice will prevail.

*

All set to follow Alice, Joe Givins abruptly changed his mind. What was the point? What did he have to say to her? They hadn't exchanged a word since the trial. It wasn't as if she'd broken any law. Unless she'd taken up whale rustling. He was getting almost as bad as his old man, he thought, for suspicion. Never took a day off from the anticipation of human failure, Givins the elder; thought the worst of everyone. His own flesh and blood included. His own flesh and blood most of all. Made their lives a bloody misery.

She was probably on holiday, he thought. Or perhaps she had a position in the town. Eden was a nice enough sort of place, if remote. As he well knew. He stood some moments, staring at the door, heedless of the doorbell, still faintly tinkling. You could hardly blame her, he thought, gone to ground. He would have known her in a line-up. Had no trouble at all summoning up a mental picture of her in court. She'd been there often enough. She might have been Katya Brajkoviç's twin: two tall, pale statues of suffering and stoicism. The jury had certainly been aware of her. And the press. Hadn't been able to take his eyes off her, that flint-hearted prosecutor, Bolten. Lascivious little bastard. They were almost frighteningly alike: tall, bony, ivory-skinned, with those strange translucent blue eyes and honeyed hair. Striking. The Slav Girls, the papers had dubbed them. Foreign-looking. Stiff. Katya walking into court each day as if she had a book on her head. Giving them a lesson in deportment. Or personal hygiene, her hair freshly washed, neatly braided. When she was supposed to look done in, done for. He wanted to salute her, at the end. What she'd gone through, what she'd faced. And that before the verdict was handed down. Bloody unforgiving lot, jurors. Didn't bear thinking about, really.

He should have gone after her, he thought then, if just to apologise. He'd probably frightened the wits out of her. Though she'd made a fist of it. Sailed out of that door. Bloody good actress. She'd had some practice, he thought, at the trial.

Like his May, he thought, at the beginning of the disease. Hideously cheerful, face lit up at the sight of him standing, yet again, in a hospital doorway. But not at the end. She hadn't the strength: bloodless, shapeless, a sack of sad bones under a white sheet. He'd been glad to let her go. Like having a brute of a nagging tooth pulled, the relief had lasted a good few hours before the agony truly set in.

Alicja. Probably going by another name. Brajkoviç. Hard to get your tongue around; not that any of them had tried. Strange, he thought, that she should be here, of all places, his old stamping ground. Must be, what, eight, nine years ago now? More like ten.

He'd been in his late twenties, still wet behind the ears. A lot of water under the bridge since then. A lot of innocent kids done to death. Still, she was a hard one to forget, Caroline Emily Rathbone. Little Caro, that silky-tongued prosecutor had called her. Like those cherubs on Christmas cards. Rosebud lips, golden curls, rosy cheeks, clear, shining eyes. Innocent. No other word for it. May would have happily killed whoever did her in. A child gone to waste. The papers, of course, had a field day with Katya. Two-faced as Janus, should never have been allowed near a child, never mind paid to look after one. None of it had made much sense. He'd watched from the sidelines, still on his training wheels as a detective constable. No special insights, revelations. Just a gut feeling. Growing by the day. Too much missing, too many gaps. And the motive? May was convinced, though. Woman's instinct, she said. Which made the press a bunch of bleeding women. Or mad arsonists, desperate to stoke a fire, so they could be seen to put it out. The only thing that burned? That rope, sawing at her neck. Woman's instinct! Joe Givins snorted under his breath.

The Stolen Whale

A stolen whale, and the death that ensued, had returned Joe to Eden. Not that he was exactly unknown to the place: born and bred there, went to school there, joined the police force there, married a local girl, May Beatrice Lewis there, with no intention of ever leaving—but she'd refused to let him knock back a promotion to detective constable in Sydney. More than a few in the district would still recognise him, he knew.

Since the move to Sydney, Joe had worked cases in half the towns up and down the coast. An obvious choice for the Eden case, according to the powers that be. A local. What's more, he'd investigated many a murder, and hadn't his old man fished? What's a whale but a big fish? Everyone knew they were a tight mob, whalers. Taciturn. Unless in their cups, when garrulous. Joe suspected that all that might be required were a few free ales, a few well-aimed questions.

*

Almost the second he'd deposited his bag in his room at the Great Southern, he'd made a beeline for Asling's Beach. Then sat, for a time, on the sand, staring at the breaking waves, his memories full of broken arms, crushed skulls, a severed foot. Standard police issue. Then blinked, shook his head, wriggled his toes in his boots: also standard issue, stiffer than a corpse when new, long since worn in. Awful, he thought, eyes unconsciously following the wild wind-blown flight of a gull, how the thing still welled up. It was Asling's, of course. What did he expect? His old stamping ground, veritable home away from home. The repository of some of his most glorious memories. He'd lost his virginity to these golden sands. May, with him. Innocents. No idea how to go about the thing, ended up with sand in every orifice. He'd licked her skin. Fingers, arm, into the secret cubby hole of her armpit. Lovestruck in the blink of her blue eyes. Amazed she could ever fancy him. Bit of a runt, little Joe. A good couple of inches shorter than his old man. Only got into the force, to his abiding shame, because Big Joe had a word in someone's shell-like. He threw a long shadow, his father. Fearless, decorated three times for valour. If a drowning child were in want of rescuing, Big Joe was your man. Didn't feel fear. Couldn't. Perfect copper.

It might have helped, Joe thought—a familiar thought—if there'd been someone to share the load: a brother, sister. Diluted things a bit. The expectations, the disappointments.

May had got his number. Cranky little bugger, she'd diagnosed. Then taught him to smile, laugh, cry, spill his guts. The only person she'd ever given up on, her own mother. Bog Irish. A slattern, May had pronounced, terrifying in her unforgiveness. When she'd have fed and given home to a stray garden gnome.

Joe scooped up a handful of sand, let it trickle through his fingers. A stocky dark-haired man, too young, at eight and thirty, to die of grief. He took off his boots, then socks. Wriggled his toes in the sand. He did it for May. It felt good.

The Visit

Chancing to bump into one another in town one afternoon, Alice and Jean arranged to meet for a walk the following Sunday at Asling's Beach. The next Wednesday, Alice's half day off, they again met in town for afternoon tea. The following week, at an evening lecture convened by the Women's Auxiliary, Alice took the plunge and invited Jean to morning tea, at a time that Max was sure to be out rowing. She was eager to show her new friend the house. Along with a particularly fine stand of coastal banksias growing nearby, Jean having a more than usual interest in botany.

On the appointed day, Jean paused some moments, on approach, to study the place. It might have been drawn by one of her young pupils, she thought, with its oversized portholes, whalebones dangling from almost every eave, wind chime made out of whales' teeth. With even a flagpole made from what appeared to be a ship's mast. Becoming aware of some slight movement at one of the windows, she smoothed down her skirts and knocked.

Just as the clock in the hallway chimed the hour.

Alice scrunched up her face in an agony of distress, hand on the doorknob. She'd hardly slept, rehearsing all the questions Jean was bound to ask. She opened the door to her with what she hoped was a welcoming smile.

More grimace, Jean thought, taken aback. 'I hope I've the right time?' she said, slightly flustered. 'You did say ten o'clock?'

Alice nodded. 'I was worried you wouldn't find us.' She ushered Jean in. 'Here, let me take your hat.'

Us? Jean glanced round, but they appeared to be alone.

Hat stowed on the coat-stand, Alice shepherded her, with what seemed to Jean to be undue haste, down a central hallway and into the kitchen.

'It's a bit hard to miss,' Jean said, of the house. 'I saw it going up. It's far nicer than I imagined,' she added. 'A proper sea house.'

'Airy,' Alice said.

'An airy eyrie,' Jean agreed.

Alice smiled properly then. 'I sometimes worry,' she said, 'that it'll float off. At high tide. When the moon's full.'

'It seems pretty well tethered,' Jean said mildly. 'What with all the whalebones.'

'Mr Carver's doing. Max,' Alice said, rueful.

'You call him that?'

'Unless we've visitors. Though we hardly ever do.'

'I'm surely not your first?' Jean teased.

Alice flushed pink, then nodded. 'And a very welcome one.'

She was more at ease, Jean saw, in the kitchen. Much as herself, she suspected, in the classroom. If still a little fidgety. Fingers roaming the cloth laid over one end of the big kitchen table, seeking wrinkles, invisible crumbs.

'You've been baking.' Jean gave an appreciative sniff.

'Eccles cakes. I hope you like currants.'

'Oh, indeed. Very much,' Jean said. 'Though I confess I did have some trouble with them as a child. Too much like flies.'

'Or giant ants,' Alice said. They both smiled.

Jean proposed, after tea, that they walk on the beach below the house. But Alice, concerned that Max might return earlier than expected, suggested instead that they view the banksias. As they returned to the house, Jean having duly admired the stand and confirmed the plants to be *banksia integrifolia,* Alice walked into a large spider's web, strung between trees. She cried out in alarm, furiously brushing at her face. Jean helped pick off the web, strand by strand, acutely conscious of Alice's breath on her face, her eyes so close, they blurred. Then helped re-tie her friend's bonnet. Stepping back to study her handiwork, head to one side. 'There's a tiny wee bit …' She picked a strand of web from below Alice's left ear. Hard to fathom, she thought, how she'd overlooked it. So perfectly formed.

'Thank you,' Alice said, grown quite pink.

'Don't mention it,' Jean said.

'It's …' Alice fumbled, smoothing back a stray lock of hair.

'Not always easy to spot a spider's web,' Jean supplied.

The Suspects

Joe busied himself, those first weeks in Eden, in investigating, interrogating. Familiarising himself with the official reports.

The bare bones of the case were soon established.

The stolen whale, harpooned, according to all accounts, late in the day by one of the Sullivan brothers, had been left overnight in Calle Calle Bay, safely secured to floats. Only, come morning, to have vanished. No sign of the beast. No blood, blubber, whale detritus; no smug, lip-smacking orcas. Just four ropes, formerly attached to the creature, now neatly sliced through.

That same week, Ted Price, a local whaler, was found dead, half buried, and minus his boots.

It needed no great powers of deduction, Joe found, to narrow the suspects to four local identities: seasoned whalers and known to be serious tipplers for the most part, and all close associates of the late Ted Price, being members of the same Sullivan whaling crew. Joe didn't hesitate to bring the four—Ron Goodley, Bert Williams, Phil Featherstone and Jim Carew—in for questioning.

As luck would have it, the barely seventeen-year-old Ron Goodley, first to be interrogated and with a visible tremor to his bottom lip, had barely taken his seat before he began to spill.

They'd had a bit of a run-in, he volunteered, unprompted, with Ted Price, after the whale was stolen. He'd seemed more than usually flush, Ron said, and sporting new boots, though he swore they were well worn. Suspicions aroused, all four had upended their mate, Ron said, to check the boots. Virgin soles, barely a scratch. Ron swore that, once righted, Ted had seemed good as new. Only, moments later, to drop down dead. What they'd planned to do if he'd lived, Ron did not divulge.

It was Jim Carew, he said, who'd suggested they mark his passing with a jar of grog.

Far from intending harm, Ron vowed that all four had been fervent in Ted's praises.

It was, once more, Jim Carew, Ron said, who thought to bury the body and burn the boots. A funeral pyre, he'd said, a mark of respect.

Or an attempt to destroy the evidence?

They'd had something of a struggle, Ron confessed, to get the boots off the corpse, Ted having already begun to stiffen.

It was only, having returned to town for a final nightcap at the Great Southern, he said, that Phil Featherstone realised that it couldn't have been Ted who'd stolen the whale because he'd been with him and his missus at the pub all that night, and not left until it had gone twelve.

They'd been about to part company, Ron said, when Phil, unprovoked, suddenly turned his full wrath on Bert Williams. 'Didn't see you in the pub, that night,' he'd accused.

'Too busy rooting,' Jim Carew had said, in an attempt to hose him down. 'Rooted Lloydie Parker's missus, what I heard,' he'd added. 'Yours, too,' he'd muttered, unthinking.

Phil, who worked part-time in the knacker's yard, felling horses, had downed Bert Williams with a blow.

It was pure chance, Ted Price's final resting place being in dense bush miles from town, that a wood-chopper, taking an unfamiliar route home in the dark, had stumbled upon his remains.

*

A man might be excused for thinking the whole thing a joke, Joe reflected, as the four, the now tearful Ron Goodley among them, were summarily arrested to be charged with the murder of Ted Price, but for the carnage.

One man dead.

Another as good as.

A pair of charred boots.

And still no clue as to who stole the whale.

Charmers

Her second visit, Jean brought the southerly. Max heard some commotion in the hall, raised voices, laughter, moments before it slammed into the house, setting all the windows rattling.

Holed up in his study, he was reminded of Paulo and the sister, the chatter emanating from the kitchen.

He'd heard quite a bit, those past weeks, about Jean Tennyson. That she was a teacher, and Alice in awe of her learning. That, coming from England, she had a fine, well-modulated voice. That she was partial to Eccles cakes and took two spoonfuls of sugar in her tea. Though hard to credit, Alice said, from the fineness of her figure.

*

'An admirable profession,' Max pronounced of Jean's vocation, when introduced.

'Sorely lacking in a woman's touch, I fear,' he demurred, when she admired the house.

A wily old fox, Jean summed him up. Though evidently fond of Alice.

Alice judged the meeting a success. 'He hardly ever talks to anyone.'

'Quite the charmer,' Jean said.

'You did really well.' Alice beamed.

'Passed with flying colours?' Jean teased.

All the same, she was pleased. Almost as pleased, she was surprised to think, as some importuning suitor, come to call.

Jean paused some moments on the path after she left, to look back at the house. The windows black and impenetrable. She wondered if Alice was standing there, watching. Watching her? And wondering? She was not the only one, Jean thought, with a secret. Alice was certainly concealing something. As, no doubt, was Max Carver. And as for Trehearne, it was hard to conceive what horrors might oppress the man: you only need come within a foot of him to smell brandy.

She cast a glance at the sky. Pale, rain-washed, lovely as Alice's eyes. The colour would deepen, she knew, as the day wore on. Grow dark and broody if an afternoon storm blew up. Like Alice, she thought, if she imagined a dish not up to scratch.

*

Her mother's eyes had been dark, Jean recalled, reflecting on her life back in England as she walked home. Even sickness hadn't dimmed them, though it had taken her almost a year to die. The worst year of her life, Jean thought at the time. Wrongly, as it turned out.

She'd done what she could for her mother; surely, Jean thought, she could console herself with that. She'd fed and dressed her, daily bathed her, careful to dry every crevice and crack. Within months, the skin had hung on her frame. Jean used to sometimes imagine her mother stepping out of it, her skeleton let loose upon the house. The nearer her mother came to death, the stranger her imaginings. The stranger her mother became too. A flaccid doll with heavy bones, flinging her legs about, kicking like a mule. Jean had dripped droplets of water into her mouth, she recalled, at the end. Had forced her mother's lips apart. Cruel. Cruel. She'd given up teaching, friends, lectures at the Royal. Thought nothing of it.

Her mother had been buried two months when he knocked on the door one afternoon. She'd answered reluctantly, red-nosed, red-eyed from crying. 'A head cold,' she said, when he enquired. 'I'll do my best not to sneeze over you.'

He smiled, opened a little suitcase, immaculately fitted out with his wares. Lace, ribbons, gloves. He was slight, wiry, dark-eyed, with a neat moustache; and handsome, most definitely handsome. Not to say attentive. She noticed his hands, the nails closely trimmed. She'd hardly seen a soul all year, but for Irene, her sole remaining friend. He obviously noted the mourning, because he was back the following week with black gloves, black-edged handkerchiefs. A black lace mantilla. She admired his enterprise.

He called again a few weeks later. And again. She found herself looking forward to his visits. She told him about her mother, surprised at how much she had to say. He'd been calling some months when, on impulse, she asked him to tea one Sunday. Then, in blind panic, asked Irene along at the last moment. He made them laugh. Irene was quite taken. Tea became a weekly event. First with, then minus Irene. Tea, a stroll around the garden, a few hands of cribbage. The time seemed to drag terribly in the intervals. She made tentative plans to return to teaching, increasingly filled with dread at the thought.

Then he proposed. She'd barely set down the tea-tray one afternoon, when he was down on one knee. She tried to tug him to his feet; they ended up in a tug-of-war, and laughing. She turned him down. Gently, but firmly, offering next to no hope. He seemed to take it in good humour, and she liked him all the more for it. He returned, the following week, with a special consignment of Spanish lace.

Teach? She could barely get through the day. She saw her mother everywhere. At the window, waving; frowning over the letters page in the newspaper; peering over her glasses, absentmindedly stirring her tea, though she never took sugar. She'd known she was going to die. Had taken to puzzled, frightened glances that cut Jean to the quick. They'd done their best to keep up the pretence. Jean had read to her: Tennyson, Blake, Keats, all the old favourites. They used to complete each other's lines if ever either faltered.

He invited her on an outing to the London Zoo, one Sunday. They admired the lions, ate the peanuts intended for the chimpanzees, laughed when the elephant took a fancy to his bow tie. She'd never had a beau. Never been kissed. For a time, she'd mooned over the boy next door. Cyril Harding. They'd barely passed the time of day. Always given to fancies, she'd seen him bent over a book as she passed his window. Of poetry, or so she was convinced, though it might well have been the rules of wrestling. A handsome boy: saturnine, dark-eyed as Byron. The salesman might have been his older brother.

Outside the camel enclosure, he once more went down on a knee. She was hardly able to get the words of acceptance out quickly enough. For a moment, he seemed stunned. And herself hideously embarrassed.

'You mean it?' he asked.

'And you?' she returned.

Both nodded furiously, then burst out laughing.

'I do,' he said fervently.

'I do too,' she replied.

He took her in his arms, grazing her lips almost reverentially with his own. They walked on in a daze, arm in arm, squeezing, almost as if to reassure one another. She felt a wave of tenderness for him: as nervous, it seemed, as herself.

'Mrs Boynton,' she said gravely, turning to him.

'Mrs John Boynton,' he said, with a proud grin.

The Book

Passing the Eden Subscription Library, Joe went in on impulse and procured a copy of *Moby-Dick*. He'd heard tell it was a whale tale for the ages.

He hadn't a great deal of knowledge about the beasts, or how to kill them. More, as a copper, about his fellows. And though he might, only at a remove, know what it was to kill a man, he knew first-hand what it was to steal. The year he turned ten, more eager than most, as a copper's son, to transgress, he'd skived off school and borrowed his father's boat. He'd lost both oars and been headed for Tasmania when an old-timer, fishing off the point, saw him float past. He'd been up to his ankles, bailing, by the time the local tugboat, under full steam, caught up with him. Showed a lot of nous, they said. His father, less impressed, gave him the belting of a lifetime.

*

His second week in Eden, Joe paid Max Carver a call. He'd heard in the bar of the Great Southern that his man, Trehearne, a notorious tippler and near impossible to rouse of a morning, had been sighted rowing, at the crack of dawn, way out near Boyd's Tower the day the whale was stolen.

Carver answered the door himself. No maid? Ushered into the study, Joe glanced quickly around the room. Unremarkable. Comfortable. A collection of scrimshaw in a glass cabinet. Carver seemed not to mind the scrutiny, a hint of amusement in his dark eyes. A handsome man, gone to fat. Not from these parts, from the accent. A tippler? No smell on his breath. No tremor in the large, surprisingly soft-looking hands, the nails neatly clipped.

'You've quite a collection,' Joe said, standing before the scrimshaw cabinet.

'All carved by me,' Max said, with a shrug.

Joe peered at the contents. Hard to make out on this cloudy day, but he could see that the work was fine.

'You've quite the gift.' He found himself, as often with tall men, raising himself a little on the balls of his feet. 'I've an admiration for those with patience, having little myself.'

'It helped pass the hours, lacking whales.'

'So you were a whaler?'

Max nodded. 'A long time back.' He fixed Joe with a slightly guarded, enquiring gaze. 'What can I do for you, Mr Givins?'

'I'm here to make some routine enquiries—'

'About the stolen whale?' Max supplied.

'Be good to sort the thing out.' Joe decided that moment, and for no particular reason, that he liked the man. 'Devilish hard work, so I've heard, whaling. Slippery customers.'

'Known to grow legs, and walk,' Max said.

Joe found it hard to suppress a smile.

'You've made some progress?' Max fished.

Joe held his gaze. 'Some.'

'And Bert Williams?'

'Still seriously unwell,' Joe said. 'Though thought to live. You've no objection,' he went on, 'if I've a few words with your man, Trehearne?'

'None at all, but he's out in the boat at present.'

'Fishing?' Joe said.

Max nodded. 'You're at the Great Southern?' he enquired.

Joe nodded.

'You'll doubtless find him there tonight.'

'Fond of the grog?'

'Devoted,' Max said.

'If you do hear anything …' Joe began.

'You'll be the first to know,' Max supplied.

Hardly the most original of lines, Joe thought, as the door closed on him. What would Mr Melville have made of Max Carver, he wondered. Swarthy, for sure, but no Queequeg. He'd grown quickly fond of Queequeg. Dear God, he thought in some amazement, was he, overnight, turned literary man?

And what of the town's insistence that Max Carver was single and solitary?

It wasn't his imagination, Joe knew, that through a gap in the closing door, he'd glimpsed the flouncing hem of a dress.

Gone

At first, Joe had trouble with *Moby-Dick*. Not the whale, he reflected, gloomily eyeing the tome that occupied a good half of his nightstand, but the old bloke, Ahab. Too much like his old man, for his taste. He'd have bet his pension that things would end badly. That old Ahab would land his fish. Like his father, Joe thought, down on the jetty of a summer's night, hauling in flathead, like crims. His mother used to wince, him coming up the path, lantern swinging, bucket brimming. Fish. More fish. And more. Never knew when to stop.

Like himself? Writing to touch base with his superior, Joe slipped in the matter, in passing, of the Katya Brajkoviç case.

'The thing's dead in the water, Joe,' his superior wrote by return post. 'It'd have to be a good ten years ago now, by my estimation. I can't see the point in stirring things up. It's not as if you're going to bring her back. She's gone.'

Gone. A word all too familiar to Joe. He remembered, held back at school for talking in class, how he got home late one afternoon to find his father gone, his mother anxiously fiddling with her apron ties. 'Where were you, lad? He's gone. Couldn't wait any longer.'

He'd been promising to take him out fishing in the boat since he was born.

'Why? Why couldn't he wait?'

He thought of May.

Gone.

Gone, he thought, staring at the ceiling of his room in the Great Southern, *Moby-Dick* propped on his chest, didn't mean forgotten.

*

They never had any kids, he and May. Not live ones. He hadn't minded, really. But May had. He wouldn't have been surprised if she'd been planning the layette as they walked down the aisle. She'd even looked like a mum, the sort every kid wanted: chubby cheeks, fair curls, warm blue eyes. There wasn't a kid alive who wouldn't have entrusted her with his piggy bank. It was all they'd talked about, those first years—he'd listened, mostly, chiming in now and again with all the stuff he was going to do with the lad. Always a lad. Always the stuff he'd never done with his father. Funny how he'd turned into him. Might have taken up farming, joined the army—but had to be a copper. Not that there'd been a lot of choice: crap at school, useless with his hands.

May had been top of her class. Smart. Good. Innocent. The sort that invariably got bludgeoned, blamed, frisked, accused, dredged up from the bottom of Sydney Harbour.

In the early years she had a couple of miscarriages, the second worse than the first. Not just the mucky stuff, but the worrying, and longing, the pretending not to long, not to worry. The third time was it; they didn't say a word, studiously avoided remarking upon the growth of her belly. What was there to say? There'd be everything to say once it was born. No he or she about it. Didn't trust themselves to give it a name, a sex. She almost carried full term. Eight months, big enough for twins. Making up for lost time, wolfing down seconds, hanging around the larder half the night. He used to smile. To himself, that is. She'd lost her sense of humour, after the first couple. She watched her every step, easing herself downstairs as if she was seventy, hanging on to the banister. Please God, he thought. Please.

She was knocked over by a dog, a German shepherd. Brute of an animal, big as a horse. Friendly, though. Like a lot of killers. She toppled onto the rocks they'd been sitting on only minutes before, might well have been sitting on still if he hadn't suggested they go and get ice-cream. She went into premature labour, bled—he couldn't believe how much. Just as well he wasn't the queasy sort. It was touch and go, and they let the baby go: a girl, so he hadn't lost a son. What a thing to think, he'd thought, yet he'd thought it. Then thought, Christ, never again, I'm not going through that fucking nightmare.

He reckoned it was all the fiddling with her insides that caused the cancer. All the mucking about, sucking stuff out, trying to stuff it back in. You wouldn't treat cattle the way she was treated; some of those doctors, they'd be struck off if they worked for the force. A year after she lost the little girl she had a pain in her belly, and the thing just took off, nothing to stop it, no hope. When she had the surgery to take out her womb, that was it. He had his work, she said, bitter then. And she, what did she have? Him, he wanted to say. Wasn't he something? Just as well he hadn't a wandering eye or he might well have been tempted around about then. Knew how crims felt in the dock: judged, condemned, only need blink, look a bit shifty. She was right, and wrong, about the work. He couldn't do it without her.

Naturally, his mum had come good. Even his dad, somewhat surprisingly. Model in-laws. Not a murmur of lost grandkids, lost hopes. The third time, his mum had set up shop beside May's bed, knitted her way through the whole thing.

Still did. And the old bloke, pushing seventy, life's work done, had taken up building model boats. Happy as Larry, after a lifetime of righteous persecution of wrongdoers, making bits of balsa wood turn in mindless, ever-decreasing circles on the lake at Wentworth Falls. He hardly got to see them since they'd moved up to the Blue Mountains. A blessing. Only need look into his mother's eyes to see May.

The Change

Max noticed the change in Alice.

Not just that when she rushed home late from meeting Jean in town, the gravy had lumps. Or that the breakfast milk for his porridge boiled over. Or that his boots sported flecks of mud, Alice having neglected to oversee Mary Kathleen's polishing of them. But that the 'dog' resurfaced, when he'd barely heard a whimper out of it in months.

And then the toast.

He came into breakfast one morning to find her at the window, pale, distraught, furiously flapping her apron to try to clear the room of smoke. As if the whole house was aflame.

Trehearne smelled it, of course; paused, turning over a bed of peas, to lean on his fork and sniff. Something burning. A sudden familiar churning in his gut. Chimney fire? Bushfire? He ticked them off. Toast. He turned aside to clear his nose. Burned. Blackened. Acrid. On the nose. On purpose? To fucking torment him? He glowered at the kitchen window, long moments, before he resumed digging.

*

Day-long, Alice would keep an ear cocked for the sound of Joe Givins's footstep on the path. Imagined the sound of the door-bell in the cry of every passing parrot. Rehearsed endlessly what she would say to him. Only to stumble and falter. Because what did she have to say to him? That she'd had no choice but to lie? No alternative but to forge letters of recommendation? That she'd been compelled—and by what?—to assume false identities?

What with Joe Givins and Max and Jean, Alice would hardly have got a thing done if she hadn't rationed the time she spent thinking of them. She allotted Givins the dark, sleepless three o'clock slot. Which allowed Jean to pleasantly materialise during the more mundane daytime tasks: stirring a sauce, sorting the table linen, policing Mary Kathleen's efforts with the silver. Max she reserved for the cooking of dinner.

But there was no rationing unsettling dreams, or fancies. Passing the grocery store, Alice thought she saw Joe Givins peering out at her only to find herself reflected in the glass. Deliberating on a leg of lamb in the butcher's shop, she was beset by a vision of Katya, golden hair let loose upon her shoulders. Pausing one evening to admire a particularly fine spotted gum, she discovered her mother's mournful face in the darkly shadowed canopy above. She resolved to redouble her nightly prayers.

It was more obvious to her by the day that she should leave. Just slip out, early one morning, leaving her bed made, the breakfast table set, with perhaps a cold collation in the larder for Max's lunch. Covered, in case of ants. Then found that she couldn't; couldn't even bear the thought. Not just of leaving Max. Or the house, or the evening walk along the beach in search of shells, or the twisted banksia trees that she'd grown to love, or the call of the bellbirds. She knew she couldn't leave Jean. Jeannie. She'd been Jeannie, in her thoughts, some weeks now.

Alice only need see her, walking towards her along Asling's Beach, for her heart to pound.

Arriving early in town one afternoon to meet Jean, Alice took a walk along the bluff overlooking the sea, drawn to the spot they'd first met. But there was no solace to be found today gazing out to sea, no surcease of apprehension or troubled thoughts. Only the dark waters, overshadowed by cloud, breaking against the rocks with such constancy you might have thought it a bell tolling. Tolling for whom, Alice wondered. Then suddenly thought of how it might be to just step off. Step off and not return. Only the upward whoosh of air. The view from on high. The one God must see. And did He ever tire of it, though He saw it every day?

The day they'd met, Alice recalled, a little mournfully, everything had seemed so very bright and sharp and clear. Even the sea hadn't seemed the sea, but an open hand, outstretched to gather her up.

What a fright, she thought, purposefully taking some steps back from the edge, she must have given Jeannie that day. How hard *her* heart must have beaten in that immaculate bosom of hers. What it must have taken to get her to lift those impeccably starched petticoats and run. When every task—untying her bonnet or totting up the daily attendance in class—Jean performed with such calm. The calm of the sea on a still day, when it seemed almost solid. So you quite forgot about currents and tides and the seething world beneath. She thought about Jeannie all the time. The sleek gloss of her hair; the little pinch at the end of her nose; her endearingly stern, headmistressy glance. The way she frowned, lips pressed firm, studying maps, or marking books. And closed her eyes, leaning back a little, to recite one of the many poems she knew by heart.

*

She'd started dreaming about Katya again. Now and again, then more and more often, until it happened almost every night. Achingly familiar dreams. With the same sweet rose-petal soap smell of Katya, fresh from the bath. Only it seemed to grow ever more sickly and cloying. Until, finally, it was nauseating.

Even awake, she could smell it. Even in the kitchen. Most of all there.

Caution

Jean daily urged caution on herself. After all, she hardly knew anything about Alice. But that she was more than usually secretive, with unusual looks, and that it was vexingly hard to remember the colour of her eyes. Unlike her face, which was paler than a moonstone. Even if moonstones, as depicted in the school encyclopaedia, did look rather cold and remote. And Alice far from either.

What she did know, with some surety, was that she herself was in need of a friend. A confidante. And had been since leaving behind Irene, and losing her mother. An only child, she'd often felt the lack of a brother or sister, someone her own age, with similar tastes, thoughts, feelings. She knew only too well, from recent experience, that she was more than usually gullible. That even as a child she had imagined things that didn't exist. Not matrimonial happiness, perhaps, but that fairies lived at the bottom of their garden. She'd often been lulled to sleep by the thought of them snug in the tangled thicket of her mother's rose bushes, safe from the human world and everything in it. The way she felt, blissfully alone with her mother, when her father was away travelling or at work. The way she felt with Alice, in the kitchen, late on Wednesday afternoons, light streaming onto the well-worn table between them, with its little maps formed of old stains, its little hollows and ruts, blackened from old mishaps, and herself, in contrast, warm and safe and whole.

She found herself constantly wondering about Alice. Why she worked so hard to impress Max Carver. Why she was seemingly all alone in the world. Like herself. Why she was so devout and nightly prayed. Often, just before she slept, Jean thought of her, picturing her on her knees on the little mat beside her bed, hair let down from her cook's bonnet, fingers clasped, face turned upward to God. She wondered what she prayed for. What sins she asked to be forgiven. As for herself, she found it impossible to pray. And even if she had been able to, Jean knew, she would have prayed for all the wrong things. That he be wiped from the very surface of the earth. That he burn in hell for all eternity. But Alice, Alice was innocent. Jean need only look into her eyes to know. There was no malice there. Even their most inconsequential conversations seemed filled with goodness and light. What Alice was to make for Max's lunch, supper, afternoon tea. Some new method of creaming butter. They never talked of the past. Or the future. Content, it seemed, to be exactly where they were.

The Slav Girls

Joe Givins did the rounds.

First up, the Davidsons, doyens of the bay, out of respect. Then the rest. Blow-ins, upstarts, adventurers—more than any occupation's fair share of miscreants and shady characters were to be found among the whalers of Eden. All eager to pass on, to anyone with an ear to lend, complaints of diminishing whale catches, shrinking returns, the Davidsons getting the first choice of the best crews, blackfellas included.

It was Trehearne who alerted him to the fact Alicja Brajkoviç was in Max Carver's employ. 'Seen her in the papers,' Trehearne told him, leaning against the bar of the Great Southern, breathing near-combustible fumes into his face. 'Her and that murdering sister of hers,' he added, hardly able to offload the words quickly enough from his treacherous tongue. 'Would have known her mug anywhere.'

Joe suspected that Trehearne wasn't the only one in on the secret.

*

He made a second call on Max Carver.

As soon as the pleasantries were dispensed with, he plunged in. 'I've been led to understand Alice Binney's in your employ, Mr Carver.'

Max hesitated the barest fraction, then nodded. 'She is that. And these past four years.'

'Can you tell me what you know of her?' Joe asked.

Max thought a moment, shrugged. 'That she's a more than usually fine cook. And no whale rustler. That I'd vouch for. I'm not much of a one for gossip, Mr Givins,' he added coolly.

'Nor I,' Joe said mildly. 'I'll take the truth, any day.' No point beating around the bush. 'It being,' he went on, 'that Alice Binney isn't who she purports to be. Her name isn't Alice Binney, but Alicja Brajkoviç.'

He awaited the response, but aside from a slight upward shift of an eyebrow, there was none.

He waited some more.

'It's hardly a crime, at least in my book,' Max finally broke the silence to say, 'to change your name. Else half the whalers I'm acquainted with would be behind bars.'

'No crime at all.' Joe nodded agreement. He leaned towards the taller man, almost conspiratorially. 'Speaking of such, some ten years ago I happened to witness a celebrated trial in Bathurst, involving the death of a child, more infant really, barely two years old and brutally murdered. I'd just been made detective constable, so with no real part to play in proceedings but to observe. Unsurprisingly, there was intense interest in the case.'

Max had grown very still.

'Alicja's sister, Katya Brajkoviç, was nursemaid to the child at the time of her death. After the inquest and a brief investigation, she was charged with her murder. I confess, like many who attended the trial, I was deeply affected by proceedings. Not just that the child was a fetching one, and the parents distraught, but that it took so little pressure from the prosecutor for Brajkoviç to admit to her guilt. When the evidence, if anything, seemed to point to the contrary. It had me deeply puzzled, I confess. Only later,' he added, after a pause, 'did I learn that it's not entirely unknown for someone to believe themselves guilty of a crime they didn't commit. Insist on it, even.'

Max continuing silent, Joe went on. The jury took but a few hours to bring down a verdict of guilty.' He paused to clear his throat. 'She was sentenced to be hanged for the crime,' he said. 'A sentence carried out, shortly afterwards, at Bathurst.'

'Dear God,' Max said, on an outward breath.

They were both silent then.

'And Alice?' Max finally ventured. 'She played some part in this?'

'None,' Joe said simply. 'But that of a devoted sister. For which she was daily pilloried in the press. I'm surprised no-one in Eden's recognised her,' he added, fishing a little. 'She was in the papers often enough. She and Katya, both. The Slav Girls, so they were known,' he added, with a faint snort. 'When the pair were born and raised barely a mile out of Bathurst.'

The Past

It was barely light when Max opened the chest, and unwrapping Antonio's whale journal, began to read it for the first time.

Not that there was a great deal, he was pleased to discover, within its close-written pages, unfamiliar to him. Stories he hadn't heard, events he hadn't witnessed for himself. Men swallowed up by whales, who lived to tell the tale. Shipwrecked souls who, believing them islands, lit fires on their capacious backs. Curious whales that swam with ships. Furious whales that stove them in.

What was unfamiliar to him was his brother's voice on the page. Not his reading to them after supper, or declaiming a psalm in church to the congregation voice. But his squinting at a page in the dying stub of a candle voice. His head propped sleepily on an arm at the table, elbow beginning to slide voice. His fingers curled a little tighter around the cover of the journal voice. As if the words might escape. As if they lived. Max had often wondered at Antonio's enchantment with words, with barely comprehensible shapes on a page. Now he saw it. More. Felt it.

Just as he felt a tear trickle down his face. And another. He let them fall.

On he read, and on. Right through the day, stamping his feet when the pins and needles jabbed, rotating a wrist when cramp set in. Easing his grip to rub his raw-rimmed eyes, book helpfully propped on the windowsill. Feet braced, as on board a ship. Facing directly into the gale. Mount Imlay rimmed with what looked like fire as the night drew in.

'I'm busy,' he shouted, to Alice's increasingly insistent knocks. 'I won't be needing lunch.' Or afternoon tea. Or supper.

He read through to the end.

And again. Almost daily, for some weeks. Mostly the pages contained simple accounts of whales and the whaling life, though the drawings, dotted throughout, were surprisingly accomplished. A few seemed to be of him. Tall, dark, arms rippling with muscle. Like a god. Could he really have been so very handsome? There he was at the prow, harpoon raised, hat safely stowed on his head, fearless. And on the dock, flensing. It looked like a scimitar in his hand, nothing like a flensing knife. Perhaps Antonio hadn't known how to draw one. Yet he knew enough to draw a whale, right down to the correct blow. And Max wasn't the only one immortalised on the page. There, almost dwarfed by the soaring arch of a whale's jawbone, was a man he was pretty sure must be Uncle Tomás. With, at his side, and holding aloft an umbrella, the Aunt, Palmira.

He hadn't expected to find himself in a book; it took some getting used to. He acquired the habit of taking the boat out after he'd been reading. Rowing as far as his arms would take him, to sit, staring back at the house. Occasionally, if she was out in the garden, Alice would wave and he'd raise a hand in salute. But mostly there was nothing to be seen, only sky, land, sea.

He shared the occasional snippet with her.

'Did you know a whale can live for over two hundred years?'

'Goodness!' Alice exclaimed. 'Just imagine.'

'Bow-heads. In the Arctic.'

'Two whole centuries,' Alice marvelled. 'Just think of all they'd have to remember.'

'Remember?'

Alice saw an eyebrow shoot up.

'They'd have to remember some of it,' she added. And after a moment's thought, 'Their babies; the mothers would never forget them.' Triumphant.

'No evidence for it,' he retorted crisply. 'Nothing in the books.'

But hadn't he seen it? Felt it? Heard for himself, when a calf was taken?

*

Sleepless, he recalled that only nights before the wedding on Fogo, he'd woken to the sound of Paulo crying. Whereas Margarida had hardly ever cried. But lain, night-long, staring at the ceiling. He hadn't dared try to console her. Or him.

The Climb

It was Doctor Culligan who laid the seed.

Told by him that a rare species of boronia, unique to Mount Imlay, was in particularly fine bloom due to recent rain, Max mentioned it to Alice who, in turn, told Jean.

Eager to sketch such a botanical rarity, Jean immediately proposed an outing.

'I'm sure we'll be able to manage it,' she said breezily, pausing at the far end of Asling's Beach one afternoon to cast an appraising eye over Mount Imlay's crooked peak, soaring clear of the clouds buffeted by a stiff nor'-easter. 'People climb it all the time.'

'Climb it?' Alice said, doubtful.

'It's not so very high,' Jean assured her. 'Though it might be a bit steep in places. It'll be an adventure,' she coaxed. 'We could make a day of it. Take a picnic.'

Alice's eyes lit up at the word.

Jean smiled to herself. A prized specimen. And a picnic. With Alice. What better?

*

On learning of the plan, Culligan immediately offered himself as guide, along with the use of his horse and carriage. Only, on the eve of the planned excursion, for the good medic to be laid low by a flare-up of gout.

Trehearne, with some misgivings all round, was appointed to take his place, if only to convey the adventurers to the foot of Mount Imlay.

Locked away in his study, Max fretted. No good could possibly come of the venture, he thought, reminded, in all the fuss, of his and Paulo's aborted trip to Little Fogo Island. He worried that the weather might break. That Culligan's carriage, which the doctor had insisted they take advantage of, might lose a wheel, or the horse bolt, or be lamed.

He already knew, courtesy of Culligan, whose special interest it was, quite a bit about Mount Imlay. With the aid of the telescope, he had observed it closely under all weathers. Had witnessed what he knew to be people on its slopes, though so small and indistinct were they, it was impossible to say if they were going up or coming down. He knew, from the good doctor, something of its history. That, like much in Eden, it was named for the Imlay brothers. That it was close to 3000 feet in height and formed of sedimentary rock, quartzite, siltstone and shale. That the local Aboriginal people knew it as Balawan and it was of great significance to them. It was said to require a certain sensibility to safely climb it. Max wasn't sure, though he knew her to be a superior cook and housekeeper, if Alice qualified.

Alice was also apprehensive. Plans had been complicated by the need for an early start on the ascent. It appeared that the climb would take some hours. They made arrangements for an overnight stay at Kiah, with Mary Kathleen's mother, Mrs O'Brien. Reluctant to be away for more than a night, Alice insisted they return home after the climb, regardless of the hour. Even one night's absence would involve no little effort: meals prepared in advance and, in atonement, a quince and apple pie.

*

Max spent much of Alice's absence worrying. Familiar territory. That Alice would fall. That she would be crippled for life, like Ana. Halfway through his solitary supper, he felt impelled to check that Mount Imlay was where it ought to be. It seemed more than usually distant. He went outside to reassess the weather, though it continued clear, and the stars seemingly more numerous than ever. He was more than happy for Alice to enjoy a special outing. He'd been more shaken than he liked to admit to hear of her sister's cruel demise. Lying sleepless, he tried out Alice's real name, Alicja, under his breath, then aloud. Then Katya. Alicja and Katya. They seemed to almost naturally conjoin. Then reminded himself, sternly, that the affair wasn't any of his business, and that it had all happened a long time ago. As if the passage of time counted for aught.

*

'Mind you don't overtax the horse,' he'd told Trehearne on departure. 'And be sure to water and feed the creature promptly on arrival.'

Not a word, Trehearne had thought, sullen, of his grub, his refreshment. Taking his time to spit out a plug of tobacco, he'd nodded in reply.

*

They left at first light after a pleasant evening at Kiah, Mrs O'Brien proving attentive to their every need. Mount Imlay's wooded slopes were still in deep shadow by the time they arrived at its base, the air refreshingly cool. Anticipating the day's heat, they discarded their coats, Alice glancing back as they started up the gentle slope of the lower reaches, to see Trehearne nonchalantly leaning against the carriage, smoking. She waved, but he glanced away, blowing out a plume of smoke.

It was a strenuous climb. Alice was glad of the riding habit she wore, borrowed from Jean. Even so, she had to hitch up its skirt at various points, particularly when they crossed the saddle-ridge and began the challenging ascent of the peak. Even Jean was soon pink and perspiring. They helped each other over the trickier bits. Held hands some moments longer than was needed. Like giant stepping stones, the boulders they clambered over had to be taken at full stretch. As they climbed higher, they noticed clouds of a delicate pink flowering bush poking up in the fissures. Mount Imlay boronia. Jean's look of delight was perhaps only equalled, Alice was surprised to think, by that of Katya in possession of a new bonnet or frock.

Jean, her manner scientific, verified the specimen in a small book on the botany of the area, brought along in her satchel; Alice experiencing an odd feeling as her friend boyishly swung the bag off her shoulders. A great warmth enveloped her, swelling her chest, surging into her throat, making it hard to swallow. She worried that it was the beginning of a nasty head-cold, or even, perhaps, the dreaded influenza.

She sat quietly watching as Jean deftly sketched the various components of the plant. In truth, she was too frightened to move, unwilling to disturb the moment that seemed to connect them more intimately than any touch. Then thought of how she might spend a lifetime watching Jean capture such delicate specimens on the page, their loveliness equalled only by her dark eyes, intent, conscious only of the object of her gaze.

Alice having duly admired the likeness, they continued their ascent, stopping near a forest of lush palms for a late morning tea, large slices of passionfruit sponge, supplied by the ever-generous Mrs O'Brien. Then again pressed on, faintly conscious of Trehearne waiting below.

It was some time before it truly sank in that they were alone. That there wasn't another soul on the mountain. And very few in the vast landscape that had opened up below them: the sea to one side, smooth as pewter, and on the other bushy peaks and valleys with a hazy plateau of towering rocks in the far distance. Far too close for Mount Kosciusko, Jean surmised, mildly disappointed. Nothing moved but for the birds, small wrens twittering in the undergrowth, and a slight breeze in the canopy. A sublime vista, Jean thought, of the kind most often depicted in great books, or paintings. One that few but the first explorers would have seen. Had their breath been taken away? Had they, too, felt themselves meek and chastened? Or puffed up at the thought of conquest? What would Mary Kingsley, the intrepid traveller in West Africa, one of her chief heroines, she wondered aloud, make of such a vision? They pressed on, passing a stand of Mount Imlay mallee, Alice dumbfounded, as often, by all that Jean knew.

Having plumped for a likely peak as the elusive summit—it becoming clear as they clambered over boulders, only to encounter further expanses of rock, that it was impossible to say precisely where the top lay—they sat at the foot of a large outcrop to eat egg and cress sandwiches. Jean, compass in hand, attempted to identify various landmarks.

'You're a born teacher,' Alice said, her voice warm with pride.

'I can't imagine you as anything else. You were probably counting beads in your crib.'

Jean laughed. 'Now that you mention it, I do have a faint memory of some bright colours, just tantalisingly out of reach.'

'I was hopeless at sums,' Alice said. 'Though I always loved to read.'

'Tennyson was my first love. Might very well be my last. As far as poetry is concerned,' Jean added, then flushed. Glancing down, she saw that the hand she leaned upon was only inches from Alice's. Close enough surely to reach out and touch. As possible, she thought, to reach out and touch the far-off phantom of Kosciusko.

Head back, eyes closed, voice grown soft and dreamy, she began to recite, Alice studying her face all the while.

I met a lady in the meads,
Full beautiful—a faery's child,
Her hair was long, her foot was light,
And her eyes were wild ...

She took me to her Elfin grot,
And there she wept and sighed full sore,
And there I shut her wild wild eyes
With kisses four.

'I used to read rhymes to Ka—my sister,' Alice said softly.

'You've a sister?' Jean's eyes opened in surprise.

'Had,' Alice said. 'She passed away when young. Of the diphtheria.'

'How very sad,' Jean said. 'I would have loved to have a sister.' Surely, she thought, the perfect moment to take Alice's hand, squeeze it in commiseration. 'Not that I wasn't fortunate,' she went on hastily, 'in my mother. She was my dearest friend.'

'She's …?' Alice began.

'Also passed away. Some years ago now,' Jean replied. 'Goodness,' she added, shading her eyes against the sun, 'there's not many hours of daylight left. We really ought to be getting back.'

The Slip

Jean slipped. Or so she told Alice, and Max, and Mary Kathleen, and would have Trehearne, if he'd been there to tell.

A loose stone shot from under her, she said (fortunately not at the steepest part of the descent, but just before the fork leading to the lower reaches), and she found herself falling. Only to collide with a large rock, severely bruising her arm, before once more tumbling on. It was only that Alice managed to snatch a handful of her riding habit that her descent was slowed.

'Jeannie!' The word was ripped from Alice.

A shrill declaration, ricocheting off rocks and trees, shattering the glassy stillness of the late afternoon.

Jean heard. Even in her falling, in her alarm, she heard the love and longing in Alice's voice. The knowledge almost instantly wiped out by an excruciating pain in her left ankle as she made a last desperate grab at a tree. She lay, some moments, unmoving, then groaned.

*

She hadn't slipped. Jean was quite certain of it, at the time. As with the cliff incident, when she knew there had been no whale, Jean was determined that something or someone had shoved her violently in the back. It wasn't just that she was more than usually sure-footed. That, since childhood, had been known as something of a mountain goat. That her late father, a surveyor, though tiresome in a hundred different ways, had engendered in her a more than usual interest in geographical phenomena and geology, dragging her along on excursions to dig for fossils. Jean was at home in the great outdoors; knew good rock from bad. Knew to test each and every one, to gauge its weight-bearing abilities. She had been pushed, of that she was sure. Propelled forward with such velocity she'd felt driven into the air by something almost pure in its single-mindedness. None of which she confided to Alice. And barely to herself, aware that no good could come of it, only upset and confusion.

So she held her tongue.

(Wisely, as Jean was later only too happy to concede. Having by then concluded that it was no bodied or disembodied agency that had propelled her forward that day, but the revelation, on descent, that she was in love with Alice, and possibly on the verge of the second-worst misstep of her life. Again!)

*

Jean attempted to rise, only to find her left foot unable to bear her weight. Around them dusk was falling. A soft amber light suffusing the bush, the eucalypts turned billowy, bars of golden light slanting between their silken trunks.

Though fully aware that they were in a tight corner, that she might very well have broken an ankle, what was that compared to 'Jeannie!'?

'Badly sprained, I think. But not broken,' Alice pronounced, after a gentle examination. 'Else ...'

'I'd probably be sobbing,' Jean supplied.

'Or screaming,' Alice said.

'Or both,' Jean said, so Alice knew that she would be all right.

'We'll have to take it slowly,' Alice said.

'Snail-like,' Jean agreed.

'Tortoise-like.'

'Because if you, too, were to fall ...'

'We'd be in a terrible pickle,' Alice supplied.

'Done for,' Jean concluded, with a brave smile. 'As opposed to only minorly incapacitated.'

*

They began the descent, Alice's arm around Jean's waist, easing her every step of the way down the vertiginous slope, only stopping, over what seemed like hours, to rest and allow Jean to take small sips of the little water that remained. The evening grew cool, then cold, then icy. Jean began to shiver, Alice chafing her arms, hugging her, brushing her lips against her hair as if inadvertently. But Jean nuzzled her head purposefully against Alice's lips in return, before pulling away to search her face. 'Dearest Alice. You're so very pale. I'm sure, if we could find a stick, I could hobble.'

'No,' Alice said. 'No hobbling. I'm fine. Truly. I could walk all night.' Surprised to realise that she could.

The moon emerged, full, over the sea, sufficient to throw strange, unnerving shadows, as well as light the way. They were grateful for it.

*

Stationed at the foot of Mount Imlay, Trehearne watched the shadows lengthen. Smoking, picking at his nose, scratching at his crotch, sucking at the socket of an empty tooth. Staring warily into the bush, fortified by occasional shots of rum from the flask concealed in the inner pocket of his jacket. Bottle drained, he took out a plug of tobacco. Chewed solidly for a time, then spat. Saw the gob sucked up by a thirsty layer of she-oak needles. Bone dry. He scanned the bush for smoke. The first faint tendrils.

The sun sank behind the trees, plunging the clearing into gloom. He saw a kangaroo lurking on the periphery. Thought of the rifle, left behind beside his bed. Weighed up the odds of wrestling the roo to the ground before it could disembowel him. If he were starving. If he were forced to stay put all night. It took off, bounding through the trees. Spooked? He'd seen a mob, once, try to outrun a fire. Seen them, one by one, ignite.

He lit the lamp as it grew darker. Wandered halfway along the path they'd disappeared up. There was a stand of tree ferns. Giant umbrellas. He wouldn't stand a chance, he thought, if caught on the road out, cut off by flames. He'd seen a man covered in whale oil go up in smoke. Then wondered, idly, if something had occurred. If they might not have gone and got their throats slit. Two women alone, traipsing through the bush. What were the odds? There were bound to be bushrangers. Then thought of the hotel in town. How they'd still be serving, and all the lamps turned up bright. It was so still he could hear his own breathing. Whistling out his nose. He turned aside to clear it. Then took a piss against a tree. Looked up into the canopy to find a possum staring at him.

He waited a while longer, then drove off, chilled to the bone. Geed up the horse and set off at a clip along the long snaking road to Eden. Felt, all the while, the bush closing in. Something about to spring. Gone for help, he told himself. Knew something was up, so went for help. Would shortly be returning for them.

*

Jean said that he'd obviously gone to secure aid. That, aware something was amiss when they failed to return, he'd gone to summon reinforcements. Knowing him better, Alice wasn't so sure. Jean's ankle was now badly swollen. Alice tore the scarf from her hat into strips and bound it up. They sat, leaning against a large spotted gum, Jean's ankle elevated on a stone padded with her satchel, which, against all odds, had survived the fall. Alice put first one and then the other arm around Jean, who was still shivering badly. She pulled her close, careful of her ankle. Jean laid her head on Alice's shoulder with such a tremulous sigh that they both laughed. They sat quietly for a long time. Afraid to move, or speak, or explain, or ask.

'It'll be fine. I'm sure it will,' Jean finally murmured.

Alice didn't know if she referred to her ankle or what had passed between them. Like a current. Surely Jean had felt it. She barely moved her lips in assent. An hour passed. Another. Alice wondered if she'd slept. She didn't feel sleepy, but wide awake. She found it hard to imagine ever getting up, walking away, separating herself from Jeannie. Store it up, she thought. Don't forget, Alicja. The stars, the tree, the weight, the warmth of Jeannie's head. Jeannie's hand—how had it come to be in her own?

Found

Seldom had Max endured such a night as when Alice failed to return. It brought back all the other nights. Nights shipwrecked at sea. Nights suffering through a father's death, a brother's, a child's. Nights scarified by a man's betrothal, a wife's betrayal.

An hour passed, another. Max paced, stood sentinel at the window, summoned up a dozen times the sight of a safely returning carriage, himself hurrying to meet it. Heard, clear as the koel calling monotonously in the dark, her voice, gently chiding him for growing thin in her absence, noting that he had barely consumed more than a portion of quince and apple pie. Her insistence that, despite the hour, he eat something: another slice of pie, perhaps; a helping of pea and ham soup? Regaling him, all the while, with what had occurred.

How, Max wondered, as the night progressed, had he been snared into feeling so? Racked with fears he'd thought himself finished with. Surely he was too old, too tired, too weak, too fat, to fret about people who weren't even related to him. But Alice. Lost on a mountain. And all alone. Only to be pulled up short by a thought. Because she wasn't alone. She was with Jean. And if he and Paulo had been obliged to spend a night on a mountainside, with only the stars for witness? Would they have wanted to be found?

And Trehearne? Where, he wondered darkly, was that supposedly faithful factotum and manservant of his, Patrick Trehearne, this dark and fearful night?

There was nothing for it but to wait for morning. Still, he paced. Room to room and along the verandah, hardly aware of the night breeze off the sea, the full moon, stars and, in the distance, treacherous Mount Imlay, looming. They would find her. All would go on as before. But he could not shake a small element of doubt, of uncertainty.

Perfidy

Joe Givens, roused from sleep by some commotion in the street, peered out to see Trehearne, staggering wildly, being steered none too gently into the local police station. More than a little curious, he dressed quickly and went to make himself known to the policeman on duty. Only to learn that Trehearne had reported Alice Binney and Jean Tennyson missing on Mount Imlay. Lost or strayed was the constable's surmise. And not, as Trehearne's inebriated account would have it—encompassing as it did Alice's character or lack thereof, burned toast and just deserts—abducted or murdered by bushrangers.

Leaving Trehearne soundly snoring in the station's lock-up, Joe and the constable set out for Mount Imlay. Joe learning en route of Trehearne's perfidy. Despite the pressing nature of his mission, Max Carver's man had lingered some hours in a public house in Kiah. Then, continuing to within sight of Eden, had once more come to a halt, stepping down from the carriage to relieve himself. Only, upon re-assuming the reins, to pass out. Or, as Trehearne would have it, succumb to a bout of dizziness.

Culligan's horse, freed of all restraints and left unfed far too many hours, had made its own way home, its measured tread rocking Trehearne deeper into oblivion. Arriving at the doctor's residence to find the carriage gates locked, and without access to stable or feed, the faithful animal had attempted entry over a low picket fence, dragging the carriage with it. Only to find itself stuck fast. The doctor, woken by the fracas but still incapacitated by gout, had despatched his manservant to fetch the police. The constable on duty, more than familiar with Culligan, the medic having delivered his wife of four sons, had been only too eager to oblige.

Trehearne, for all that the carriage had come to its sudden halt, had continued in a pleasant reverie of himself rocked in a cradle by a benign hand. Only to wake abruptly and, attempting to clamber out of the carriage, find himself in the very thick of Culligan's prize roses. Where, struggling to free himself of their thorny embrace, he was discovered by the constable and duly arrested.

So it was that dawn was about to break before the two women were discovered. Alice on her feet, eagerly beckoning; Jean still seated, leaning against a tree. Both shivering but unharmed, to the relief of their rescuers, and in surprisingly good spirits.

Safely returned to Broadside, both professed themselves profoundly grateful to be so little indisposed by their misadventure.

Unlike the good doctor, with substantial damages to home and hearth. Or Trehearne, released from incarceration, pending possible charges, only to find himself dismissed.

In a lecture worthy of João, Max told him to pack his bags, leave and not come back. He was untrustworthy, Max thundered, unreliable and an ingrate. He was adamant. There was to be no forgiveness.

Eavesdropping at the door, Alice flinched at every word. Judgement and blame, falling easy as rain in a summer storm. It gave her pause to see Max so unyielding.

And Max some sleepless nights, to find Alice so censorious.

Hadn't he always forgiven? Forgiven a brother, mother, wife, lover? What more did they want?

*

Jean took up residence in the spare room. A week, then another, and still she continued to appear at the breakfast table. Ankle on the mend, she returned to teaching, driving herself, in Trehearne's absence, into town in the cart each day, surprised to find herself grateful for a father who, despite considerable shortcomings, had taught her how to handle a horse.

If Max failed to remark upon it when Jean stayed on, it was perhaps because Alice daily scaled ever more dizzying culinary heights: a bombe Alaska, a Sachertorte, a vacherin of peaches, and more.

And he still hadn't heard a peep out of the 'dog'.

He found it hard not to acknowledge love when he saw it. Hadn't he witnessed the fourteen-year-old Antonio, spurning his walking stick, almost fall into the fire in the presence of Margarida? Hard to swagger on one leg.

*

His dismissal of Trehearne came back to torment Max. And often. He knew the bare bones of the man's past: a brutal father, mother driven to an early grave, lost wife and child. Just as he'd known about the welts on Fredo's back, the lust in José's eyes, surveying Ana, his only daughter. It was hardly surprising, he thought, that Trehearne had turned sly and dishonest.

It was almost a month before the man returned to Broadside. Alice came home from town one afternoon, Trehearne in tow. Mary Kathleen had known where to find him. Standing in the kitchen, Alice took off her hat with a steady hand. Trehearne, seated in her domain, flushed, chin gone rubbery, mouth moving all ways. She made him a cup of tea, then took one in to Max, along with a favourite treat, a more than usually large wedge of a Victoria sponge; he liked the way it almost melted in the mouth, he said, so he barely need chew and could focus on the telescope.

'He's back,' she said levelly, setting down the tray. An eyebrow shot up, but she held her nerve. 'And he's truly sorry.' Surprised to find her voice wobbling. 'Surely that's enough?'

Max was silent some moments, fiddling with the telescope. 'He'd do well to mind himself,' he finally growled, with a stern glance.

'Best behaviour,' she said happily. 'Nothing less.'

'Bravo, Alice!' Jean applauded, herself consuming a generous slice of sponge cake at the kitchen table. 'You know your man.'

Fever

'Do you smell something?' Alice asked of Jean one Sunday morning at breakfast, nose wrinkling.

'Bread baking?' Jean suggested.

Alice shook her head. 'Sweeter.'

'The Cécile Brünner? It's romped away. Six months, and you won't be able to find the shed.'

Alice searched the house. She quickly grew tired of her own sniffing. Max asked if she'd caught a chill.

'There's an odd smell.'

'Flathead,' Max pronounced. 'Trehearne's been gutting them down on the beach.'

Far from reassured, Alice developed a headache so severe, she was obliged to lie down after lunch, a cold compress over her eyes.

Jean stationed herself at her bedside, book in hand, though she found it impossible to read. Alice fell asleep after a while, but lightly, eyes flickering as if on the verge of opening. When they did, she glanced around the room as if in search of something, before closing them again with a sigh.

Late in the afternoon she grew restless, picking at the sheet, gathering it into folds, smoothing it flat. As if she were kneading bread. Jean held her hands to calm her, but the moment she was released she began again.

By nightfall, she was shivering. A summer chill, Jean diagnosed, heart in her mouth. Any number of her children were down with it. She hoped fervently that she hadn't passed it on. Opening her eyes, Alice asked for the lamps to be lit, though both already were, lending a comforting glow to the room. Jean put a hand to her forehead: it was burning hot, paper dry. Alice was pale, paler even than the day they'd met. She had never pressed her about the cliff incident. Too afraid, Jean now confessed to herself, to have Alice perhaps confirm that there'd been no whale.

Looking in, on his way to bed, so concerned was Max he roused Trehearne. Despite the lateness of the hour, he sent him for Culligan.

After a thorough examination, the medic pronounced himself only mildly concerned. Mumps was doing the rounds, he said, and to call him in the morning if Alice showed no improvement. Then dosed her with laudanum. She raised her head sleepily to take it.

*

All afternoon Katya had been beside her, reading. Strange, Alice thought, because Katya hardly ever read. Alice was the reader. Katya lacked the patience. Though she had any amount for needlework. She seemed anxious, leaning over her, peering into her face, squeezing her hands. Fretful. She was always highly strung. Had almost died of the scarlet fever, when little. Perhaps that was why she was so very precious to their mother. She should never have teased her, Alice thought, in sudden anguish. Refusing, playing hide-and-seek, to be found. Refusing to appear when summoned. Katya used to grow quite desperate. 'Come out, Alicja. Please, come out!' Alicja would have to smother giggles. 'I can't find you anywhere! Please! It's no fun anymore.'

'Here I am, Katya! Here I am!' Popping up like a jack-in-the-box. Scaring Katya so she sobbed. Cruel. Cruel. Punishment awaits.

*

'We'll find it,' Jean assured her, Alice's hands in her own. 'You mustn't worry, dearest. Please, please, don't fret about your cat.' But over and over, Alice continued to call. Cat! Cat!

Jean sat with her all night. Just before dawn, Alice began to shudder, as if something had taken hold of her. The whole bed shook. Jean held her down, surprised and alarmed by Alice's strength. Alice's eyes suddenly flew wide. She stared up at Jean beseechingly. 'Katya,' she said clearly, and in apparent anguish. 'Katya.'

Jean's blood ran cold.

She had tried very hard, since the outing to Mount Imlay, not to examine too closely the moment of her fall. Not to reinforce the absurd conviction that she had been pushed. That in those chaotic moments of rapid descent, overriding even the clatter of flying stones and sibilant rush of air, she had heard clearly in her ear a name. Not just her own, wrung from Alice in distress, or that of Keats, of whom she had been thinking, but one unknown to her and now voiced by Alice in her delirium. And with such passionate longing that Jean felt a terrible pang.

For what did she really know of Alice? Of her former life? Her former loves?

*

Abruptly raising herself on an elbow, Alice stared fixedly at the window. Following her gaze, Jean saw the glass begin to shimmer. Then trickle downwards, like water. For long moments she found herself unable to move. Then leaped to her feet, sending the laudanum bottle flying. Reaching for it, so overcome with dizziness was she, she had to regain her seat. Only to find, when next she glanced at the clock on the mantelpiece, that an hour had passed. A whole hour had gone missing. And the laudanum bottle was upright on the bedside table, as before. Laying a hand on Alice's forehead, she found it cool. There was even a tinge of pink to her cheeks. She was fast asleep, face turned to the window. Someone had come in and closed the curtains, Jean saw. Mary Kathleen. Only to recall that Mary Kathleen was away overnight, visiting her mother. Then Max. Walking over to the window, she lifted the curtain and peered out. Dawn was about to break, the sky a violent, lurid red, as if a storm were brewing. She abruptly turned on her heel to scan the room. There was no-one there. Only herself at the window, and Alice soundly sleeping.

Fishing

In the general euphoria of Alice's safe return, Max, on impulse, offered to take Joe Givins out fishing. The policeman accepted with surprising alacrity. Only for Max to spend the days preceding the outing in some turmoil. Not that he harboured designs on the policeman, but he suffered some vague anxiety, after Paulo, about being alone in the company of younger men. Feared that he might, in some way, reveal himself. Perhaps brush against a man's hand in error. Glance too long at a muscled chest. If he had abandoned, these many years, the seas of passion for the safe harbours of gluttony, he was still distinctly uneasy as they set out. But was soon put at ease by Joe telling him the disaster of his stealing his father's boat.

Max found himself laughing. Then revealing his own father's response to lost hats. So a friendship began, cemented by a bountiful day of catching. As if the spirit of cod had migrated some thousands of miles across the Atlantic and the Pacific, whiting upon whiting they hauled in, bream and tailor, with even a John Dory for good measure. 'Manna from heaven.' Joe Givins grinned down at his feet, the floor awash with fish. Max spared a momentary thought for Paulo's putative son: if he had come to exist, he would be like Joe, he was certain—large-hearted, full of some joyous thread sadly lacking in his own material.

Whereas Joe wondered at the bulk of the man. The amount of room he took up, he might have been crammed in with a bear. Not dancing, but oddly restrained. Chained? And to what? There was an impenetrable denseness to Max Carver. Wound tight, the way some crims are before they spill their guts.

*

They saw whales. Max quick to point them out in the far distance. Surprised to find himself, at the sight of them breaking the smooth water, with no fast-beating heart, no sweaty palms, no uneasy fear that he might foul his pants. Only a stillness, a sort of pride, as he indicated their swift, soundless passage. Within minutes they had vanished, only the sea slapping restlessly against the gunwales.

'The orcas chase them in,' Joe remarked.

'Herd them in like sheep,' Max said, with a dismissive edge. 'Old Tom at the fore. Eager for his reward. Whale lips. A rare delicacy for an orca.'

'You don't care for the sport?' Joe suggested.

Max shrugged. 'I'd rather a fairer, more equal fight.'

Joe considered the words some moments. Did he even know what fair or equal meant? He once thought he did. Had thought it his very vocation to ensure justice prevailed. After May's death, he hardly knew what fairness meant. A splinter had wormed its way into him. If he scratched the surface of himself, what might he find?

*

The storm came suddenly out of the north-east. Not life-threatening, no tilting captains or wives. But summer storm. Full of bluster and lightning, the lid of the sea blown sideways.

'No use fighting it,' Max cautioned, at its approach. 'Or trying to row. It'll take us where it wants.'

They were swept, with great rapidity, over the wind-flattened water. All the way to Boydtown, the sepulchral sand-white bulk of the Seahorse Inn speared by a bolt of lightning as they passed. Further they flew. On and on. And on, as they grimly held on to the gunwales. Until a sudden shout of laughter split the slanting rain. Joe Givins, face turned to the sky, whooping as he might have whooped when he was ten if he hadn't been so occupied in bailing. Max grinned, half blinded, drenched through.

They found themselves washed up on the sandbar at the Kiah Inlet, sun out, rain clouds rapidly retreating to the south.

And themselves stranded. One of the Davidsons' mob rowed leisurely out after a while and towed them in. 'Bloke on horseback got took by a shark, that same spot.' He pointed to where they'd washed up. 'Didn't fancy your chances swimming it.'

They thanked him with some fish before leaving the boat safely secured above the high-tide mark, then walked back to Broadside together, their remaining bounty carried between them, shreds of mist snaking through the trees.

The Divide

Something seemed altered between them after Alice's illness. Almost, Alice thought, as if a divide had opened up. Even the night together at Mount Imlay seemed all too soon to have attained a dream-like quality. So that Alice began to wonder if she might not have imagined the intimacy between them. Perhaps it was merely that she was still a little weak from the fever, she thought, or found it hard to sleep for the guilt she felt, wishing the hold Katya had on her gone.

Jean seemed to think of nothing but Katya. Of the longing in Alice's voice, uttering her name. After yet another sleepless night she made up her mind to leave Broadside.

'Leave?' Alice half rose from the table in alarm, when told the news at breakfast. 'And go back to England?'

'To town.' Jean's tone so crisp as to remind Alice of the day they'd met and she'd imagined her a headmistress. 'To Eden, to my lodgings.'

'But who will help plant the hyacinths?' was all Alice could summon on the spot.

'I'm sure you'll be able to manage it. Besides, my ankle's healed.'

'But I'll miss you,' Alice said.

'And I you. We'll still see one another,' Jean added as encouragement. 'Just as before.'

'It won't be the same.' Then, realising her tone, Alice added, 'I'm sorry, that did sound rather childish.'

'Rather like me, I thought,' Jean agreed, with a faint smile, 'when my mother abandoned me for an outing with my father. I couldn't ever bear to be parted from her.'

Nor I from you, Alice thought. 'And now you are older and wiser than Methuselah,' she rallied, with a little smile, 'you have forgiven her?'

'Just,' Jean said drily.

'I'm sure you were a good child,' Alice pronounced, with some certainty.

'Good?' Jean pondered the word a moment. 'I suppose I was. I was certainly an obedient one.'

They both fell silent.

'You've no idea what your friendship means to me,' Alice finally volunteered softly. 'I was often lonely and miserable before we met.'

And I, too, Jean thought.

Abruptly changing tack, Alice spoke a little plaintively. 'Max will miss you. Who will listen to his whale tales?'

'Miss me?' Jean was amused, despite herself. 'You know perfectly well that he loves to have you all to himself, Alice.'

She could feel her resolve weakening, not helped by the sun slanting through the kitchen window that moment, illuminating Alice's face, as mournful as the Madonna's, and as lovely.

'I suppose,' she finally relented, 'I could stay a little longer. A week or two, perhaps. And never mind Mr Carver,' she added briskly, 'what of you? Who's going to persuade you from the kitchen for a walk along the beach? Or make you sit still long enough to finish your tea?'

'So it's decided.' So relieved was Alice, she leaned across the table to take Jean's hand, squeezing it momentarily in her own as if to seal the pact. 'You'll stay.'

The Ball

Though with no further thoughts of Jean leaving or of any divide, Alice resolved to occupy herself less with thoughts of her sister. Since Jean's advent, she seemed to have thought of little else. She also determined to return the pot, thoroughly scoured, to its rightful place under the bed.

But it was never an easy matter, as Alice was soon reminded, to silence Katya. In no time at all she wheedled herself back into Alice's thoughts.

They were always close, Alice reflected. Sorely lacking in family but for their parents, they grew closer still after the loss of their mother to the influenza. It was Alice who comforted the distraught Katya after their mother's demise, their father prostrate with grief. Alice, who gladly took upon herself the task of cooking and caring for the close-knit, sadly depleted little band. Her chief pleasure and consolation, just as it was for her mother, to be found in the kitchen. Small wonder, she thought, that she held fast to Katya's memory: had done all she could to conceal what she knew of Katya's crime, aware that its revelation could only attach to her sister's name further judgement and blame.

It was with some relief, that Alice turned her attention to

the ball, quite forgotten in the recent upheavals and excitement. Mary Kathleen, promised a surprise on the night by her beau, and with mounting expectations of a proposal, was first to remind her of it.

Arranged by the Eden Progress Association to raise much-needed funds to promote Bombala, with Eden as its port, as the new capital of a soon-to-be federated Australia, the ball was held in the town hall. Despite Alice's recent inattention, for months people had talked of little else than their town's impending glory. Everyone fretting how best to accommodate the inevitable hordes of newcomers; which investments might render the best returns; how to manage the ensuing crime wave; how to choose between Sydney and Melbourne for the odd shopping spree, both cities to be readily accessible thanks to the eagerly anticipated rail link. With Twofold Bay easily able to accommodate two navies, let alone one, and with access to the rich Monaro hinterland, Bombala and Eden, equidistant to the new nation's two largest cities, were the obvious choice.

Almost the whole town was in attendance at the ball. There were fairy lights in the trees. Even the weather, notoriously unreliable, held.

Jean, with her pupils, had helped decorate the hall with bunting. Alice, newly galvanised, had baked herself to a standstill. Then spent the whole night fretting that she should be admiring the young men and not Jean; Eden had never seen so many polished shoes in the one room. Jean was wearing a dress of midnight blue, a crimson rose pinned to her bosom. Alice had pinned it there herself, pricking her finger in the process. A drop of blood had stained the bodice. She'd dabbed at it ineffectually with a handkerchief, until Jean stayed her hand.

'Dearest,' she'd said, 'you mustn't fuss. I'm sure it will wash out.'

Though she knew that it wouldn't. And it had cost a small fortune. She couldn't for the life of her think why she'd gone to the expense. But she'd wanted to look nice, for Alice. As the band struck up, slightly discordant at first but improving as it took its cue from the increasingly frenetic enjoyment of the dancers, all she really wanted, she knew, was to dance with Alice.

She drank a glass of sherry, a mistake. She saw Alice flash by, whisked round and round in the arms of a lanky young man she recognised as the new assistant at the Customs House. She accepted a second sherry. And an invitation to dance from Mr Leckie, Harold: one of the older teachers, gingery, with whiskers and a thatch of hair on his neck. He ground her round and round the room as she tried to steer them in Alice's direction. Coming so close, at one point, they almost grazed one another. She momentarily felt the silky stuff of Alice's dress, the silky stuff of Alice herself, before she was gone. Whisked off again. She was light on her feet. Lovely to look at. She wasn't the only one aware of it, Jean knew, as she and Harold ploughed on through the assemblage, knocking people off balance.

*

Waiting for Trehearne outside the hall afterwards, Alice was about to unpin the flower, now badly wilted, from Jean's dress, when he suddenly loomed out of the darkness in the buggy. They climbed in. And, after some minutes, under cover of darkness and plucking up her courage, Alice took Jean's hand. She could only guess at her expression, the night being moonless. She tentatively squeezed Jean's fingers through her evening gloves, and feeling a returning pressure, stroked first one then another of them: around the nail, down to the base, pausing over the slight, sweet chubbiness of the thumb. Finding the buggy suddenly spotlit under a streetlamp, Jean retrieved her hand with an apologetic glance. Only to sit staring ahead into the darkness, a little smile playing on her lips. While Alice, with a smirk—no other word for it, Jean thought—on hers, fiddled with her own pearl-buttoned glove, straightening and smoothing down a seam. And not a word said.

Loss

Aware that the stolen whale would keep him in Eden for the long haul, Joe renewed his loan of *Moby-Dick*. Though he repeatedly interrogated them, all four of the accused stuck to their original account of the night of Ted Price's death.

They were released on bail. Bert Williams, more or less recovered, among them. Most nights they could be seen propping up the bar of the Great Southern and, more often than not, Trehearne with them.

Jim Carew was first to abscond: gone north or inland was the universal belief. Phil Featherstone was quick to follow. And probably halfway to Valparaíso before his absence was even remarked.

Joe kept a close watch on the remaining pair. But, sidelined to Nowra for a couple of weeks to investigate a spate of petty burglaries, he feared the worst.

Moby-Dick was his boon companion. He found it hard to sleep without a page or two at night; any man's nightmare, he suspected, was preferable to his own. The very thought of the diminishing pages made his heart sink.

*

He had barely been back in Eden a week before, chancing to see Max Carver in the barber's shop, he paid Alice Binney a visit.

She answered the door, first knock, Jean Tennyson at her side. Alice seemingly struck dumb at the sight of him.

'Mr Givins.' Alice finally found her voice. 'It's been quite some time.'

'It has, that,' he replied. 'Must be nine years, now.'

'More than ten,' she supplied briskly.

Alice gathered herself up, gaining an inch in height. 'How can I help you, Mr Givins? Mr Carver's away in town today, on business.'

'Mr Givins?' Jean abruptly queried. 'The Mr Givins sent to sort out the not insignificant matter of the stolen whale?'

'The same,' Joe said.

'Hard to imagine such a weighty creature spirited away.'

'Doubtless helped,' Joe said, a gleam in his eye, 'by the fact they all look much the same in the dark.'

Jean smiled encouragingly at Alice. But she remained unmoving, hand on the doorknob.

'I'll be sure to tell Mr Carver you called,' she said into the lengthening silence.

'Thank you,' Joe said levelly. 'It's not him I've come to see, but yourself, Miss Binney. It's something of a private matter,' he added, in an aside to Jean.

'I was just leaving for the school,' she helpfully supplied. 'Good day to you, Mr Givins. And good luck with the whale hunt.'

'If you'll give me a moment,' Alice said to Joe, indicating her soiled apron, when Jean had gone.

She showed him into the front room, then hurried to the kitchen. Hands shaking as she loosed the ties of her apron. She'd done nothing wrong, she reminded herself. Had every right ... to what? Lie? Pretend to be other than who she was? Fake references? Gain employment through deception? Surely enough to get anyone investigated.

'I saw you in the grocery store,' she confessed when they were seated.

'I know,' Joe nodded. 'It was only chance that I was there that day, after provisions. Though I suspect,' he added, 'it wouldn't have been overlong before you were made known to me, Eden being a small place.'

'And it being a popular pastime to mind others' business?' Alice said.

'Indeed. And one generally thought harmless,' he added, with a faint snort. He deliberated a long moment. 'It sometimes seems to me that even to consider harm is as good as doing it.'

'Then it would seem we're of a mind, Mr Givins,' she offered cautiously.

'Joe.' The word formed on his lips, but he let it go, pulled at his mouth as if contemplating what she'd said.

He took in a steadying breath. 'You've nothing to fear from me, Alicja,' he said abruptly, and in earnest. 'You've done nothing wrong.'

'I'm very glad to hear it,' she replied after a moment. 'And you've come all this way to assure me of it?'

He shook his head.

'I hoped to speak to you of your sister. Though with little to add to the matter, I confess. But that I have some guilt on my conscience.'

'Guilt?' She was puzzled. 'As I recall, you played next to no part in the proceedings.'

'None to speak of,' he was quick to agree. 'Though I've often wished that I had. That I'd the courage of my convictions. I thought your sister innocent from the outset. And soon became convinced. I saw them together, more than once, out of court, the Miskell girl and Doherty. The pair seemed thick as thieves.'

'It would have made little difference,' Alice said faintly. 'You can relieve your conscience of the burden. Katya would never have spoken against anyone but herself. There was no malice in my sister.'

'I never believed there was,' Joe said. 'Besides, from my experience, a woman's far more inclined, if anything, to smother or drown a child than bludgeon one to death.'

'And that's your theory of murderesses, Mr Givins?' Alice's voice was icy cold.

Abashed, he shook his head. 'I just found it hard to fathom why your sister accepted the blame when I imagine there was much more to the story, and possibly another's involvement.'

She was silent a moment, taken aback by his admission.

'Then you've never been in love,' she finally offered, bluntly.

'In love? Oh, but I have,' was his swift reply. 'And lost it, too.'

*

Love? Joe seized on the word, turned it over in his mind, unspeaking, some moments.

There'd been rumours, and not just in the gutter press, of a man. And surely he couldn't have been alone in noting the effect the handsome, self-assured footman, William Doherty, tossing back his dark hair to expose the piercing gaze of his blue eyes, had on the jury. Giving voice, in his smooth tongue, to all the many suspicions he'd harboured of the Brajkoviç girl.

He and the scullery maid, Eliza Miskell, both.

'She was often flushed and forgetful. Her behaviour odd and often unseemly for a nursemaid,' Miskell had avowed, herself flushed to the roots of her red hair.

'Highly strung?' the prosecutor had suggested.

'Nervy. Easily excited,' Miskell had been eager to elaborate. 'Else badly downcast. And sometimes both within the hour.'

She'd grown increasingly alarmed by Brajkoviç's strange ways, Miskell had borne witness. And often thought of the little one, alone in her care.

Every word a nail.

Ably driven home in the prosecutor's closing address, published on the front page of almost every newspaper:

I put it to the members of the jury that Katya Brajkoviç, in a fit of rage at the child's persistent crying, repeatedly shook little Caroline Rathbone before striking her violently on the arms and legs. After which, having failed to achieve her quiescence, she struck the child repeatedly on the head. Only, overcome by the gravity of her misdeeds, to flee into the night, leaving the child to perish alone.

*

Alice found herself wondering at the pain evident in Joe Givins's voice when he spoke of love and loss.

In court, he'd been almost indistinguishable from the rest, a small, stocky, dark-haired man in blue. But it was hard now not to acknowledge that his eyes held depth and humour, and even, perhaps, some kindness.

'I confess,' Joe went on to concede, 'it would have been a brave jury to have found your sister not guilty, faced with the anguish of a mother of such standing and editorials in every newspaper.'

'Hang her!' they'd shouted outside the court. 'Hang the murdering bitch.'

'My wife lost three babies,' Joe confided then. 'Not that I thought them of great account at the time, I confess. It only came late to me that a child's far more than flesh and blood. A child's a dream. A promise of the future. And when it's overnight snatched away and brutally ...' He cleared his throat, studying his hat intently.

'What do you want, Mr Givins?' Alice asked.

Joe met her eyes. 'What I've probably no right to ask for. To try to make some sense of the thing. It's gnawed at me, these many years, that the law, purporting to bring justice, can destroy those it's meant to serve.'

'Worthy sentiments,' Alice said. 'But I'd rather my sister was left in peace.'

'And is she?' Joe's eyes fixed on hers. 'At peace?'

Alice was silent. Fighting the familiar urge to say her name, plead her cause. Then thought of Jean and of what the future might hold, and knew in her heart that she had no choice but to let Katya go.

To the lengthening silence, Alice finally replied: 'I've heard what you came to say, Mr Givins. And believe you sincere. But if I were to tell you what l do know, what I only later learned, it would need your sacred word that it would never leave this room.'

'You have it,' Joe said, instantly and in earnest. 'I swear.'

The Letter

Alice fetched Katya's letter, kept in a little box made by her father for her special treasures.

Returned to the kitchen, she was about to hand the letter to Joe Givins when something gave her pause: perhaps the eagerness of his expression, as if a long desired prize was finally almost within his grasp.

'You swear you will not use it against her or reveal it to any other living soul?' she asked again sternly.

'I gave you my word,' he said. 'It is for my eyes only.' Then paused a moment, as if struck by a sudden thought though, in truth, one long held: 'But if a day were to come when an investigation into your sister's case was proposed, you would not dismiss it out of hand?'

Alice thought some moments. 'No, Mr Givins. Not out of hand. Not if its honest intention was to confirm my sister's innocence and clear her name.'

Tendering him the letter, yellowed and brittle with handling, Alice found herself trembling though relieved to see him receive it with almost reverential care.

She remembered, as he read, receiving Katya's few possessions shortly after she was hanged. Their mother's bible, a neatly folded pile of clothes and concealed within the lining of a dress the letter, addressed solely to herself. Her father, though aware of her possession of it, never once inquired as to its contents, knowing only that his beloved youngest child was lost to him in a brutal and unjust death. A burden that within a year was to prove unequal to an already weakened and failing heart.

'*My own darling sister ...*' Katya began, in a hand apparently unfaltering.

> *I find it so very hard to write this, knowing that, far from consolation, this missive will only add to your distress. But I feel that I owe you, who has always been so very careful of it, the truth. Though I swore under oath that I was alone in the house the night little Caro died, I wasn't. William Doherty was with me.*
>
> *I believe the moment I laid eyes on William, I knew myself lost. I remember that I had to take hold of a chair, so as not to swoon. Just like one of the heroines in those romances you were always so fond of, and that I scorned. Never for a moment imagining that I, too, might one day fall in love, at a glance.*
>
> *Far from rebuffing William's advances, I confess that I gave myself to him wholeheartedly and without reservation. And found it impossible to pretend modesty or reticence, the whole world seeming so utterly changed and made new in his presence.*
>
> *As I spoke of in court, I woke the day of little Caro's death to news that the mistress had been suddenly called away to tend to an ailing aunt. With the master in Sydney, Eliza Miskell visiting family, and William in Orange, on some business of the master's, I was that night to be sole custodian of the house and of little Caro.*
>
> *What I neglected to reveal was that, with his business concluded earlier than expected, William returned to Bathurst that afternoon.*

I remember that I was both thrilled and apprehensive, in equal measure, at his unexpected presence. So much so, in truth I barely paid any mind to the fact the little one was unusually pale, and subdued and cheerless at supper, and hardly touched her food, falling deep asleep the moment I laid her in her crib.

William and I were barely together a quarter-hour when she stirred. And with such a cry of distress, I immediately went to her. She reached up her arms to me, I recall, tears streaming down her cheeks. 'Mama!' she cried. 'Mama!' Cradling her in my arms, I did everything I could to console her, but it seemed that no endearment, lullaby or nursery rhyme could still her tears. She cried for her mother as if her little heart were broken.

It was William, quickly losing patience, who suggested he try his hand at settling her. I confess I didn't hesitate to agree. Not just that I was at my wit's end, but she was so very fond of him, always quick to laugh when he pulled faces at her, or tipped his hat to her, handing her into the carriage as if she were some grand lady.

I've no idea how long he was away from the bed that night. Only that time often seemed strangely altered in his presence, an hour seeming to pass in a matter of moments, whereas a day in his absence could seem to stretch an eternity. What I do recall is that, lying there, I was surprised by a growing sense of guilt and shame. So distressing, that to counter it I tried to persuade myself I was awaiting the return of a lawfully wedded husband, gone to console a fretful child of our own. Only to become aware of silence. And William in the doorway, a shushing finger to his lips, the light from the room behind seeming to radiate from him.

When I finally went to her, after our love-making, I found little Caro lying face down, the blanket over her head. As soon as I picked her up, I knew something was badly wrong. She was cold and strangely limp, her head lolling to one side so that the curls spilled down my arm.

I gave her a gentle shake, to rouse her, but there was no response. I shook her again, a little more firmly, but still she slept. I carried her over to the lamp then, only to find, to my horror, that her lips were blue. The faint bump on her temple that she'd sustained in a small fall earlier in the day had become so badly swollen her head seemed lopsided. I chafed her little arms and legs, but nothing seemed to rouse her. At a loss, I finally laid her back in her crib. Only to notice a bruise on one of her little arms and, drawing back the covers, another on her leg which seemed oddly twisted to one side. Injuries, I could only surmise, from her fall earlier that day which I, solely occupied with thoughts of William, had entirely neglected to remark. So appalled at the failure that I must have cried out in alarm because I suddenly found William at my side.

He stood staring down at her, long moments, before he finally bent and laid an ear to her lips. He remained that way, I remember, for some time, before he finally straightened. She's not breathing, he declared with conviction.

So taken aback was I, I recall that I assured him with some asperity that she was merely deep asleep.

He went to pull the blanket from her, but I stayed his hand. I told him that she was best kept warmly wrapped. He then demanded to know, his tone accusing, what had happened to her head. I told him the truth: that she had tripped and fallen that morning, banging it cruelly against the doorframe. That, as was often the case at her age, she was still a little unsteady on her feet. Even the mistress, I assured him, often chided her for her exuberances.

He then asked whether I'd called the doctor.

There was no need, I said, attempting a calm demeanour, though I was by now trembling all over. She had perfectly recovered, I assured him, aside from a faint swelling at the temple.

I bent and gathered her into my arms, holding her close to try to warm her. It suddenly came to me that she might have suffered some sort of fit, something to do with her injuries. I've no idea how long I stood there, but I looked up to find William in the doorway, fully dressed, hat clasped to his chest like a shield. He stared hard at me some moments, silent, then turned and left. I believe that never in my life did I feel so alone and bereft as at that moment when I heard the door close behind him.

I continued to cradle Caro, trying to imbue her with my warmth. gently chafing her little arms and legs to try to warm her. Only, as soon as I stopped, to feel her grow cold again. And heavy. Impossibly heavy for such a small bundle. I could hardly hold her. I again laid her down in the crib, laid her head on the pillow, smoothing out the curls so that they sat nicely, then pulled the blanket up to her chin. I told myself that she would soon wake up. Even though I knew, in my heart, that it wasn't true. That little Caro was dead.

I'm unsure how long I stood watch over her, but long enough to see the blue begin to seep from her lips into her cheeks.

It puzzles me still how hard I find it to remember the sequence of events. Whether it was before or after her morning nap that she struck her head. What I do clearly recall is that she barely touched her lunch that day, and that I put it down to the lingering effects of a recent cold. And so slight was her injury that I hadn't even thought to call the doctor. My thoughts, to my abiding shame, turned far more, with William's return, to what I might wear, how to dress my hair, whether to colour my cheeks a little.

I finally got to my feet, filled with fresh resolve. I must do something, I thought. Tell someone, call someone. But who? And to say what? That I'd let her cry while I was in bed with my lover?

All I could think was that I must tell her mother. And at the very thought my stomach churned, so that I barely made the closet, splashing cold water repeatedly on my face to try to clear my thoughts, but to no avail. Then found myself unable to go in to her. I instead went outside and began to walk to and fro in front of the house, all the while desperately trying to make some sense of it all.

Finally, returning to Caro's room, I sat beside her crib and prayed as I never had before in my life: that she might live, that she might wake and open her eyes. But there was no miracle. Only that little face, cruelly altered by the swelling, the whole of her left eye swallowed up.

After a time I once more ventured out, hoping against hope to find William returned. But there was no-one. No-one to advise me or give succor. I remember a crushing pain in my chest. And that, to try to ease it, I again began to walk. I walked the length of the street, returning to the gate, to the house, to the faint light beckoning, over and over. Until I found myself venturing further and still further afield. Until, almost unknown to myself, I finally made my way home to you and father.

Every day I have thought of your faces in court, my darling Alicja, filled with the absolute certainty of my innocence. As if it were only a matter of time before the angels themselves descended to proclaim it.

Whereas my sins have grown more unbearable and despicable to me with every passing hour. Believe me, dearest one, I needed no judge or jury to find me guilty; the crime is mine, and mine alone. Day and night I have repented of it, and the loss of that small innocent life. And have thought often, and fondly, of the many times you and I, when little, would confess our small crimes and misdemeanors to one another, under the covers in bed at night, and find comfort and forgiveness.

I won't ask that you not grieve for me, dearest, knowing if you were ever lost to me how I would grieve you. But only that you find it in your heart to forgive me, and continue to think fondly of me, as you always have, and keep me in your prayers at night, as you have always been in mine.

I confess I find almost too hard to bear the thought of being forever parted from you. And can only take consolation from the belief that, despite all, we will one day be happily reunited. It has always gladdened *my heart to have you for my sister. And I can only thank you, with all my heart, for all the sisterly love and kindness you have bestowed upon me over the years. I promise to remain, always, and forever,*

Your own, most loving, and devoted
Katya

Carefully folding the letter, Joe handed it back without a word. He sat some moments in contemplation of the hopes, the curiosity that had led him here today. And now? He had seen the very workings of a woman's heart. And could only think of May. Of how he never understood her pain and loss, nor ever truly tried. He felt ashamed and abashed. In a court you saw nothing, Joe thought, but the case, the questions, the possible evasions, the dodgy answers, the outright lies. You were on the scent of a confession, a revelation. It was what brought him here today. Katya Brajakoviç was to him little more than a possible 'perpetrator', a possible 'victim'. Innocent? Guilty? Who could say, thought Joe. Like Ahab's great white whale, truth was the goal, the pursuit of it relentless. As if it could ever be truly known. And now? Joe posed the question to himself. Perhaps he would one day find a way to redeem the young woman's name. Redeem himself? He'd heard Katya's true voice and could not forget it; he could never unknow her words or the love and passion and sacrifice behind them. It left him stunned.

'It is very much as I suspected. I always believed your sister to be innocent,' he said with a piercing glance, then cleared his throat, stumbling a little as he rose to his feet.

He rallied quickly, thanking Alice with all the sincerity he could muster before, reaching for his hat as a man will for the thing he hopes will save him, he gratefully put it on.

Alice showed him to the door.

The Prognosis

Max put the ache in his gut down to choux buns. Alice's attempts to perfect the croquembouche meant any number of the delectable little puffs of cream-filled pastry needed to be consumed. But what began as a dull ache turned to stabbing, full-blown pain. Max went to see Culligan for a sleeping draught. Only to find himself subjected to a thorough examination and with a referral to a specialist in Macquarie Street, in Sydney.

Max told Alice he had to go to the great city on business, and to purchase a new telescope, the existing one having ceased to properly focus. Pleased with his inventiveness. Still, she fussed: what would he eat? where would he stay? how would he travel?

On the steamship, Max reassured her. At the Australian Club, thanks to Culligan, a long-time member. And as for what he would eat …

Alice prepared lunches, fruitcake, cold collations, wrapping everything in cloth, packing it all snugly into a basket, saying a little prayer under her breath for his safe return. What was God for, after all, she reasoned, but to ask favours of? He must like it, she thought. Everyone talking to Him, asking Him questions, promising Him things. She had taken Katya their mother's bible, brought with her all the way from the old country. Every Sunday evening, after the table was cleared, their mother had read to them from the Psalms. What did it matter that they didn't understand each and every word? Of what significance was that beside the sound of their mother's voice, a warm fire, a warm bed waiting for them?

*

In Sydney, Max was surprised to discover he was to die. And far sooner than he might have thought. And not in some raging gale at sea, or shipwrecked on some wild exotic shore, but at home, in bed. In pain? Not, the specialist assured him, with generous amounts of opium. It seemed he was to end his days with barely a whimper. Of no more consequence than an empty crab claw flung into a rock pool. Of no more import than a chunk of blubber impaled on a whaler's hook. He treated himself to a new, large, prohibitively expensive telescope. Then paid a visit to the archives of the law courts, in search of information on Katya Brajkoviç.

*

Returned to Eden, he hadn't counted on the loss of appetite. Hourly, the thing whittled him away. Unlike his scrimshaw, he didn't grow elegant in relief, but gaunt, hollowed out, withered to the core. He did his best to hide it: wrapped lamb chops and sausages in handkerchiefs, concealing them in pockets. For a time, custards and soups had him stumped. Until he had Mary Kathleen move the aspidistra from the hallway into the dining room. It seemed none the worse for it.

What would Alice do, he fretted, with no-one to cook for; her home taken from her; no outlet for her demons? The dog would return.

She soon found him out. No red herring, but a fillet of snapper, poking out of a trouser pocket. Alice laughed. Then cried. Almost more tears than a cook's apron could absorb.

*

Daily, Max found himself almost overwhelmed by thoughts of the past. All manner of things came back: a day spent cleaning a room of infant blood; he and Fredo hosing down the slipway, and each other, after work; the cod he and Paulo had seen out in the bay, on Fogo Island, in vast drifts; the capelin covering the shore in spring, ankle-deep, countless in their spawning and dying.

He even found himself becoming something of a philosopher. Wherever a man went, he mused, the same sun shone, the same winds blew. And a man might die of thirst surrounded by water. Die of loneliness in a crowded room or crammed ship. Every act of commission or omission, he realised, wrought some shift. Acts as small as the nick of a whittling knife. And as seismic, as loving Paulo.

More and more, he was to be seen at the study windows, staring at some distant spouting whale in frank amazement. To think that he'd believed he'd mastered the beasts; thought he knew them better than himself! As well to think you knew a man when you'd only seen the whites of his eyes in battle, Max thought. Never once having seen him at ease at his own hearth, dandling an infant child or talking peaceably with his wife. Never once witnessing the everyday moments of his life. But only the extremes. The terror in the face of death.

He supposed he was seeing whales anew.

He even dreamed of them. Or worse, found them lined up at night before his wakeful eyes. Ragged. Bloodied. Butchered.

As for the rest of his time, he spent much of it worrying.

About the house: that it would grow desolate, the bush creeping in, the path lost to weeds, salt air seeping through cracks.

About the books: that the pages would spot with mould, the ink run, his brother's words dribble down the page.

About Alice: so much so, he paid a discreet visit to a solicitor in town. And made some unexpected purchases.

So it was that Alice, returning from Eden one afternoon, opened the door to find a gleaming sewing-machine, especially ordered by Max from Sydney, greeting her in the hallway.

But as well as fretting and fussing, chasing errant memories, and making domestic refinements, Max pondered, day and night, on what might be a fitting end to his life.

That it involved a whale came as little surprise to him.

The Birds

Three o'clock on a Sunday afternoon, a strange, unsettled hour. A grey day, a summer storm. Rain steadily falling, hard to say where sky let off and sea began.

They were at the kitchen table, a basket of mending at Alice's feet, Jean with a book open before her, when, just as the clock struck the hour, the clouds broke rank and a watery sun emerged. Wordlessly, they grabbed umbrellas and coats, and hurried down the path to the beach.

Only to be pulled up short.

It seemed they'd stumbled upon a graveyard. Dozens of mutton birds, downed by the storm, were washed up on the morning tide. Singly and in clumps they lay, the length and breadth of the small strand. Sodden, crumpled as rags, some with wings outstretched as if still in flight.

A dismal sight.

'And all within sight of land,' Jean mourned.

'And the sea,' Alice puzzled, 'now smooth as silk.'

They walked on in silence, sidestepping the fallen creatures, pausing now and then to gaze down pityingly at the devastation.

'It's so very final, death,' Jean said.

'And unfair,' Alice said. 'Not that the dead care. But the living.'

'My mother fought to the very end. She didn't want to die.'

Alice took a breath.'Whereas my sister,' she said, 'could hardly wait. But then, she was always the impatient one.'

'You said she died of the diphtheria?' Jean was puzzled.

Alice met her eyes. 'I lied,' she confessed. 'My sister—Katya—was hanged for the murder of a child.'

'Dear God, Alice!' Jean grabbed her arm. 'Hanged?'

'Keep walking,' Alice said, 'and I'll tell you all. I can't keep still.'

For over an hour, to and fro they strode across the strand. Jean matching Alice stride for stride. Never once stumbling, flinching, glancing away. Alice's arm tight in her own.

Blessed

Hands shaking, Alice unbuttoned the bodice of Jean's dress. Revealing her breasts, so often imagined.

'You're very lovely, Jeannie.' A bat's voice, nothing like her own. Jean didn't seem to mind. Or her breasts, blushing pink against their white, bleached barricades.

Everything slowed down. But for her heart. Pounding. Like the day Jean tried to teach her to swim. Swept off her feet by a rogue wave, she'd tumbled over and over in the surf only to find herself scooped up. Held tight against Jean's body. The way her mother used to hold her when she towelled dry her hair. Blissfully blind and half suffocated in the softness and warmth of her.

No, nothing like a mother.

'What's it like,' she ventured, running her fingers into the cleft of warm flesh, 'for you?' Daring, after a moment, to add 'my darling'. The words repeated, slightly alarmingly, in her head.

Jean considered her reply so long that Alice grew alarmed.

'I'm not sure. I've never felt like this. This happy. This blessed. As if I've been especially singled out. Chosen. Just as when I was little and three ladybirds landed on me, all within the hour. I never forgot. Thrice blessed.'

Alice stared at her in some surprise.

But she wasn't finished. 'And frightened,' she said. 'Terrified. That it'll end. That it must. That I'll lose you. That I won't be able to bear it.'

'Goodness,' Alice murmured.

'You've no idea,' Jean said with a rueful smile, 'how I've lost my head over you. And I used to be quite sensible.'

'Before me?' Alice suggested, smug.

Jean stroked a strand of Alice's hair from her forehead. 'Before you, Alice, I was a different person.'

*

Alice, snug in Jean's arms in the narrow iron bed, hardly space enough for breath, thought of all the rumours she'd heard over the years. Mr Aloysius, piano teacher, overly fond of laying his hand over the young master's as he practised the scales—banished. The 'sisters' Bligh. Mannish, brusque, fond of topiary: often to be seen up ladders, twigs in their hair—scorned.

Not a word of wet bits, sticky bits, things that bumped and ground and snagged, and made you laugh. Not a word, Alice thought, of love.

The Confession

Assuming her customary place at the breakfast table one morning, fixing her eyes intently on Alice, Jean said, 'There is something I must tell you, Alice. About my life in England. Something I should have told you when we first met.'

Alice experienced a feeling of dread. Much, she recalled, as in church as a child when convinced, though unaware of any crime, that some terrible judgement was about to be handed down on her from on high. Or far worse, as she'd felt in court awaiting the sentence to be pronounced.

'I really think I ought to attend to ...' she half attempted to rise.

'Please hear me out, Alice,' Jean said, a little beseechingly.

Subsiding, Alice sat very still, hands in lap. She heard Jean take a deep breath.

'What I didn't tell you, reveal,' she added the emphasis, 'was that I was married in England. Am married still,' she added, seeming to flinch, 'though I wish with all my heart that it was otherwise.'

'Married?' Alice said, faintly.

Jean nodded. 'Some months after my mother passed away, I met a young man. He proposed.'

Alice stared at Jean some moments then, conscious of a sudden lump in her throat, down at her plate. She'd only just been contemplating the prospect of a piece of buttered toast, and Jean was suddenly married. And not just wed, but from the sound of it seeming to think it perfectly reasonable to accept a proposal, when proposed to. When a person could always say no, Alice thought, bleakly.

*

Jean knew on her wedding night that she'd made a terrible mistake in marrying John Boynton.

He'd pushed into her so violently, she told Alice, with so little warning, she'd cried out in agony. He hadn't paused. Like some mechanical tin monkey, he'd beaten at her maidenhead until he'd broken through, uttering an animal grunt of release.

When she was unable to respond to his advances the next morning, he slapped her face. She was sulking, he pronounced. It was soon standard punishment. An overcooked egg, a cinder on the hearthrug, an over-starched collar.

And the drink. Before the wedding, he'd refuse a second sherry. The alcohol he imbibed nightly after they were married seemed to loosen something inside him: loosen his hands, his member.

Day and night, she tried to make sense of it. To bring her reason to bear. How could someone be so utterly changed? What could she do to right matters? It was some time before it dawned on her that there would be no change. Could be no change. Nor any help. That she had been duped, lied to, made a fool of, her vulnerability used against her.

They'd been married barely a month when he came home drunk one night and, climbing onto her in bed, tried to flip her onto her stomach. When she resisted, he punched her in the face. Hard. She was halfway out of bed when he dragged her back by the hair, banging her head against the headboard. She fought in earnest then: fists, nails, teeth—striking out with all her strength. Managing to secure both her hands in his, he shoved her over and anally raped her. Then fell asleep.

Afterwards, Jean lay awake for hours, staring into the dark. Utterly numb. Even the beat of her heart seemed muffled and distant. Barely aware of the pain, and that she was bleeding. Only a pressing need to relieve herself finally propelled her to her feet. She used the closet and then, in the kitchen, took out a knife, one of a set given to them by Irene for a wedding present. She stood staring at the blade. Conscious of the heft of it in her hand. The full moon sparking off cold steel. Momentarily, she caught a glimpse of herself in it. Jean. Small Jean. Shrunken, diminished, hardly anything left at all. She returned the knife to the drawer.

He ran through all her money; her mother's money. It had been the whole point, of course. The sex a mere sideline.

It became an almost daily event. Every morning as soon as it grew light. As soon as he'd relieved himself, opened the curtains, stood scratching his chest, under his arms, his swelling crotch. He'd turn that particular lascivious look on her, as if she was the Sunday roast.

'Look at it,' he'd grin. 'Fancy a bit of that inside you?'

Mr Johnny, the girls called it, he told her. The whores. You're a bit of a whore yourself, doll-face. On the QT. Do it for nothing. Do it for anyone. My mate, Fred, could do with a bit. Might have a word in his pearly.'

He liked to talk. A geyser of filth.

'Heave ho, over you go.' Flipping her onto her stomach. Lifting up her nightdress, straddling her, bringing all his weight to bear upon her, so she was pinned to the bed. He'd force her head down into the pillow, so deep she couldn't breathe. 'That's a girl, bum up. Don't you try to flip, that won't do the trick. Ooh, you've got a tight one. Nice tight little hole for Mr Johnny.' She'd never been frightened of anyone before, not even her father. 'Knew, the second you opened that door. Acting like you were a lady. Ladies don't beg for it. Come on, let's hear it. Please, Mr Johnny, put your cock in my hole. Please, Mr Johnny, put your big cock in my hole. That's it. That's the way. Fucking whore.'

She couldn't remember when she decided to remove herself. Refused to fight, struggle, to acknowledge his existence in any way. Lay limply, reciting lines of poetry to herself, as he pounded her into the mattress. Recalled the plots of favourite books, pieces of music, plays she and her mother had seen together. Transported herself to another place and time, one he had no knowledge of, and never would.

And all the while plotted her escape.

*

They'd been married almost two years when she finally made good of it. She'd made her escape her life's work, in the interim, studying her captor's habits, routines, weaknesses. She knew that he went out at ten o'clock each morning, returning in the late afternoon. That he kept loose change in his pockets, and the spare key to the house was concealed in an old tobacco tin, at the back of his chest of drawers. Every day she had to fight the urge to retrieve it, to force patience on herself. Then woke one morning to find him leaning over her, his sour breath in her face. And with such a look of loathing, and sly speculation, she knew that something had shifted, and that she was in peril of her very life.

She waited until midday before she retrieved the key and, opening the door, walked out. Tread measured, head held high. No-one would have suspected that she struggled for every breath. That she could hardly keep the contents of her stomach, for fear. She had formulated a sketchy plan that, if he tried to intercept her, she would throw herself to the ground, as if in a fit. That she would writhe and scream, and claw at anyone who tried to soothe her. That she would pretend madness, in the hope that someone would call the police who would take her away and lock her up. Somewhere safe, away from him. And if with the truly insane, it could not, surely, be worse than her incarceration, day and night, with the sane and vicious? But no-one stopped her. No-one paid her the least attention, so she kept walking.

For some months, she'd rifled his pockets while he slept, taking the odd coin, so as not to arouse suspicion. She now used the money to take an omnibus to the part of town known as home to people of ill-repute. People she had once privately damned as weak-willed, weak-minded, incapable of making anything of themselves. Much like the person she now found herself to be. She spent more of the coins, rapidly dwindling, in a tea-room, on an iced bun and pot of tea.

Then she walked the streets. Almost deserted when she set out, rapidly filling as dusk fell. She had never seen so many strange and disturbing sights. And was surprised to find that, far from repulsed or frightened by them, she felt almost at home, and safe.

She'd been walking some time when a man came up to her and laid a hand on her arm. It took all her will not to recoil or lash out at him. She reminded herself sternly of what she intended. And that every first time was like this. The man's request, after what she'd lately endured, seemed almost naive. All that was required of her, it seemed, was a simple transaction of the flesh.

She earned enough that night for food and lodging for some days. She went out again the very next night, and the one after. And every night for over a year. And never once questioned herself; never once condemned her actions. She would have done far worse, she knew, to be free of him. Her only concern, that he find her. That he wreak upon her some hideous vengeance.

Not for a moment did she let down her guard: not once venture out before dusk, or stray from the familiar, bustling, well-lit streets. She kept her distance from everyone, from the other women like herself, from her customers, some of whom were soon regulars. Having taken pride in performing her duties diligently since she was a child, it came as a droll surprise to find that her work ethic extended to formerly unimagined, nay unimaginable, scenarios.

Her savings increasing, she formed a plan to go abroad, to put as much distance as she could between herself and her husband. Even if it meant leaving all that was familiar and dear to her, not least her mother's grave. There was much in the newspapers, at the time, of Australia. Touted as a land of milk and honey, it was said to offer ample reward to those prepared to work hard and with a yen for adventure. Its chief drawback, a propensity to swallow people up. A prospect which, for Jean at least, held next to no fear.

She left on a bitterly cold midwinter's morning. Right up until the moment they sailed, she anxiously scanned the crowds on the dock for a sight of him, then remained on deck some hours to watch the land recede. Only when England was no more than a speck on the horizon did she breathe a little easier.

By the time they docked in Melbourne, she was already well established as Jean Tennyson, spinster, teacher, only daughter of an elderly mother who'd recently died. Still, she was vigilant. After all, she reasoned, if she could venture so far afield, so might he.

As a safeguard, she made up her mind to apply for teaching positions in remote regions. One such arose in the small coastal town of Eden, in New South Wales. The reply came by return mail. The school would be very pleased, the principal wrote, to offer her employment, one of the teachers having recently left to be married. Eden. The very word seemed a balm. She had prepared for her journey north that same day.

*

Her confession at an end, Jean abruptly rose and walking over to the window gazed out to sea.

'I never thought to ever share the sorry tale,' she said, her back to Alice. 'But that I would take it with me to the grave.'

Alice had given little indication, listening to Jean's account, of her thoughts and feelings. But the more she learned of all Jean had endured, the more a feeling of anger rose in her, such a rage as Alice never before felt in her life. And such pity. Such sorrow. As if her very heart would break. And not just for Jean, but for Katya, for all the pitilessly used and disgraced.

Walking over to the window she put an arm around Jean though she remained stiff and unspeaking.

After a time Alice gently asked, 'Can you hear it, Jeannie? Can you hear the sea?'

Jean gave a faint nod.

'How very calm and peaceful it is?' Alice suggested. She stroked Jean's hair as if she were gentling a wild creature. 'As if it's whispering.'

Jean was silent. Then very softly, 'And what does it say?'

'That you are safe now,' Alice said. 'That you are free. That he will never again hurt or harm you.'

A faint tremor passed through Jean, but Alice felt her lean a little closer.

'And that it will go on, as always?' asked Jean, her tone lightening a little. 'Despite all suffering? It will never cease?'

'Oh, it will never stop,' Alice assured her. 'It is like my love for you. It is never ending.'

They were silent for a time, Alice stroking Jean's hair as she leaned close.

'I was foolish to marry him,' Jean finally murmured.

'No. You were merely trusting. As is your way,' Alice said.

'I was lonely.'

'You were waiting for me,' Alice said, with surety.

And Jean's monster? Alice thought, as Jean's hand sought her own. Was he now to appear nightly in her dreams? Was he always to be there now between them? Victorious, despite all. No, Alice thought. Never, her fierce unyielding thought. Alice was done with monsters.

The Calf

Max, out rowing in the bay one morning, sighted them. A calf, half grown, and a cow, its passage oddly halting. Lamed? Harpooned? Weighed down with rotted ambergris? Something was amiss. He thought he caught a glint of metal. An old barb? He remembered the certainty in Gonçalves's voice the day the whale had stranded on Pico. The cow looked to be headed straight for shore, calf at her side. It couldn't have been more than five minutes before the first whaleboat hove into sight. The McIntyres, an unsavoury mob.

Let them be! The thought came from nowhere. And was surprisingly loud and fierce. Let them be! There's few enough left.

The first harpoon fell well short. Time enough for the cow to gather up the calf and flee, whaleboat in pursuit. Max rowed in a fury, had almost caught up with the scene, when the second harpoon found its mark. The cow bucked to throw it off. Again and again, as the calf splashed and cavorted at her side. Unable to fathom why its mother writhed. Max was barely two boat lengths off when the third barb went in. He heard the whoosh of iron, the cow's bellow of pain. Felt the stab in his gut. Or was it his heart? Then she was still. All the fight gone out of her. Until she felt the calf at her side and stirred. Now, Max silently roared. Now!

Newly revived, she charged. Max saw the boat shatter, tossing men and oars into the air.

He waited until they had all safely landed in the water before leisurely rowing over. Even managing, by dint of cunning effort, to give Jim McIntyre a hefty whack on the noddle as he reached out to him with an oar.

'Take hold, man! Hang on there, lad!' He was everywhere at once. It was a good ten minutes, his oar dangling like a hook in a pond of thrashing fish, before the last man was hauled in. Time enough for the calf to make good its escape. Unlike its mother, mortally wounded and sounding into the depths of Twofold Bay only to be dispatched by a marauding band of orcas.

*

Joe Givins heard the tale in the bar of the Great Southern that night. That Max Carver, an ailing man, had single-handedly saved an entire boatload of whale fishermen.

Ailing?

*

The calf returned that same evening. Max saw it through the telescope, searching for its mother. Alice and Jean, at the kitchen window, feared it might strand. But no. To and fro, to and fro, it swam, unwilling or unable to give up. Only knowing, as the young do, to keep its mother close.

'The poor creature,' Alice said to Max, her voice mournful and small. 'All alone. And motherless.'

The idea came to Max that same moment.

*

He was up, next morning, before first light. He lit the lamp in his study, hauled everything out of the chest and onto his desk. Then sat for a time, considering the pile. After a while, he retrieved a whale tooth from it, the first he'd ever carved at sea, incised with a woman clutching a bible to her heaving bosom; a girl with streaming hair in tiny, chiselled strands; a boy labouring over oars. He studied the scene, clutching it momentarily to his heart, before replacing it on his desk.

'Amends,' he finally muttered, getting to his feet. Or perhaps it was 'Amen'.

He piled everything back in, closed the lid.

Then went and roused Trehearne.

The Rescue

Trehearne was snoring, deep in his throat, gurgling like a river. It was the dawn chorus of kookaburras that finally woke him. That, and Max pounding on his door. He opened it with a curse, peered blearily out.

'Over time you were up and about,' Max said. 'There's work to be done.'

First light had already begun to rim the cove.

They'd be wide awake across the bay, Max thought. Such a day for it, such sport to be had.

He found Alice in the kitchen, stirring porridge. Jean at the table, smoothing down the cloth. They both stared at him as he walked in.

'I thought we might take the boat out.' He attempted nonchalance.

'I thought I heard it crying,' Alice said.

Max hesitated a moment. 'There was some noise,' he conceded.

'Porridge?' Alice suggested then.

Max shook his head.

'You'll need your strength.'

'A small helping,' Max said.

Jean bit down on her lip.

Trehearne appeared in the doorway, yawning. He glanced incuriously from one to the other, before pulling up a chair. Alice pushed a brimming bowl of porridge at him. All three watched, in apparent fascination, as he ladled down big gulping spoonfuls.

Hearing a disturbance, Alice went to the window, only to find Joe Givins, on horseback. As if of one mind, she, Jean and Max trooped outside, leaving Trehearne to his porridge. Dismounting, Joe stood some moments, turning his hat in his hands.

'I see you survived,' he finally said to Max. 'What I heard, you were quite the hero.' All the while searching his face. The man had lost weight, he saw. And with an unnerving pallor.

'Hero?' Max grinned. 'Villain. You ask Jim McIntyre.'

'I saw his bandaged head,' Joe said, with a smile.

'Perils of whaling,' Max said drily.

'You're up betimes.' Joe glanced at the rapidly lightening sky. 'You're taking her out?' With a nod to the boat.

'We're going fishing.'

'Good day for it,' Joe said.

'None better.'

Joe ran an admiring eye over the freshly oiled boards. 'She's come up good.'

'Freshly caulked,' Max said. 'As per your suggestion.'

They were silent some moments, staring at the boat, the two men acutely conscious of what the day might bring.

He should have said more, Joe later thought. But what? Don't go out? You've not the strength for it? As if he were the arbiter of what a man could bear.

'You've breakfasted, Mr Givins?' Alice broke the silence to ask.

Joe shook his head.

'A helping of porridge?'

'Would be greatly appreciated. I've had an early start of it.'

'I've some few things to attend to, in my study. If you'll excuse me?' Max absented himself.

Closing the door, he leaned against it, staring at the chest. Then, walking over to his desk, reached for pen and ink.

Joe was starting back along the road by the time he emerged.

'It appears he has some further questions for the whaling crews. About the stolen whale,' Alice told Max. She was clutching something tied up in a cloth. 'Sandwiches.' To his enquiring glance. 'Just in case.'

'In reserve,' Jean murmured.

She'd put her arms around Alice in the pantry.

'We can but try,' she'd said.

*

Alice was first to climb into the boat. She stared into the middle distance when Max suggested she might like to climb out again. Then patted a space beside her, for Jean who climbed in without comment. Max hesitated some moments before, with a sigh, he climbed in and took up an oar. Trehearne pushed them off, then stood knee-deep in the water as if undecided, before he, too, climbed in and took up an oar, Max surprised at Trehearne's strength as they began to row. He had no trouble at all keeping time. With almost the same smooth rhythm as Fredo.

Mount Imlay looked much as it had the first time he saw it, he thought, awash with pink clouds. He would never scale it now. Or Pico. It seemed Joe Givins was on their side. Why else try to buy them time by questioning the whaling crews? It'd be hard to miss the youngster in the morning light.

Gulls floated like spots before his eyes, the sea shining, a smudge of haze on the horizon. A moment later, the calf was making straight for them, block head up like a periscope.

Then 'Boat!' Alice was first to point out the pursuing vessel. Jean reached for a spare paddle. Handed Alice the other.

She drenched them all, first stroke.

'Bloody oath!' Trehearne exclaimed.

'Like this.' Jean scooped water neatly aside. 'Like stirring soup.'

Alice smiled with sudden comprehension.

They could see the whaleboat clearly now, on the other side of the bay, almost parallel with their own small craft.

Max began to row in earnest then. They immediately picked up speed. Time and again, the whale calf headed towards them, only to veer away at the last moment. Both drawn and repelled. Or perhaps undecided. Alice looked up to find its head looming above her like a cliff. Her heart gave a little gallop, then steadied. It means us no harm, she assured herself. It's what whales do. Jean, pale and endearingly dishevelled, never missed a stroke.

Max was surprised to realise that in all his years whaling he'd never been so close. Almost in the pocket of the creature, the hand. And so vast! Surely it would swamp them? But no.

They were close to Boyd's Tower when he got to his feet, setting the boat rocking. He pulled off his shoes and socks, tore at the buttons of his shirt.

'What are you doing?' Alice was shrill with fear. 'Mr Carver! Max!'

Jean glanced away as he began to unbutton his trousers.

'Close your eyes,' Max ordered.

'No,' Alice moaned. 'Don't.'

'It's for the best,' he said. 'Trust me. I wouldn't do it otherwise,' He sounded quite reasonable. 'Everything's in order. And legal. Look after the books for me, Alice. And yourself.'

And in a startling expanse of naked flesh, he flung himself into the water. The boat almost capsized as Alice sprang to her feet.

'No!' she cried again. 'No!'

Jean grabbed her by the hand, yanking her down. 'Row,' she ordered. 'Row, Alice.'

Max was already some distance off, heading for the horizon, when next they saw him. He appeared to be swimming strongly. Alice saw the whale turn and surge towards him. To attack? To kill and maim? To swallow him up, like Jonah?

To follow him.

The whale's wash sent Max flying. Soaring above the water, then plunging. Down, down, then up, until he broke the surface. Long moments before he could take a breath, regain his rhythm.

'It's following him,' Jean cried in astonishment.

'Of course it is!' Alice crowed. 'Of course! It's all it knows to do.'

*

Every time the gap looked to close, the whale came between them, setting the boat plunging and bucking. Still, they kept on. Drenched through, hardly able to see for salt water. Alice's and Jean's paddles constantly flailing and flinging water over each other, and Trehearne, in their haste.

Max gave it all he had. Not that he could see much, waterlogged, plunging up and down in whirlpools of whale. But he could sense the calf. Close behind. Following? Now and again he found himself flung forward at immense speed. Exhilarated. Flying. The calf was strong. Even if an infant. Surely it must live.

He'd forgotten how water could hold you up. When it didn't drag you down. Had Antonio cried out? Gone under without a sound? Sad? Grateful for the time he'd had? In the end, nothing but water. Like himself. Like every man that lived.

He saw it clearly that moment. Staring at him, with a small, inscrutable eye. Then it was gone.

*

Alice was first to put down her paddle, Jean following suit not long after. Only Trehearne kept doggedly on. Now and again Alice caught sight of the other boat, still making its way out to sea. Would Max make it? Would the whale follow him? Was there the remotest chance?

Moments later they came to a shuddering halt, the boat wallowing badly in the swell. Trehearne was slumped, chest heaving, over the oars, head down, eyes on his boots.

Shading her eyes, Alice turned to peer at the distant shore, the long, smooth curve of the bay, but there was nothing to be seen. Unless some small movement at the foot of Boyd's Tower. Someone waving? A branch, stirred by the wind. The wind! Come from nowhere. Turning the whole bay, in moments, to a sea of whitecaps. With nothing to be seen. No Max. Or whale. Or whaleboat, either.

She suddenly felt badly queasy. She'd never been much good at wallowing, she thought. Fix on something solid, she told herself sternly. But what? What in that mad, shifting kaleidoscope of breaking chop? The horizon. Fix on the horizon, Alice, she thought fiercely. Fix on the thought of them swimming towards it. Not for a moment thinking to look back.

It seemed to help.

Case Closed

Much as expected, the case of the stolen whale was closed, for lack of evidence. Not to mention perpetrators. Ron Goodley and Bert Williams having scarpered while Joe was in Bega.

He applied for a permanent transfer back to Eden.

That same day he wrote his final report.

Concluding that, in their cups, any one of the four accused might have delivered the fatal blow that felled Ted Price. That every last one of them, to all intents and purposes, was guilty of the crime. Or innocent as a babe in arms. There was no mention of one Patrick Trehearne.

Of the stolen whale, Joe wrote, in language both comfortingly familiar and consolingly vague, that the beast had vanished into thin air, doubtless cut up and sold off by person or persons unknown.

Not every crime is solved.

*

He read the final chapter of *Moby-Dick* that night. Somewhat to his surprise, he'd come to a grudging accommodation with the old man, Ahab. Poor, mad, stubborn bastard, thinking a fish to blame for his ills. As well to think a man's father was to blame for his every mis-step, he thought drily.

Closing the covers, he imagined the great white whale swimming free. And Ahab, captive to the end.

Beset with whale-ish thoughts, he reached to extinguish the lamp beside his bed, and, plunged into darkness, slept.

A man at peace.

The Lure

There were the odd days, still. Days when Alice felt the lure of the pot. Picked it up, sat with it in her lap, staring into the depths. Despair. All was lost. Always would be. And forever. As antidote, she'd rub at the thing, trying to summon up some hope, some genie. Her Jeannie. Slipping a finger into her mouth, she'd suck. Think of Jeannie's tickling tongue, wicked grin, looking up at her through a spill of dark hair. Feel, on cue, a stickiness between her thighs. Then sigh. It wasn't enough. Would it ever be? She'd stick two fingers down her throat, retch, spew on cue. But it was strangely hollow now, when once there'd been sweet relief, the bile more bitter than poison. With a sigh, she'd return the pot to its rightful place, blow out the lamp.

No-one knew her secret, she thought, moments off sleep. No-one ever would. There was that.

The Lotos-Eaters

Almost a year to the day of Max's presumed death by drowning, Alice found herself once more afflicted by dreams. No smell this time. Just Max, standing in the middle of the road to Boyd's Tower, beckoning her.

*

Alice and Jean rowed out one morning, the chest balanced between them on the transom. Then sat for a time, motionless, in the calm.

'You're sure?' Jean finally asked.

Alice nodded.

They manoeuvred it, with some difficulty, overboard. It landed with a terrific splash, then bobbed just proud of the surface, as if held there. They exchanged looks. Then, very slowly, it began to sink. A bubble broke the surface, then another. As if it were breathing out. A small gurgling noise issued from it. Like a lowered flag, it went down in inches. Alice saw

LO.DO.
BO.TON

swallowed up.

*

She'd read the whale book and Antonio's whale journal. Unable, at the last, to relinquish either, she'd placed them in Max's study, on his desk. Jean's desk now, she corrected herself: piled with schoolbooks, children's drawings, more than a few sketches of herself.

*

Trehearne had helped load it onto the boat.

'Like a faithful dog,' Jean said, as he stood watching from the shore. 'Minus the wagging tail,' Alice said drily.

They hadn't felt able to let him go. Hard to tell if he was grateful for it.

*

Alice said a brief prayer for the departed, then scattered some geraniums on the water. The plants under her window had made a full recovery.

Jean followed with some lines from her namesake:

Surely, surely, slumber is more sweet than toil, the shore
Than labour in the deep mid-ocean, wind and wave and oar;
O, rest ye, brother mariners, we will not wander more.

'He always feared it wouldn't sink,' Alice said. 'That it might get caught up in a gyre. Circle the globe for all eternity.'

'Like himself?' Jean murmured.

'There are worse fates, I suppose,' Alice said.

But it did. Sink.

The sight of it smaller and smaller, the bubbles fewer, then fewer still, and it was gone.

NOTE

I met a lady in the meads: from 'La Belle Dame sans Merci' by John Keats

Surely, surely, slumber is more sweet than toil: from 'The Lotos-Eaters' by Alfred, Lord Tennyson